TOM AND HUCK'S DEATHLY RIVER

CHAPTER 1

Monday,
October 22, 1849
St. Petersburg, Missouri

"Me and Hucky been surmising why they ain't no villagers still afeared o' them big hairy monsters," Tom Sawyer greeted Zane Rasmussen who stepped up onto the boardwalk to join the boys returning from school.

"That's so," Huckleberry Finn nodded. "They ain't discussing it no more—kinda like all that scary stuff never happened this summer."

The three boys clumped along the boardwalk toward the center of the village. Tom and Huck had resumed wearing shoes with the advent of chilly weather.

Zane shrugged, holding the wool jacket with missing buttons close around his throat. "Since there's been no alarms in several weeks, maybe everybody just decided those Bigfoot creatures never existed." He reflected that most scientists in his former life in the twenty-first century gave no credence to the Bigfoot, Yeti, Sasquatch-type giants. "Most folks in my time still don't believe there is any such thing," he added. "Some think he's real, but most say he's just a myth—a folk legend."

"If the hairy brute ain't real, then maybe them villagers that're a sight more religious are right to blame Satan for mauling and killing Gus Weir," Tom scoffed.

"Well," Huck said, thoughtfully, "folks that know about black magic and witches and fallen angels and such . . ."

"Like Jim and most o' the blacks hereabouts?" Tom interrupted.

"Yeah, and it ain't just hereabouts. Talk is, they's plenty o' voodoo and witchcraft down around N'Orleans. Anyways, they all say the devil can throw on any old disguise and it'll fool even folks as smart as Judge Thatcher or the preacher, but he can't hide his cloven foot. I used to think that word 'cloven' had sumpin' to do with clover, but that ain't so. It just means . . ."

"A 'cleft' or 'divide,' " Tom finished.

"I know what it means, Tom Sawyer. I been to school a good while now." Huck gave Tom a disgusted look. "As I was saying, the devil can't hide his cloven hoof that's like a sheep's foot, so that trips him up every time. And Sheriff Stiles swore the prints around Weir's body was more like a bear or a big human foot. So it couldn't of been the Dark Angel his own self."

"Too bad the rain washed out the tracks before anyone could make an impression of them," Zane said. "But then, we faked some tracks ourselves, so I guess somebody else coulda done the same."

"Afore he died a few days later, Weir told the sheriff the thing that come at him was big and dark, but it warn't no bear," Tom said.

"Coulda been that six-foot, nine-inch runaway buck he was trying to capture," Zane offered. "It was night and Weir was likely scared outa his wits. He could've imagined anything. That black slave had a fearsome reputation as a prize fighter and brawler."

Tom shook his head. "Weir was a mean, tough slave catcher. He warn't likely scared of anything much. And Weir had a pistol. Besides, Sheriff Stiles said 'twas bright moonlight, and the attack happened out on an open sandbar. Weir told Stiles the thing was huge and furry, stunk like a privy, and walked on two legs like a man."

The boys paused on the corner where Tom had to turn up Hill Street to his house and Huck had to break off toward Cardiff Hill where he lived with the Widow Douglas.

A cool, October wind gusted down from the wooded hill, whirling red and yellow leaves around them along the dirt street before fetching up in small, rustling piles against the wooden storefronts.

"Well, whatever kinda ferocious critter it was, I guess folks just decided to forget about it and go on with their daily lives," Zane concluded. He looked sideways at Tom. "Unless, of course, you want to stir it up again and make us all heroes like before." Without realizing it, Zane was gradually falling into the idiom and speech rhythms of these nineteenth century Missouri boys.

"Naw," Tom said. "I reckon once was enough. We was almighty lucky our conspiracy warn't exposed. Reckon it's best to let sleeping hounds stay put. Besides, I ain't taking no chances on stirring up one o' them real creatures."

"If there *are* any real ones," Zane said.

"You recollect that Becky saw the outline of one moving in the trees on the island that night," Huck said. "That's what the river pirate's dog was barking at. And Becky ain't much on lying, like some girls I've knowed."

"You and me ain't no slouches when it comes to practicing that art form," Tom observed.

"That's right," Huck said. "But girls generally lie about little things that don't amount to shucks."

"When Becky puts her mind to it, she can tell a whopper as good as any," Tom said. "After she wormed her way into our conspiracy, Becky took an oath to keep mum about it," he declared, "even though I knew it was bothersome to her conscience to get up in front o' the whole town and her father, Judge Thatcher, and agree to the whopper we made up. That big lie laid it over any little white lies her girlfriends coulda told."

"Yeah," Huck agreed. "She stretched her natural ability considerable."

They paused for a few moments and Zane stared off at the big river a short block away. The chilly wind was ruffling dark patches on the green water.

"Wal, what're we gonna do for excitement now?" Tom wondered. "Winter will be clomping down on us afore we can turn around. And it's likely to be long and cold and dull."

The three of them looked at each other. Zane knew Tom loved adventure better than pie. If there was any way to keep winter at bay with some kind of excitement, Tom could devise a plan to do it.

"Since all of you started back to school nearly a month ago, I've been bored to death," Zane said. "I've explored this village from end to end and read all the books and newspapers I could borrow or lay my hands on. You don't have television or computers to fool away the time, so I don't know how I'll ever make it through this winter stuck in that rooming house. I ain't much on winter sports like sledding or ice skating."

Since things had quieted down, Zane was beginning to miss his family and his former life in twenty-first century Delaware. But he still had no idea how to return there. He'd had no intention of traveling here to 1849 St. Petersburg—had actually considered travel through time impossible. It was all an accident. After a soccer game, he'd slipped away to a favorite creek and eaten a peanut butter/dark chocolate candy bar. It contained the two ingredients he was violently allergic to, but he'd given in to temptation. He became nauseated and vomited before passing out. When he awakened, disoriented, he'd found himself on Jackson's Island in the Mississippi River, and shortly afterward, discovered it was early June, 1849.

He was found by two boys who called themselves Tom and Huck; they were accompanied by a black man who was identified as a freed slave named Jim. Their clothes and demeanor appeared to be out of a long past time. Zane thought he was dreaming or someone was playing a practical joke on him. But, after comparing all available evidence, he was finally forced to conclude these three were actually human embodiments of Mark Twain's famous characters. They, in turn, reluctantly agreed that Zane was a boy from some future time and place. None of them understood it. Jim blamed it on witches. The boys admitted the world was strange, complex, and mysterious, and many unknown realities remained to be discovered. So, they just left it as a mystery of the universe and accepted what they saw before them.

Since that week in early June, Zane, who had no idea how to return home, had shared two mighty adventures with these three and Becky Thatcher—adventures he would not trade for anything in his former world.

As he stared vacantly across the river at the colorful leaves on the trees lining the far shore, he realized that most lives were not a series of grand adventures, one after another, so why should he expect his own life to be?

"There's always dull times," Tom said, voicing Zane's own thoughts. "The trick is to make sure they don't last."

Huck was gazing expectantly at his friend.

Zane had been here nearly five months—long enough to learn that Tom was the thinker, the schemer with imagination, while Huck pretty much reacted to whatever came his way.

"I been studying on a plan," Tom continued.

Zane waited.

"You know what this month is?" Tom asked.

"Sure. October," Huck said.

"It ain't just any October. This is a blue moon month."

"What's that?" Zane asked.

"It's a month that has two full moons in it."

"Why is it called that?"

"I ain't rightly certain, but that's what everybody calls it, anyhow. Ain't you ever heard someone say, 'Such-and-such only happens once in a blue moon'?"

"Sure, but I thought it was just an odd figure of speech," Zane said.

"No. Whoever says that means whatever they're talking about is mighty rare and only happens every now and again—like blue moon months. There's two full moons this month—one was on October 2nd and there will be one on Wednesday night, October 31st, which just happens to be Halloween."

"So, what about it?" Huck asked, a bit impatient.

When telling a story, Tom always went a roundabout way before arriving at the point he was making.

"It means that this Halloween is special and lots more spirits than usual will rise from their graves. Them two full moons draws ghosts outen the ground like the full moon draws the tides, 'cepten the pull on them uneasy dead folks is twicet as strong in a blue moon month—'specially when one o' them full moons falls on Halloween—the night spirits is likely to be roaming about, anyways."

"How do you know that?" Huck asked, sounding skeptical.

The thought occurred to Zane that anyone who believed an incantation involving stump water, or hurling a dead cat after a retreating devil could cure warts, was liable to believe anything. But he kept silent.

"I got it from Ted Gardner who got it from Ben Rogers who was told in confidence by Homer Johnson. Homer got it straight from his father who got it from a black slave he just bought in Orleans that was shipped fresh from Haiti. There now! That's how I know," he finished triumphantly, as if that settled the matter. "You don't think I'd make up sumpin' like that, do you?"

"I reckon it's true, then," Huck said. "I just ain't heard of it before."

"Likely one o' them secrets that comes from Africa where the tribes of natives live closer to nature," Tom said.

"So what's this got to do with us?" Zane inquired.

"It ain't but a fortnight 'til Halloween. We got that great sailing yawl now and can go dern near anywhere we have a mind to on the river, without 'borrowing' a skiff or buying a ticket on a steamboat. Halloween falls on Wednesday night this year. Let's stock the boat with a little food and fishing gear and a couple o' lanterns and shovels and maybe a pistol or two and go downriver to that place where Hucky got mixed up in the feud last year. What was the names o' them families, Huck?"

"The Grangerfords and the Shepherdsons," he replied with no enthusiasm.

"That's it. We'll raise some Cain, go yowling around, let slip a peek or two of light in the woods from the lanterns. Anybody with any sense will figure it's spirits that ain't resting easy and 're coming back a haunting and dissatisfied on Halloween night. You know they's been a bunch from both families killed over the years in that feud, so anyone still in that house will know for sure it's some o' their kin that died by the gun and ain't settled comfortable, and maybe looking for revenge on one side or t'other."

"That ain't such a good idea," Huck said.

"It's perfect," Tom declared. "And we can throw in some other things like rattling chains or sumpin' to give it more style as we go along."

"No," Huck demurred, shaking his head. "I got away from that place oncet and I sure ain't going back. I still have nightmares about it now and again."

"We'll have the boat close by so we can quick-like shove off downriver."

"First off, we couldn't get within shouting distance of that Grangerford log house," Huck said.

"Why not?"

"They keep a pack o' hounds round about for coon hunting and such. Those dogs set up a powwow of howling the night I was jest trying to walk past the place quiet-like. Woke up the whole family. That's how I got hooked in there." He paused a moment. "Besides, they have triple locks on their doors and keep their muskets loaded and primed. They been at this feud a good many years and is always on guard. Ain't no Shepherdson or nobody else could sneak up on that place. I ain't hankering to get shot just for the fun and excitement of it."

Tom paused for several seconds and then said, "It won't be the same as it was last year when you was there. You told me yourself, the boy, Buck, and his nineteen-year-old cousin, Joe, and Buck's father and two older brothers was killed the day you and Jim escaped from there on the raft—the day they had that rip-roaring battle with the Shepherdsons after Buck's sister, Sophia, run off with Harney Shepherdson."

"It happened just so," Huck said.

"Then how many of them Grangerfords could be left? Maybe a few o' the womenfolk, but it ain't likely they's gonna stay around without no protection from the men."

"I don't know."

"And the slaves . . ." Tom went on, "With their masters all dead and gone, they'd scatter like chaff and probably head for the nearest free state."

"Could be some o' Buck's cousins or uncles moved in since then to keep the feud agoing," Huck said. "Buck talked like they was a whole passel o' them Grangerfords."

"Here's all I'm saying—let's go down there Halloween night

and take a look-see," Tom persisted. "Poke around a little. We'll pretend we're the downtrod French citizens storming the Bastille. Stir things up amongst the prison turnkeys." He glanced at Zane. "What about you? Might be a sure cure for boredom."

"I'm game for just about anything at this point."

"Jest recollecting all them hateful words and shootings and murders 'most gives me the fantods," Huck muttered with a faraway look.

"Then you stay with the boat and we'll take Jim along to explore."

"You can bet Jim don't wanta go back there."

"Wonder if Becky would be up for it? This would be a lot more fun and exciting than any Halloween party."

"She told me her father wants her to start spending more time with her girl friends and not hanging around the boys so much," Huck said. "She's kept mum about our conspiracy, but she thinks the judge still suspicions we had something to do with all that business this summer."

"We can ask her. And maybe I can persuade Jim to go, too."

"Come to think of it, I don't reckon I could even find the place again," Huck said, by way of further argument. "It was the middle of the night—the dark just thick-like, with no moon. An up-bound steamboat had just plowed over our raft and me and Jim had both dove over the side. When I come up, I couldn't find Jim or the raft and had to catch hold of a floating board and make for shore. The current was taking me to the left toward the outside of a big bend in one o' them long, slanting crossings and I had to swim upward of two mile afore I finally got to the bank and pulled myself out at a low spot." He paused a moment. "Truth is, I doubt I could pick out that place again if I was to be whipped for it."

"If we can't find it, we can't find it," Tom shrugged. "That don't mean we can't try. We'll calculate how many nights you and Jim drifted and figure about how far along you'd got. But we'll sail and row by day and cover the same distance a lot quicker than a raft could. Come to think of it, we don't have to calculate much at all. You said the Grangerfords was rich with a good bit o' land and owned upwards of a hundred slaves. Well, if that's the case, it had to be south of Cairo, in Kentucky, where slaveholding is legal. We'll just scoot on down past the Ohio River and go to looking from there. We'll be traveling by daylight, so we can likely spot that log house built with a dogtrot. Was it near the river?"

Huck nodded. "But it's upslope above high water."

There was a pause, then Huck said, "It ain't no short jaunt down that far. I reckon it's upward of three hundred miles by river."

"Hmmm . . ." Tom put a hand to his mouth. "Then we'll skip school for a week. We need a break from old Mister Dobbins, anyway." He looked at the other two. "So, what about it, Huck? Zane says he's game for it."

Huck looked down and was silent for several seconds. "I reckon if you're bound to go, anyhow, I'll go along. But I'm taking a pistol and I ain't getting too close to that place."

"Good." Tom was all enthused again. "Maybe I can talk Jim into going. He likely won't miss much work time. If he does, we can make up his wages."

"If he agrees to go—which ain't likely—you gonna tell the widow where we're headed?"

"Of course not. She's used to him going off with us fishing and camping and such."

"And getting him into dangersome trouble," Huck added.

"Huck, a body would think you're as old and fidgety as Aunt Polly."

16

"I ain't but a few months older than you," he replied, taking it literally.

"You used to be up for any project afore the widow begun to civilize you."

Huck squirmed a bit at this. "Well, I'm still up for it. But fooling along them Grangerfords jest appears t' be asking for trouble."

"Wonder if I should get Becky to go with us?" Tom mused. "No," he suddenly decided. "I know she'd want to go. But the judge would be mighty aggravated if we was to persuade her to miss that Halloween party Amy Lawrence is throwing."

"We was invited to that, too," Huck said. "You gonna pass up a chance to dance with Becky?"

Tom grimaced. "Like as not there'll be other chances for that. A blue moon Halloween don't come along but once in a flock o' blue moons."

CHAPTER 2

"Jim, you recollect if this was about where the steamboat run over us that night?" Huck asked.

"Lawsy, Huck, I ain't sho. It uz dark as sin that night." The muscular black man looked around, scanning the shoreline in the slanting rays of the late afternoon sun. "It likely could be. De river was wide and dat big steamer hit our raf' just b'fo a big bend like de one down yonder."

Tom had doused the mainsail and it lay piled on the boom while the jib barely stirred in the dying breeze near sunset. Zane was at the tiller holding the twenty-foot yawl steady as it drifted in the mid-channel current.

It was Wednesday, October 31—Halloween—with a clear sky and a full moon in the offing for their adventure. They had benefited from a gusty autumn wind from the north and northwest, but it had still taken them three full days from sunup to sundown to reach Cairo and the confluence of the Ohio River. Each night they'd beached the boat on a towhead. Too tired to fish, they'd eaten supper of ham and corn pone, and fallen asleep around the campfire before rising at dawn and starting again. When the wind had subsided or been blocked by trees, they'd rowed hard with the aid of the current.

Huck was right, Zane realized. It was, indeed, a long ways.

Since Huck was reluctant about this expedition, Tom and Zane had finally managed to persuade Jim to come with them.

Tom had accosted Jim at his work earlier that week behind

the widow's house and confided the purpose of their excursion. "You're big and strong. We're just going to have some fun and want you to be part of it. We ain't expecting no trouble, but it's good to have a big strong man along just in case," Tom added.

"Dat's what you said de las' time. Ah ain't so sure ah wants to come along on dis venture," Jim said when he'd heard the plan.

"Jim, you likely been bored to death around here since all the excitement this summer," Tom said. "Besides, it'll take your mind offen the judge making an offer to buy your wife and children. Judge Thatcher is going to ride over to Logansville next Thursday to see the owner again."

"Yassuh. Ah been pooty anxious 'bout dat since you and Huck tole me." The black man rested the scythe on its long, curved blade, and mopped the sweat from his face in the warmth of the Indian summer day. The deep weeds inside the fenced yard were nearly cleared.

"This will give you a chance for a little fun."

Jim was silent for several seconds, then said, "You boys be axin' fo' trouble, same as always. But ah'll go on dis trip, providin' ah kin stay in de boat, jest like ah stayed hid in de marsh wid de raf' last time we was dere."

"Fair enough," Tom said, grinning at Zane. "Now, let's go see the widow."

Widow Douglas consented to let Jim take time off his job if he was of a mind to go, since work on her place was light just then. The summer vegetables and fruit had all been harvested— pickled, dried, and preserved for winter, and some sold fresh at market. There was little for him to do at the moment.

Zane and Tom assured her Jim would be back within a week, without mentioning the object of the trip. "We're just going downriver apiece to camp and fish. Maybe we'll bag a duck to bring back for Sunday dinner," Tom said as they left her house.

Playing hooky from school was another matter. Rather than ask permission from his Aunt Polly, Tom had just left a re-assuring note for her to the effect they'd be gone only a few days and excused his action by explaining this was the last chance they'd have for an outing before winter. He and Huck would be in for a painful switching from the schoolmaster when they returned, but Tom was firm in his conviction this excursion would make it worthwhile.

Now, as Halloween night approached, they were in danger of not finding the site at all. Tom stood up in the boat, unsheathed a spyglass, and put it to his eye. "Huck, the Grangerford place gotta be somers along here in Kentucky. You said both families shared a steamboat landing. I ain't seen no sign of one since we passed Cairo a few miles back. Was it a ramp or a dock to tie off to?"

"They just run the gangway offen the deck to the low bank. This here warn't no regular stop—only a woodyard mostly. Or, a boat would put in to answer a hail. They's a little store about a quarter-mile back in the edge o' the woods there. Lots o' cordwood stacked this side of it for the boats. That's where I clumb a tree to hide when I seen Buck and his cousin shootin' at the Shepherdsons that last day."

They drifted silently along for another half-minute, the shoreline sliding slowly past. Tom was holding the glass steady against the mast.

"We ain't near far enough downriver yet," Huck said. "Lemme see that map."

Tom handed over the folded map with the rough drawing of the Mississippi he'd bought at the village mercantile. Huck spread it out on a thwart. "Look." He pointed. "The river makes a big double bend below Cairo. See how it loops back on itself? Right in the midst of this big oxbow in southern Kentucky is Shepherdson's territory that stretches down a ways to the Tennessee border. See the state line drawed straight across there? O' course there ain't no marker or fence on the ground. But Buck called this here Compromise Landing 'cause it straddles the line and both warring families used it. About two mile south of that is the Grangerford house."

"Oh." Tom straightened up. "We been doubling around some mighty tight bends for the last hour or three. I reckon we's just now coming around the last bend in this oxbow 'cause the river runs straight south for a ways now, and the sun's on our right," he said looking ahead, then squinting at the orange ball sinking into the western haze.

"Yeah," Huck said. "Keep a sharp lookout. I figure it's only about three mile more. We should make it afore dark."

"The wind died off. Reckon we'll have to row," Zane said.

Without being asked, Jim climbed into position and unshipped a pair of oars and began pulling hard with the aid of the current. The boat fairly flew along at a steady speed. Zane kept the boat in the strongest mid-channel current.

Tom leaned against the port shroud and kept the spyglass steady on the unwinding shoreline.

"Ha! There's something!" Tom cried, about three-quarters of an hour later. "I can see part of a log building back upslope."

"Lemme see." Huck took the spyglass.

"Yeah. That's the store, all right. Don't appear to be nobody around." He lowered the glass and handed it to Jim to look. "The house is about two-mile downstream from that store."

The broad river was sweeping into a wide right-hand bend ahead of them. Zane squinted into the bright sheen that the dying sun was reflecting from the surface.

"And this here must be the big bend I swum across," Huck said. "A road runs alongshore back in the trees."

"Good. What about the graveyard?"

"Lemme see . . . Me and Buck used to go there when we

21

wanted to be alone and talk and smoke our pipes. It's about a half-mile below the house, just off the river road. The grass don't grow none too tall there 'cause the place gets a right smart amount o' business that keeps it tromped down," he added.

"Dat graveyard jest be a short ways above de swamp and de crick where ah hid de raf," Jim said.

"Is there room to slide this yawl into the crick and outa sight?" Tom asked.

"Sholy is. But de mas' might catch up in de vines and branches."

"Hmm . . . Then we'll drop the mast. Not likely to be any wind tonight, anyway. We want the boat pointed toward the river and the oars shipped in case we need to make a fast getaway."

Zane's stomach clenched at this, wondering what Tom had planned.

A few high clouds glowed red and gold in the last rays of the vanished sun. A peaceful evening heralding a coming night fraught with supernatural possibilities.

Jim continued to row. "We gots to hurry to be dere befo' dark."

Ten minutes later, Tom spotted the Grangerford house.

Huck took the glass and looked intently.

The boat was sliding along about six miles an hour now with Jim at the oars and slowly the trees parted to reveal the double log house with the dogtrot between. To Zane, it looked like a fortress. Twilight was reflecting opaque light from the two front windows so Zane could not see inside.

"Don't see nobody around," Huck said, moving the telescope. "If they's any horses in the barn, I can't see no sign of 'em. Nor dogs nuther." He lowered the glass. "Gives me all-over shivers jest to see the place again." Tom motioned for Huck to join him and they unstepped the mast and lowered it on the sail, gaff and boom across the thwarts, just out of Jim's way.

Zane didn't know the details of the plan, but he guessed Tom probably didn't either; he was making it up as he went along. Huck and Jim each carried a pistol. Jim had again "borrowed" the widow's small revolver. Zane had no weapon.

"There's the graveyard," Huck said pointing. He turned to Zane. "Keep'er in the current that swings toward the left bank up ahead here."

Zane caught a glimpse of a few scattered wooden headboards before they disappeared behind the trees.

"De crick ain't but a little way now," Jim added, glancing over his shoulder as he rowed.

The yawl was moving quicker than Zane realized as they came closer inshore. Jim stopped rowing and backed water with the oars to slow them.

Dusk was settling over the river. Zane glanced up and saw stars beginning to wink on. Apparently, it would be a clear night to give a complete view of the full moon.

"Dere she be!" Jim pointed toward a break in the trees.

Zane thrust the tiller away from him and the boat pivoted to port. Jim worked the bow upstream with the oars and then with several dexterous thrusts backed the boat, stern first, out of the current and into the mouth of the creek. Twenty yards inside the arching tree tunnel, the boat rocked gently to a stop, the rudder just touching the overhanging limbs and brush. Zane tied off the transom to a thick sapling.

"Nice piece o' work," Tom nodded.

The boys all took long swigs of water from their canteens. Tom struck a lucifer to both lanterns. By the slivers of light that leaked out around the loose shutters, they checked both of their revolvers.

"Shall we leave one of the lanterns with you, Jim?" Tom asked.

"Nossuh. Ah has a stub o' candle in my pocket and can light dat if ah needs it." He waved them away as he settled himself. "You boys have fun and ah'll be ready to cast off when you shows up."

Zane noticed no aggravating mosquitoes and assumed the frost several nights earlier had put a serious dent in their numbers.

Tom took up a four-foot length of chain to which he'd attached one of the iron wrist shackles he'd saved from his summer imprisonment. "Since I escaped, I figure that shackle will bring me good luck," Tom explained. "And rattling it will be even scarier for anybody hears it."

"Don't get in no trouble," Jim cautioned. "Hoot like an owl if you needs me." He sounded relieved to be staying under cover. Zane was hoping Jim had forgotten their promise to let him stay in the boat. Superstitious as he was, Jim had always proved a reassuring presence when danger threatened.

Tom stepped ashore and began forcing his way noisily through the clinging brush, whacking the willows and dead brush with the doubled chain. He muttered savagely under his breath when a thorn bush caught his jacket and ripped a four-inch gap in the sleeve.

Huck followed with a shuttered lantern and Zane was last with the second lantern and extra matches.

As the boys broke into the clear beyond the dark vegetation bordering the creek, they realized there was still a little daylight left and they didn't yet need the lanterns. The graveyard lay about two hundred yards ahead. A few bare trees stood among the scattered headboards.

As they trudged along, single file, Zane noticed a brightness coming from his left. He glanced that way. A giant orange moon was rising above the trees on the Missouri shore. It was an awesome sight. He paused to look and sucked in a deep lungful of the unseasonably warm, humid air, smelling the river and damp mold. What a night!

The lunar light grew slowly as the moon detached itself from the horizon and slid upward, losing its orange cast.

When they finally paused at the edge of the graveyard, Zane could not see the house.

"It's more'an quarter-mile farther up," Tom said to a whispered query.

Whispering instead of talking aloud seemed natural, given the eerie setting. It wasn't as if they feared being overheard by any humans. But Zane thought it likely their presence could be sensed by dogs. He whispered his concern to Huck.

"Even if they's about, ain't no harm in a hound, nohow, nor even a pack of 'em."

Maybe the baying of hounds is exactly what Tom was counting on to get humans in the house stirred up, Zane thought. But if the Grangerfords were no longer on this place, someone else could have brought in a vicious guard dog. He also wondered about the presence of snakes. Rattlers and copperheads were nocturnal hunters. But his own limited experience told him they'd probably retired underground after the first or second hard frost and were only out when the sun warmed them.

Zane's eyes had now become accustomed to the dim light and he could see the headboards—twenty or more of them scattered about in random fashion among the few bare trees. Rising above the haze, the moon was now bright yellow, casting a pale light and etching sharp black shadows.

"Let's take a look at some o' these headboards as we work up toward the house," Tom whispered.

"I wonder if they found Buck's body and buried him?" Huck said, sadly. "I dragged him and his cousin out of the river afore I lit out."

Tom unshuttered his lantern and went creeping among the headboards, holding the light to each as he passed.

Zane knew there was no need for stealth or whispering since the benign face of the full moon was the only observer of their activities. But Tom liked to make everything as exciting as possible; he never missed a chance to create more drama.

Zane opened his lantern as well and they went exploring.

"Lookee here," Huck said. " 'Silas Grangerford 1804–1831. Shot from ambush by a Shepherdson ward.' What's a 'ward'?"

Zane held the light closer. Some of the paint had weathered off. "I think there's two letters missing. Looks like 'c' and 'o.' A Shepherdson 'coward.' "

"I reckon Silas ain't the only one here with a marker like that," Tom said.

"Do you reckon any o' these long-gone souls might be rising up along about midnight?" Huck wondered. "Ole Silas might be looking for revenge."

"He's had plenty o' time to git it afore now," Tom observed. He turned away toward the next grave and fell flat, dropping the lantern. "What's this?" He pushed himself up from a small pile of dirt.

Huck picked up the lantern, which was still burning. Tom was trying to brush off the fresh dirt that clung to his hands and knees.

Huck held the lantern up to reveal an oblong black hole.

Zane caught his breath. He knelt and held his lantern down inside. An empty wooden coffin lay in the bottom, its broken lid askew.

Chapter 3

"Well here's one that's already on the prowl," he said, his heart beginning to pound.

The boys looked at each other, and then quickly over their shoulders, to make sure nothing was behind them.

"What's the headboard say?" Zane asked.

"They ain't one."

"This dirt is recently dug since the last rain."

"Likely a fresh grave then," Huck said. "Ain't no place safe from grave robbers, even way out here."

"I hope that's all it is," Tom said.

Zane felt damp with sweat. Maybe it was just the dew forming. He wiped a sleeve across his forehead, swallowed hard, then drew a deep breath to calm himself.

"Let's look around and see can we find the body or see if any others are missing," Tom finally said to stir them out of their collective shock. He led the way.

"Let's call Jim," Zane said, not moving. "No telling what we're likely to run into out here."

"What can Jim do?" Tom asked.

"He's big and strong and he's got a gun, too," Huck said, apparently opting for reinforcements as well.

"Okay." Tom took a dozen paces to the edge of the graveyard and, facing the creek, cupped his hands around his mouth. "Hoo, hoo. Uh, whooo! Uh, whooo!"

He paused. All was still as death. He tried again. And then a third time, even louder.

"Jim likely can't hear you," Huck said, coming up behind him. "Besides, he might think it's a coyote. That's likely the worst owl hoot I've ever heard."

"It's a barred owl. They use all kinds of barking calls and screams," Tom retorted.

Huck tried his own version of a barred owl call.

Dead silence for at least a half-minute. Then the brush lining the creek two hundred yards away stirred and a figure emerged.

Tom gave the call another try, then stepped out into the moonlight and swung the lighted lantern. The figure homed in on the boys and came trudging toward them through the deep grass.

"Huck?" came a hoarse whisper as Jim approached.

"Yeah. It's us."

"What be de trouble?"

"We need you to keep guard whilst we look around this graveyard. Lemme show you what we found." He led Jim by lantern light to the gaping grave they'd discovered and knelt to hold the lantern down inside. "What do you make of that?"

Jim put his hands on his knees and peered down at the open coffin.

"Fresh dug," Huck said. "And no headboard."

"Likely de work o' witches," Jim said, looking quickly around in the deep shadow and patchy moonlight.

"We wuz thinking grave robbers," Tom said.

"Away out here?" Jim was skeptical. "Most o' dem resurrection men does dere work near villages and towns where dey can sell de body."

Zane had not thought about that. On the other hand, he didn't hold with the explanation about witches. Yet . . . in this time and place, he couldn't entirely rule it out, either; he'd witnessed some very strange things since he'd mysteriously found himself in 1849 Missouri.

Huck was still looking down into the hole. "Tom, you recollect when we saw Injun Joe and Muff Potter dig up Hoss Williams that night Doc Robinson was murdered?"

"I ain't likely to forget it."

"They hoisted up the coffin and then dumped out the body. I reckon that'd be a lot easier than trying to snag the body outen the coffin from the bottom of that hole."

"That's so. Maybe they didn't have no rope."

"See how that lid is split right down the middle? I'm thinking that body come busting outa that grave without no help. Notice how the dirt is all thrown around instead of in one pile?"

"Naw. Jesus was the onliest one done that . . . on Easter Sunday a long time ago," Tom said. "Everybody knows that."

"Not so sure. When we was studying scripture in Sunday school last year, I recollect something about when Jesus was nailed on that cross by the Romans, all kinds o' things happened—an earthquake, the curtain o' the temple was torn in two, and bodies of the saints come outen their tombs and walked around in the city."

"Mebbe so, but that's because Jesus was murdered. Nothing like that happening now. On Halloween the onliest part of the dead rising up is their spirits—not the bodies, even though I've heard tell of zombies with bodies rising up, but they only got the brains of a wood tick. This here's gotta be grave robbers."

"Witches likely done it," Jim repeated, "Or mebbe de devil come to haul him off to de hot place."

"Well, we ain't gonna figure it out standing around discussing it," Tom said. "You and Jim keep your hands on your pistols and stay behind me whilst I inspect some o' these other graves. Mebbe we can find this missing body."

"Ain't no animals coulda dug that deep and pried the lid offen that coffin," Huck said. "Excepten maybe that big hairy monster."

Now it was Zane's turn to be scared. Witches didn't bother him, because they were mostly ethereal; the thought of a physical Bigfoot did.

Jim trailed along behind as the boys went creeping from headboard to headboard, examining the sunken graves, none of which had been disturbed.

Near the upper end of the graveyard Huck stumbled over something in the dark and nearly fell. "Here, Tom!" The lantern was held low and they saw Huck had tripped over a partially buried human skull. The rest of the skeleton was nearly washed out of the ground by rain. Apparently, it had been in a shallow grave and without a coffin.

"Oh!" Huck gasped.

"What's wrong?"

"That skull bone is mighty narrow and it has long white hair still hanging down the back of it. That's old Colonel Saul Grangerford, for sure. Look here . . ." He pointed at the rib cage. "He's even wearing what's left of his white shirt or waistcoat. And them bones has gotta be over six foot long. There ain't no doubt it's him. Lordy! He was tolerable slim when I knowed him. And I still reckonize the old gentleman even as skinny as he is now."

"That's what comes o' not eating no vittles for fifteen months," Tom said dryly.

Huck ignored the comment. "Musta been buried quick, maybe by the womenfolk who couldn't dig a grave deep as needed."

"Like enough, especially if the slaves run off and warn't nobody to do the work," Tom agreed. "Since these murdered remainders ain't planted and comfortable, the old man's spirit's likely walking abroad in the full moon tonight, looking for revenge."

"Don't touch dem bones," Jim warned. "Dat be de wust kind o' bad luck."

Zane could see the whites of Jim's eyes in the lantern light as the big man moved back a step.

No one made a move to touch the skeleton. Zane thought the boys' guess as to what happened was as good as any. It didn't appear wolves or coyotes had dug up this corpse because the bones weren't scattered.

Fanning the coals of their active imaginations, a night breeze sprang up from the direction of the river, rustling the dead leaves that still clung to the trees. The limbs of the elms and sycamores bent in the sudden stirring of air, their black shadows writhing on the ground like outstretched arms.

"The spirits of the dead are restless." Tom sounded awed. "It must be getting near midnight."

"Naw. I doubt it's much past ten o'clock," Zane opined, forcing down his own uneasiness.

They moved on and cautiously surveyed the remaining gravesites but found nothing unusual.

"We come here to stir up any folks in that house yonder," Huck stated. "But it's us that's being scared outa our wits. I didn't wanta come, but now we're here, I say we get up to the house and see if anybody's home."

Thus shamed, Tom and Zane assumed a confident air. "Let's go, then."

Huck, the only one who'd been here before, marched ahead through the trees by the intermittent light of the full moon and a few spangles of light leaking from the shuttered lantern. Jim reluctantly followed up the rear.

The house came into view as an indistinct hulking presence. All trees and bushes had been cut away from the sides and front of the place for about fifteen yards around. Even the stumps had rotted and fallen in, creating depressions here and there in the deep grass. Zane estimated the house had been there for more than fifteen years. Pale moonlight illuminated the house and open area around it.

The boys paused, subdued, in the deep shade of several big oaks, and watched for any sign of life. Each side of the double log house had a second story and a stoop in front—no wide porch. Zane guessed it was to keep anyone from getting too close without being seen from inside.

"No hounds," Huck muttered. " 'Tain't natural."

Zane noted the waist-high grass and weeds covering the wide yard, some of it gone to seed and drooping over. It didn't appear to have been cut all summer. The whole place had a forlorn, deserted look about it. There was no sound except the soft rustling of the night breeze that had sprung up. Apparently, the feud was over and the house deserted. But then Zane thought of the empty grave with the fresh dirt. Maybe the house wasn't being lived in, but someone had been around here very recently.

After a few minutes of silence, Tom leaned toward them and whispered, "I reckon the Almighty has let these fools all kill each other off, and the devil take the hindmost."

"We come all this way for nothing," Huck said.

"We best be getting on back to de boat," Jim said.

The boys ignored him.

"I'm surprised somebody hasn't come along and moved into this nice house," Zane said.

"Likely it's got a reputation for death and despair, and nobody wants to live with all these ghosts 'round about." Tom gave a shudder as if to shake off the spirits on his back.

"Well, maybe we ain't . . ."

Bang!

They all gave a start at the sudden slamming of a door somewhere inside.

"Shh!" Tom grabbed Huck's arm and they crouched down behind a thick oak. Jim was leaning against a nearby elm, pistol in hand, breathing heavily.

The indirect glow of a candle or lamp lit up the front window as someone entered the parlor.

Zane's heart was beating faster. "I reckon there's someone here to scare after all," he whispered.

Three men entered the room, one of them carrying a smoky coal-oil lamp he set on a table. The other two threw themselves into armchairs, crock mugs in their fists.

The one who'd carried the lamp remained standing and began talking, pacing around as he gestured. His voice carried to the boys as only a low muttering.

"Them three don't favor no Grangerfords," Huck whispered. "They's shorter and wearing rough clothes. Not like the gentry I met."

"Likely some river rats or raftsmen who found the place empty and using it for a hotel," Zane guessed.

"You want we should set up some howling, like lost souls, and scare the livers out o' them?" Huck whispered.

"Hold on a minute or two," Tom replied in a low voice. "They's having some kind o' meeting. Let's slide up under the window and see can we hear what it's about."

Huck considered this proposal in silence. "I don't know," he finally said, but then added, "But I reckon it ain't no more dangersome than when me and Jim landed on the wreck o' the *Walter Scott* and run into them murderers."

"Wisht I'd a been with you that night," Tom replied, his eyes wide with excitement in the moonlight. "But this here's the same kinda thing. I ain't passing up no chances for a grand adventure."

"You coming, Jim?" Zane asked.

"Ah kin see all ah wants from right here." He remained standing behind the elm, pistol in hand. "Ah be on guard 'case you needs me."

The boys crept away to the right, out of sight of the window, and then to the corner of the house. From there, they hugged the log wall and catfooted slowly along the front, until their heads were inches below the wavy window glass.

"I plan to finish this operation before winter sets in," a voice came to them so clearly, they all jumped and held their breaths.

Then Zane pointed to a louvered panel just below the sealed window. The slats were cranked open to admit fresh air. Zane noted these slots would also make good gun ports for a feuding family.

Another voice mumbled a reply.

"What's the rush?" a third voice asked.

"You're from Loosiana," the first man said. "The river up here will be icing up in a few weeks. Deck passage won't be practical. Liable to lose some to the cold."

"We made a good pile awready," one of them said. "Why not get out while we're ahead?"

"There's plenty more to be made. You want to just leave all that cash unclaimed?" the first man sneered.

"A good gambler knows when to leave off bucking a lucky streak," the man answered defensively. "On my last job me and my pardner pushed things too far, and wound up losing everything. Lucky to get away with our hides."

Zane thought the voice sounded vaguely familiar. He wished he could get a look at the faces.

"Look, you want to get out now, I ain't gonna stop you. But you'll hafta light outa here to somewhere you can't be found," retorted the first man—apparently the boss. "Three more weeks'll wind up the operation, anyways. I already contracted with Wilson in Keokuk for two more shipments, so we quit now, we're on the hook for that. I don't favor losing that much from our profits."

A pause. "Okay, I ain't easy about it, but I'm in 'til we run outa time," the objector said. "We funnel 'em through this place, same as usual, I reckon."

The look the boys exchanged plainly showed a shared recognition. It was their old adversary, Chigger Smealey. But they dared not speak.

"Yeah, this is the best staging area we coulda found."

A few seconds of silence followed.

"Remember what I said about drinking," the boss continued. "Lay off the tanglefoot until this is over. I don't want anybody getting drunk and blabbing. Got it?"

The other two grunted their assent.

Then Zane heard another strange noise. It sounded like scratching.

"That dog's gotta go. Let him outside."

Whining and growling. More scratching.

"Likely smells a coon or a possum."

Fear shot through Zane as he heard a bolt being slid back and a latch click. The boys scuttled around the corner of the house.

They heard the door open and close, and Zane held his breath as they hugged the side of the house, out of sight.

A low growl got louder as the dog approached, sensing their presence.

Suddenly Tom jumped out of hiding swinging the four-foot chain with the shackle on the end. The dog gave two sharp barks, ears back and bared fangs snapping before he attacked. It was just enough time for Tom to whip the chain forward. It wrapped around the dog's forelegs the instant it lunged. The timing of the leap was thrown off and the animal fell hard on its face and chest at Tom's feet.

Huck yanked his pistol. As he tried to cock the big hammer, his thumb slipped. The shot exploded in a streak of flame, the bullet shivering the front window, which collapsed in a jangle of falling glass.

"Run, boys!" Jim was suddenly beside them and threw something at the stunned dog while it was kicking free of the chain.

Zane flung his lantern at the dog. It struck the animal's head and bounced off, igniting the spilled coal oil. A rivulet of flame ran along the ground. Zane didn't wait to see more as he turned and sprinted away.

An uproar of shouting and cussing erupted from the house and the front door slammed back on its hinges.

A gun roared and a slug tore up the dirt ten feet ahead of Zane. Even on the soccer field in his other life, he'd never run so fast. His feet fairly flew over the ground, barely touching.

Two more shots blasted the night.

Jim was already ten yards ahead of the boys and pulling away with his longer stride.

Just before they went over a rise down toward the graveyard, Huck slid to a stop and pulled his pistol. Chest heaving, he braced his arm against a tree to steady himself and fired three times at the distant house. Then he turned and raced after the others.

The shouts sounded farther away.

They reached the graveyard, out of sight of the house, but never slowed. Zane's lungs and thighs were burning. His foot dropped into a sunken grave and his ankle turned. Momentum threw him forward and he tucked his shoulder and rolled, coming up on his feet. He had to stop or die. Leaning hands on knees, he labored to suck in enough oxygen. Sweat dripped from his nose. The only one who could catch them now was the dog, he thought, but he could do nothing about that now.

It was almost a minute before his heart and breathing slowed enough to continue. There was no sound of pursuit.

The three boys straggled, nearly spent, across the open field beyond the graveyard. Jim was fifty yards ahead pushing into the willows and brush bordering the creek.

The last hundred yards were the hardest, and Zane wondered if his heart would explode and he'd collapse in the tall grass and die before he reached the boat. He assumed he was still in condition from soccer, but several months in this nineteenth century world must have softened him to a different life.

Fear and panic spurred him on. He was the last one to tumble into the boat, exhausted and scratched.

Tom cast off. Jim dug in his oars and thrust the boat down the creek toward the river.

CHAPTER 4

Nobody spoke until the yawl was out in the current. Jim laid on his oars and all of them were still panting and wiping sweat.

The full moon shone on the broad river, silvering the surface. With no one rowing or steering, the inshore current spun the boat sideways and they drifted silently near trees, hidden from anyone onshore behind them.

Two minutes later, Tom stirred himself. "Hucky, I reckon we oughta step the mast so's we can hang up our signal lantern."

Huck didn't reply but got to his feet and the boys awkwardly hoisted the mast, sliding it down into its step, and then fastened the forestay and shrouds. Huck took the lantern and tied it off as high as he could reach.

"What kind of dog was that?" Zane asked.

"Dunno, but he had big teeth," Tom said with a shudder.

"De pointy ears and long hair be like a wolf," Jim said.

"Coulda been one o' them sled dogs from up north," Zane guessed. "How come he didn't chase us? That chain that tangled his legs and the lantern I threw at him wouldn't have slowed him down for long."

"What did you hit him with, Jim?" Tom asked.

"You know dat ham we been eatin' on? I shoved de bone in a sack and tied it to m' belt."

"Good thinking."

"A hambone wif meat on it always come in handy—fo eatin' or throwin' hounds off de scent. Ah spects dis dog likes meat same as bloodhounds."

"Jim, you're a wonder." Zane was amazed at this man's foresight. He could only guess how Jim had experience escaping from bloodhounds.

"If ole Jim was still at de widow's, ah spect you boys be back at dat house, shot dead or chewed up," he added.

Zane had even more respect for this freed slave and knew why Tom and Huck always included him in their dangerous schemes.

Zane looked at Jim, who was pivoting the oars inboard along the gunwales. "How come you didn't use your gun on that dog?"

"No need. He only be actin' like a dog and doing his duty. Not like a man who can hate."

"But he was probably trained by men to be a guard dog and kill any strangers."

Jim nodded. "Ah spect dat be agin his nature, but if ah seen him hurtin' you boys, or comin' fo' me, I'da busted him 'cross de nose. Dat be a dog's tender spot."

"You wouldn't a'shot him?"

"Don't speck so, lessen to save m'life. Ah don't believe in killing none o' God's creatures lessen it's a cow or a pig if you gots to have sumpin' to eat."

"Well that adventure didn't go as planned," Zane said.

"No," Tom replied, apparently recovered and brash once again. "But we couldn't a planned it no better."

"How so?"

"Now we got a mystery to figure out."

"That was Chigger Smealey in that room," Huck said.

"It was for sure," Tom said. "What do you reckon he's doing back here? Up to no good, I'll wager."

"Well, you heard what they said. They got some kind of illegal scheme working."

"Shipping something to New Orleans for pay," Zane said.

"You reckon we should tell Judge Thatcher and let him and Sheriff Stiles handle it?" Huck asked.

Zane thought about this.

"I don't recollect them saying they was doing nothing agin the law," Tom said, slowly. "For all we know they mighta been talking about shipping sheep or beef cattle or something. He said they couldn't do it after the river begun to freeze 'cause they might lose some to the cold on the deck of a steamboat."

"He's paid somebody named Wilson at Keokuk for two more shipments," Zane said. "If this was something on the up and up, why would Smealey have said he wanted to get out now—afraid if he stayed in too long, he'd lose everything?"

"Dunno. But it sounds fishy to me," Tom said. "Howsomever, since they didn't say exactly what they was doing, nor mentioned breaking any laws, I don't reckon we can go to the judge 'cause we ain't got nothing to tell him."

Silence while they absorbed this.

"Do you reckon them three can track us?" Huck wondered.

"Don't see how. They never seen us in the light. And the chain and the lantern we left behind coulda belonged to anybody."

"And the hambone don't have no names on it," Zane smiled.

"Hucky, was you trying to shoot that dog?" Tom asked. "If so, you likely need some more practice."

"My thumb was sweaty," Huck muttered defensively. "Mighty stiff spring on that gun."

"Your chain snagged that dog's front legs just in time," Zane said. "Musta been your lucky shackle attached to it."

"No," Tom replied somberly. " 'Twas a clear case of Providence stepping in to protect us. That hambone and coal oil fire was likely Providence distracting him, too."

"Likely so," Huck agreed. "Anyways, we're still in one piece and ain't leaking nowheres, except from a few scratches."

"We best be looking fo' a towhead to camp," Jim said, after a pause.

"I don't want t' stop nowheres near that house," Tom said.

"We already drifted near a half-mile," Huck said. "Let's get the sail up. There's still a bit o' breeze. And we can row. Scout out a towhead toward the Missouri shore another mile or two downriver. Them three likely won't come looking for us, even if they got a boat. They ain't gonna risk running into an ambush. We could be the remains of the Murrell gang for all they know."

"Or the spirits o' the dead rising in the full moon," Zane said.

"Spirits don't shoot out windows," Tom said.

They hoisted the mainsail and caught the light westerly breeze. With Zane at the tiller they tacked across toward the Missouri side, angling downstream.

"The house is hid from here," Tom said, looking back and sounding nervous. "They can't see us unless they walked down to the shoreline."

The moonlight showed what appeared to be a narrow island and Zane steered the yawl toward the chute on the back side if it.

Only when the boat had rounded the wooded upper end did he realize his mistake. Moonlight revealed the chute to be only a long, swampy slough of tangled vines and overhanging limbs.

The breeze was cut off by trees on the Missouri shore, and the boat coasted into the labyrinth. As the near shoreline bent back, Zane realized the swamp was wider than it first appeared.

"This ain't no towhead," Jim said. "We needs to back out and go 'round." He climbed over the thwart and began to unship the oars.

The yawl drifted forward into tendrils of mist. Then fog became thicker, damp, and smothering in the stagnant, moldy-smelling air.

Jim rotated his oars, expertly pivoting the boat nearly on itself.

As the hull swung around with the help of the rudder, a bright shaft of moonlight made the fog ahead appear to be thick smoke.

"Look!" Tom gasped, pointing.

Zane and Huck swiveled their heads. There, dimly silhouetted in the moonlit fog, was the outline of a steamboat.

"How'd that thing get in here?" Zane wondered.

"Is it real?" Huck asked. "Looks all shadow-like. Mebbe a ghost ship."

"It's the fog," Tom said, looking around at the swampy tangle. "Might be an old wreck that's caught up in here."

"No! It's moving," Zane said. "Look!"

"It's some kind of reflection," Tom said, apparently struggling to find a logical explanation to calm them all. "The moonlight's casting the steamer's shadow on the fog from the other side."

"Shh! Listen!"

Zane held his breath. At first, the only sound was the lapping of water against the hull of their boat and the throaty croak of a frog. Then came the steady swishing of a paddle wheel and the image slowly faded from the fogbank.

Zane exhaled with a mighty sigh. "You're right. Must be on the lower end of the chute."

About thirty seconds later, the churning noise of the paddle wheels ceased and a half-minute later, the slight ripples from it rocked their yawl.

"See there!" Tom said in a relieved voice. "Ghost ships don't make no wake."

Jim, who'd remained silent during this exchange, finally said, "Musta gone 'round de bottom o' de island, and we ain't able to see it or hear it no mo." He dug in his oars and thrust the boat ahead to retreat from the overgrown chute.

As he rowed the yawl out into the river once again, they saw a stern-wheeler steaming upstream, angling across the current, apparently to look for easy water near the Tennessee shore.

"Dat be de boat, sho enuff," Jim said. "It warn't no side-wheeler."

Tom pulled out the spyglass and trained it on the retreating steamer. The full moon lit up the river and the bulk of the steamboat with a pale light. The only illumination showing on the boat was the larboard running light. "I can just make out the name on the side," Tom said. "Looks like S-T-Y-X." He snorted in disgust, lowering the glass. "Reckon the owner ain't never been near a schoolroom. Can't even spell STICKS."

"No," Zane said. "That's named for the River Styx. In ancient mythology, that's the river that divides this world from the underworld."

"Is dat so?" Jim seemed surprised. "I ain't never seen a boat wid dat name on dis river."

"Don't see no home port painted on her, neither," Tom added. "Can't tell where she's from."

"You know how they put those big copper pennies on dead people's eyes at funerals?" Zane asked.

"Sure," Tom said. "What about it? It's to keep their eyelids shut."

"That ain't the reason," Zane said. "That custom is really old, too. It's to give the dead person some money to pay the boatman who ferries him across the River Styx to the underworld."

"Whew! That gives me all-over shivers," Huck said.

Zane felt secretly proud he was able to enlighten these boys about something that went back many centuries—far longer than the nearly two hundred years he'd traveled back in time to get here from the twenty-first century.

"You boys look sharp fo' a towhead so's we can make camp,"

Jim said, pulling across the current with strong strokes. The wind had nearly died again.

"Reckon we best go downriver a ways," Tom said. "Ain't enough wind now to offset the current so's we can tack upstream."

"Dey be lots o' towheads around," Jim said. "Me and Huck didn't have no trouble findin' one befo' daylight every night when we was fixing to tie up de raf' and hide it," Jim said.

Sure enough, a quarter of an hour later, they grounded on a big sandbar that was thick with willows. They hopped out and dragged the bow up the beach and tied it off to a thick sapling. In another fifteen minutes, Zane and Jim had a fire of driftwood going while Tom was laying out the blankets and what was left of their food.

"Since that dog's likely gnawing on our ham right now, I'd best see if I can catch us something to eat," Huck said. "Hoecakes and greens ain't much of a meal."

Hardly ten minutes later, he hooked a good-sized catfish, weighing at least three pounds. Jim snatched it off the hook and got busy gutting, skinning, and filleting it on a flat rock.

Zane was always amazed at Huck's ability as a fisherman. He seemed to know the right place, right bait, and technique for luring a bass or catfish just when they were needed.

"I could never catch a fish that quick," Zane said as the delectable white meat was sizzling in the frying pan.

"We brought a can o' coffee grounds with some grubs and nightcrawlers for bait," Huck explained. "Ain't nothin' them mudcats like better—'lessin' it's a stinky doughball. In this bright moonlight, them fish is usually awake and ready for a midnight snack."

"Speaking of midnight, I wonder what time it is?" Zane asked.

Jim glanced at the moon. "Ah s'pect it be 'round about one in de mawnin.'"

Cold greens, hot fish, hoecakes washed down with canteen water hit the spot, Zane thought while he was attacking the food a few minutes later. "Now if we just had some ice cream for dessert," he sighed, finally setting his tin plate aside.

"Lot's o' folks be glad to have what we gots right heah," Jim said solemnly, wiping the grease from his plate with a last bite of hoecake.

"Amen to that," Zane agreed, thinking of the homeless beggars he'd seen on the streets in his own time. "Didn't mean to sound greedy or ungrateful."

They lounged on their blankets, content to rest after their adventure, listening to the night sounds of the river swishing along past a nearby dead snag, feeling the damp air beginning to chill. The earlier breeze had calmed and a light mist was rising from the river.

It seemed to Zane the earth was resting between seasons, drawing a deep breath before it continued rolling over into the hard cold of winter. Flies and mosquitoes were about gone, along with late summer heat. The air off the water would be cold enough for a blanket tonight. The moon was far over in the night sky now, but still silvering the river and their camp in the space between the tall willows.

Jim and Huck had loaded and fired up their pipes and were leaning on their elbows, puffing contentedly in the silence.

"What d'ya think we oughta do about Smealey and them other two?" Huck asked directly.

"I been studying on that," Tom said.

Zane would have been surprised if Tom had said anything else. He was always thinking ahead, planning, conjuring up some scheme or other, workable or not.

"Anybody heard about any big robberies up north lately?" Zane asked. "Maybe they're shipping gold coins to New Orleans."

"Ain't heard of none," Tom said. "Besides, if it was gold bars or coins they was shipping, they wouldn't need but one boat and one trip. Mine and Hucky's twelve thousand in gold fit into two heavy sacks."

"Mebbe we should let blame well alone," Jim suggested.

Nobody paid him any mind.

"Livestock rustling?" Zane guessed.

"Could be, but I don't think so," Tom said.

"Yeah," Huck agreed. "We come to know Smealey pretty good when him and Weir was holding us prisoners last summer, and he don't seem like he'd fool with no animals. That takes work. And he's lazy. You notice he was taking orders from that other fella tonight?"

"Maybe they're hauling expensive minks or stolen beaver pelts that's all the rage for men's hats now," Zane thought aloud.

Tom considered this. " 'Tain't likely. The trappers out west bring them beaver pelts down the Missouri River to St. Louis to sell them. That fella tonight talked like it was sumpin' come from Keokuk or farther upriver."

"Then maybe it's some kind of perishable food," Zane said. "Stolen off the warehouse docks up north. Boxes o' stuff that could be ruined by extremely cold weather."

"Hmmm . . ." Tom mused. "Would you take so much trouble and expense as them fellas seem to be doing for a bunch o' food put up in cans, or fresh corn or cabbages or melons? A whole boatload o' that truck ain't worth shucks. Maybe fresh-killed beef, but that won't keep unless they shipped it in winter. And he especially said cold weather might ruin whatever it is they was discussing."

"I'm not from this century, but if something valuable was stolen, and it was big enough that it couldn't be hid and had to be transported on the main deck of a steamboat, wouldn't the law be looking for that steamboat?" Zane reasoned. "It's a long way by water to the gulf, so how could they do it, unless they slipped around and traveled at night like Huck and Jim did on the raft? And a steamboat is too big to hide in the daytime like a raft."

Tom and Huck appeared to ponder that.

Finally, Huck spoke up. "The law wouldn't be after them if they didn't know nothing had been stole—or, if it was sumpin' could be hid in plain sight."

"Hucky, you likely hit on it," Tom said. "That's gotta be the answer. Now, we just have t' be detectives and find out what it is. Then we'll see can we throw sumpin' big as a church steeple into the paddle wheel to stop it."

They were interrupted by a muffled snore. Jim was stretched out on his back, blanket over him, his old coat rolled up for a pillow and his hat over his face to keep off the moonlight.

"Boys, I'm getting mighty tired, too," Zane said, standing up and stretching. "Think I'll hit it myself. We can talk about this some more tomorrow on the way home."

CHAPTER 5

Next morning, just after sunup, they passed the Grangerford house on their way north. Tom examined the place through his spyglass and said there was no sign of life. The broken front window had not been boarded up.

"It's still early," he remarked, lowering the glass. "Mebbe they's still sleeping. And the dog, too. Don't see no boat or canoe along the shoreline."

The disturbed graves they'd discovered were not visible through the bare trees and tall grass.

"We likely shook them up some last night," Huck opined. "They mighta left early this morning afore dawn."

"If they come here by steamboat, they had to hike two mile to the landing or rode horses they had hid in the barn," Tom said.

"Naw, I think a steamer could put in just below the Grangerford house," Huck said. "The bank is low enough there."

The sails began flapping as the boat luffed up into the wind. Zane thrust the tiller away from him and the boat swung slowly away from the shore on the starboard tack. "You reckon that stern-wheeler we saw last night might be their own private transportation?" Zane wondered. "We shoulda waited to see if it put in below the house."

"Wow! I never thought of that," Tom said. "We missed a chance to find out if that boat had sumpin' to do with them crooks. I'll wager it does. It might have picked them up last night. Jim knows nearly all the boats that steam up and down the river above St. Louis and he says he ain't never seen one with the name of *STYX*."

"Dat's so," Jim nodded.

"Mebbe that steamer is the one them crooks is using to haul their mystery cargo down to Orleans," Huck said.

"Best we not jump to no conclusions," Tom cautioned. "We'll just keep an eye out for that boat for the next week or two, even if it don't stop in St. Petersburg." He turned to Zane. "You ain't in school, so I appoint you as lookout to stay down by the levee with the spyglass and watch every boat that goes past or lands."

Zane was watching the curve of the mainsail and nodded. "It'll give me something to do and fend off boredom."

A stronger puff of wind heeled the boat and Zane yanked the mainsheet out of the jam cleat and let it slip through his fingers to spill some air from the main. The boat straightened up, but still clove the green water with a rushing sound as a bow wave spread out on either side.

The voyagers arrived back in St. Petersburg just at dusk, Sunday evening, November 4th. It had taken them four days to sail back upstream.

Tying off their yawl just below the cobblestone levee, and carrying their gear, the four trudged wearily up the street past shuttered stores. Lamplight was beginning to wink on in windows of houses here and there.

Zane held the collar of his jacket close around his throat with one hand, thinking it would likely frost tonight if the wind died. Daylight hours were shortening with the approach of winter, even though there might still be a mild spell ahead. Except for the general forecasts in the *Farmer's Almanac*, there was no way of predicting the weather. Though outboard motors didn't exist yet, Zane was grateful for the gusting west wind that had aided their quick return upstream under sail.

They stashed their utensils and blankets and sails in the woodshed behind Tom's house until they had time to haul it all up Cardiff Hill and put it in the Widow Douglas's barn.

The voyagers promised to meet and make further plans the next afternoon, then separated and went to their various homes—Jim and Huck to the widow's, Zane to his boarding house where no one was waiting for him, and Tom to face the wrath of his Aunt Polly for taking off without permission and leaving only a note. Zane guessed both boys would also be in for a switching the next day at the hands of the schoolmaster for playing hooky for a week. As a visitor to this time and place, Zane was relieved not to have any real responsibilities, but he did miss his family, and the parents who cared about him.

He was thinking again of trying to figure out a way to go home. But these thoughts were quickly banished when he opened the front door of his boarding house and caught the aroma of roasting meat. He was just in time for supper.

CHAPTER 6

Near Keokuk, Iowa
November 3, 1849

Margaret Fayberest glanced across the campfire at her fourteen-year-old daughter, Arminta Lucinta, who was stirring stew in a pot resting on an iron spider over the flames.

"It's ready," the girl said. She dipped up a portion into a bowl and handed it to her mother.

Margaret accepted the stew and set it on her voluminous skirt to warm her lap. Her mind was elsewhere and she had no appetite. She had to make a decision and she had to do it this very night. Her stomach tensed at the thought. If she made the right choice, it could save her daughter for a better life than she had here. But no one could predict the future. She could only do what she thought best.

The girl dipped up a bowl for herself, blowing on its steaming contents, then knelt down on the blanket to eat.

"How are you ladies this evening?" A tall, bearded man appeared in the firelight. "That stew smells mighty appetizing." He glanced at Margaret as if expecting an invitation to eat.

"Hiram," she nodded, acknowledging his presence. She pretended to stir the steaming stew, hoping her aversion didn't show. Since her husband had died of a strange fever a month earlier, Hiram Lester, forty-six-year-old head of this group of ten dozen Mormon converts, had been eyeing her. He already had two wives, and she purposely made herself unattractive so

51

he wouldn't try to make her the third. But only in the last week had she begun to realize he was actually more interested in her black-haired, blue-eyed daughter, Mint. And this alarmed her to the point of desperation.

With her husband gone, Margaret had no defense against this Hiram Lester. And without sufficient money of her own, she couldn't leave the group with winter coming on. Why had her husband been so attracted to this new religion? He had convinced her to join up for the trek to Salt Lake. So enthralled was he by this faith, he likely would have gone without her and their daughter if she had refused to join. So, quietly and reluctantly, Margaret had stayed with him. She really had no choice since he'd sold his sawmill and paid off the mortgage, leaving only enough money to buy a secondhand wagon, two mules, and a month's supply of food.

Fate had intervened a few weeks later in Nauvoo, Illinois, and he'd contracted some kind of fever from which he died within three days. Margaret had seen much of death in her forty years, but the quick, unexpected loss of her husband, Joseph Fayberest, seemed to devastate her. She and Mint were now on their own with no close relatives or friends nearby she could trust.

After burying Joe, followed by ten days of grieving, she got hold of herself and reassessed the situation just before the travelers crossed the Mississippi on flatboats to the Iowa shore.

Her husband, Joe, was the only one of the three who had espoused this new religion. She had kept her eyes down and her mouth shut among the group, planning to escape as soon as she saw an opportunity. Mormon teachings were not for her. Women did not seem to have much of a show with the Latter Day Saints. This new doctrine, except for a few odd twists, seemed to be a throwback to Old Testament times. The group was now camped on the edge of the village of two thousand souls—a place named

Keokuk—preparing to move on the next day. But the late season guaranteed they would not reach Salt Lake until next year. Hiram Lester had indicated they would cross Iowa before the worst of the weather set in and winter at a place called Kanesville on the Missouri River.

"It's only squirrel stew," she heard herself saying without looking up. "Used up the last o' the onions and potatoes. When this is gone, we're outa vittles."

Hiram removed his slouch hat and squatted on his heels, staring into the fire. The gray was tingeing his beard and tiny wrinkles fanned out from the corners of his eyes. He cast a couple of surreptitious glances at the lovely teen who had not spoken.

"I'll see to it that you get fresh supplies," he said, still eyeing the daughter.

Only a week before on the bluff above the Mississippi, Hiram Lester had addressed the group of one hundred and twenty recent converts. By the light of a roaring bonfire, he had stood on the tailgate of a wagon and outlined plans for their long trek.

Among many other things, he'd announced that no one need fret if an individual or family could not afford the long trip to Zion. Only this year the LDS church had formed a corporation called the Perpetual Emigration Fund Company. It was designed to ensure that even the poorest would be able to trek west to join their brethren. But money from this fund was only a loan to those in need and was to be repaid with cash or goods or services once the converts were settled in the Valley of the Great Salt Lake.

Now that her husband was gone, Margaret Fayberest and her daughter, Arminta Lucinta, fell into the category of destitute travelers.

"Margaret"—he had taken to using her given name since her husband's death—"we must all cooperate and get along if we are to reach the promised land." He glanced up at her. "We must do all we can for each other and set aside our own likes and dislikes for the good of the group. I need the help of each and every one to fulfill my duties." He again glanced at Mint, as if to include her in his statement. But Margaret defined the look as lustful rather than courteous. *You already have two wives. Why do you need my daughter?* she thought, biting her lip, and casting her gaze down to the bowl in her lap. But she knew the answer to that rhetorical question. Arminta was rapidly growing into a stunning beauty who would turn the head of any man.

"Captain Lester"—she used his honorary title—"we must excuse ourselves. Mint and I have a lot to do to prepare for our decamping in the morning and need to get as much sleep as possible."

"Certainly." He rose and put on his slouch hat. He looked at each of them. "Margaret, you and I must have a confab soon and discuss the future of your family." He touched the brim of his hat. "Ladies," and turned away into the darkness.

When Hiram was gone, Margaret handed her bowl to her daughter. "Mint, I've lost my appetite. Put this back in the pot and we'll save it."

The girl did as requested.

"You feeling all right, Mama?"

"I'm fine. But when you're finished eating, step into the wagon. We need to talk."

Ten minutes later, Margaret tied the wagon cover shut and sat down facing her daughter.

"Mint, that man intends to force you into marriage," she said, without preliminary.

"I know," Mint nodded.

"You're only fourteen, but men like Lester don't care."

"I'd rather die than marry that old man," the girl shuddered. "Ugh."

"I'm afraid he'll use his authority to force it. We'll be obligated very soon to that Mormon Emigration Fund for our sustenance."

"He can't force me. It's against the law."

"Maybe civil law, but not Mormon law," Margaret said. "I think polygamy is the main reason Mormons are being hounded out of established society." She reached into a nearby trunk. "Your father left us only a little money, and we must use it wisely." She paused with a small poke in her hand and looked fondly at her daughter. "Are you willing to take a chance on getting away from here?"

Mint's eyes grew wide. "What? How?"

"The train will move out tomorrow across Iowa. I have enough money for you to slip off and escape right now—tonight."

"Just me? You're not coming?"

"I'll join you as soon as I can, but I must first make sure you are safely away from his clutches."

"How?" She seemed on the verge of tears.

"Take this poke of gold coins I've been hoarding. After midnight, slip out of here and hike the two miles into Keokuk. Stay hidden until the steamboat ticket office opens early in the morning. It's likely near the river. Buy yourself a one-way ticket to New Orleans on the next southbound steamer. There should be at least two southbound boats a day. There's enough for a ticket and a little more. Your ticket will include food for the trip, so you won't need much cash."

"Why New Orleans?"

"I've written to your Aunt Rowena Medlin, who's the headmistress of the Saint Agnes Female Academy there. I'm mailing her a letter to explain everything."

Arminta looked anguished. "I barely remember Aunt Rowena. I can't leave without you."

"Don't worry, Rowena will take good care of you until I can break loose and join you. I may not be able to get away with our wagon and mules, but they're not worth a great deal, anyway. And I might have to forfeit them to repay the loan from the Emigration Fund. Fifty dollars of the money in that poke came from the fund. Guard it carefully." She leaned over the open trunk again. "Here. Take this as well. It was your father's." She handed over a small Colt revolver, butt first. "And here's the extra powder, balls, and caps for it."

The girl still looked distressed.

"Mint, when your father died, I knew you'd have to grow up quickly and take responsibility. Now I'm asking you to do this for me, but mostly for yourself. You have your whole life ahead of you, and I don't think you want to ruin it by starting off as the third wife of this Lester character."

Tears appeared in the girl's eyes, but she silently nodded.

"Life is a gamble, but we must make the best decisions we can and follow through with them. Will you do this?"

"Yes."

"Lester won't know you're gone for at least two days. I'll make excuses that you're not feeling well and are sleeping in the wagon. I can stall him until we're so far from here that he won't be able to come back looking. Then I'll tell him you ran off when I was asleep."

"Oh, mother, I'm scared."

Margaret hugged her daughter. "Just have confidence that Providence will protect you. And I have confidence in both you and the Almighty."

Arminta sat back and took a deep breath, wiping her eyes with her sleeve. "I'll do it."

"Take a few clothes and a blanket and I'll pack enough food to keep you going for a day. Keep that loaded pistol and your money in a safe place under your clothes—not in your handbag.

In this cold weather, you'll be wearing your big cloak with the hood much of the time."

They hugged each other again.

"Get some rest and I'll wake you after midnight. I'll see you again very soon—likely in a few weeks—and we can celebrate Christmas with Rowena in a warm climate, free of all this."

CHAPTER 7

Tuesday, November 6th

St. Petersburg, Missouri

Zane Rasmussen was pacing along the top of the levee trying to warm his chilled extremities. If he stayed in this village much longer, he'd have to find himself a proper coat to replace this ragged secondhand jacket, and maybe a wool hat as well.

He shivered in the north wind that was stinging tears from his eyes. It was time to hunker down in some protected spot. He jogged down off the raised levee and ducked behind several hogsheads of cured tobacco leaf stacked near the landing, awaiting shipment.

Hands thrust deep in his pockets, he glanced at the gray sweep of river to the south. No boats in sight. At Tom's instructions, Zane had spent the last two days watching the river, noting the names of boats that passed or, more often, landed at the village. But he'd seen no sign of the mysterious stern-wheeler, *STYX*. Maybe it operated only on the river far to the south or on the Ohio. Was it engaged in commerce or carrying passengers? Perhaps it was under private ownership and contracted to the three men they'd discovered at the old Grangerford place. But Chigger Smealey had never struck him as a big money operator. He was more of a sneak thief and opportunist—strictly small time. His scheme to extort the gold ransom from Judge Thatcher earlier in the summer had eventually backfired on him and his partner, Gus Weir.

Then again, maybe the *STYX* had nothing at all to do with the three men. He regretted they had not followed the boat in their yawl that moonlit night to see if it had stopped anywhere near Compromise Landing or the Grangerford house.

This day Zane had observed two northbound steamers and two southbound that had stopped at the cobblestone landing. Only one of the southbound boats had seemed interesting to him. And it wasn't the boat itself, but rather a passenger standing at the rail on the second deck that caught his eye. It was a girl about his own age wearing a dark-blue hooded cloak. Even from several yards away, he could see she was unusually pretty, with fine features, and thick black hair.

He sat down and leaned against one of the barrels, hugging his knees for warmth as he tried to recall the details of this unknown passenger. He'd observed her for only a few minutes as the boat discharged and took on freight. She looked too young to be traveling alone. But teens in this era seemed to be given much more leeway and responsibility. He pictured himself traveling alone on a train or airliner in his own day. It was a possibility, but unlikely. It was the girls in 1849 who seemed to be more protected. She probably had an older family member nearby. He wished he'd hurried aboard, avoiding the clerk, and introduced himself during the twenty minutes the boat was docked. But to what end? He sighed, dismissing the pleasant daydream.

These thoughts aside, he concentrated again on the three men he and the boys had discovered at the Grangerford house on Halloween night. He and Tom and Huck had agreed that Chigger Smealey was present. But Zane had been thinking about the voice and dialect of one of the others—the man who seemed to be in charge. He wished he'd gotten a glimpse of the face because he had a strong hunch he'd heard that voice before. But where? Zane hadn't lived here long enough to meet a great number of people. Yet this voice rang a bell in his recent memory—the sardonic manner of speaking, the cadence and deep quality. The slight dialect seemed more western than Missouri. But the identity hovered barely beyond his recollection, like a slightly familiar face in the shadows, beyond the circle of firelight.

The battery in his wristwatch had died a month ago, so he'd dropped the useless timepiece into a drawer at his boarding house, knowing no batteries for such things existed here. The sun was covered by an overcast, but he estimated it was nearly time for Tom and Huck to join him after school.

Sure enough, about twenty minutes later, the boys turned up at the landing.

"Nothing doing," Zane reported, standing up and stretching his stiffened limbs.

"Then Jim was right," Tom said. "No boat named *STYX* operates along this stretch of river."

The trio trudged away from the river toward the village, Zane relieved to be going somewhere indoors to warm up. He was hungry, but it was still a long way from six o'clock when the landlady at the boarding house would have supper on the table. She was as punctual as the grandfather clock in her parlor. Her boarders were on time or they waited until the next meal. And there were no snacks or sweets in between.

"I reckon it's up to us to bust open this mystery," Tom said. "I figured that boat would show up here, and we could snoop around and get a clue as to what it was about. Since it ain't put in an appearance, we gotta figure some other plan to keep them no-goods from smuggling their cargo to Orleans."

"Like what?" Huck asked.

"I dunno yet. Lemme think on it a spell."

"Maybe we could go back down to the Grangerford house," Zane suggested.

"Too dern far," Tom said, "and those three might not even be there this time. We'd likely have to set around and wait a few days hoping they'd show up again, and we can't afford the time. Mister Dobbins about wore out his arm and his stock o' switches on me and Huck for skipping school for a week. I don't favor giving him no more exercise like that for a while."

They had reached the corner of Hill Street and paused near Tom's white frame house.

"Mars Huck . . ."

The boys looked up at a light-skinned black girl standing on the sidewalk nearby.

"Lola," Huck said. "What're you doing here?"

Zane recognized her as the house slave of the Widow Douglas.

"The missus sent me to fetch you and Tom . . . and your friend," she added, taking in Zane. "She'd be obliged if you all come to the house for supper this evening. Vittles be ready in 'bout an hour."

A very unusual request, Zane thought. Something must be up. But he welcomed the prospect of a hot meal an hour earlier than usual. And it would likely be topped off by one of the widow's pies. She was a great pastry cook and did most of the baking herself.

"I'll ask Aunt Polly," Tom said. "Don't reckon she'd mind."

"Judge Thatcher coming, too," Lola said.

Now Zane was sure something was afoot.

"I'll be up directly," Huck said. "Tell her we'll all be there."

Lola, clutching the headscarf under her chin, ducked away into the cold wind.

CHAPTER 8

The widow's mantel clock had just chimed a musical five o'clock when Tom, Huck, Zane, Judge Thatcher, and his daughter, Becky, sat down to an elegant supper. The flames in the clean glass chimneys of the chandelier were casting a warm glow over the white tablecloth and gleaming silverware.

Lola, in a white apron and calico dress, carried in a steaming tureen of chicken and dumplings and set it in the center of the oblong dining room table.

The widow stood at one end and led the blessing. It was brief—a fact that Huck and Tom very likely appreciated.

Zane felt his attire was rather mean in this setting. He had few clothes and had only washed his face and hands and combed his hair to prepare. He noted Tom and Huck had on clean shirts. Did Huck and the widow dine like this every night? Unlikely she would have brought out her best china and silver flatware for an everyday meal. As the food was passed and conversations began, Zane glanced at Becky Thatcher. He hadn't seen her for several weeks. Huck and Tom saw her every day, because they all went to school together. She looked as fresh and lovely as ever.

As the meal progressed, Zane filled up on fresh white bread, green beans, home canned tomatoes, and chicken and dumplings. By the time dessert was brought out and served, Zane had nearly forgotten to speculate about the underlying reason for this gathering.

Lola served each of them a slice of lemon pie, with flaky crust. When Zane finished, he was stuffed, and only sipped at his coffee.

The widow dismissed Lola for an hour and the maid left the room, closing the dining room door behind her.

Widow Douglas stood up. "You boys are probably wondering why I asked you here," she began. "Actually, Huck doesn't get to invite his friends here often, but I do like your company now and again." She smiled at Tom and Zane and Becky.

"There is something the judge wants to tell you, and I thought I might as well make a pleasant social occasion of it. Since this also concerns Becky, I asked the judge to bring her along." She held out a hand toward Becky's father. "Judge, it's all yours."

Instead of rising, Judge Thatcher leaned forward on his elbows and looked at all of them. "I have some news concerning Jim's family." he began. "It's rather serious news."

Zane felt his stomach clench.

"No . . . nobody's sick or anything like that. But I actually wish it were nothing more than that. A couple of weeks ago, I rode over to the farm of Horace and Constance Albertson ten miles beyond Palmyra. I casually mentioned that I was looking for someone to look after Becky and my house and property when I'm not around. It seemed to me Jim's wife and two children had proven they were trustworthy and I'd like to buy them if they were for sale. I've known the Albertsons for a long time. They're getting up in years, and don't have the income they used to generate from that farm and figured they might be willing to give Jim's family up for a decent price. I hinted to the old couple it could relieve them of the economic burden of supporting three slaves they had no further need for now that the farm work has dwindled." The judge paused, cleared his throat, and took a sip of water. "Well, they were open to the idea and we discussed price. I made them an offer that was somewhat below market value. They said they'd think it over and to come back and see them this past Tuesday. We left it at that, and two days ago, I rode over there again. This time, I fetched along enough gold coin from Tom and Huck's stash to buy them, even if I had to wind up paying the going price, or even a bit more. I wasn't prepared for what I found." He paused and shook his head. "They told me all three of their slaves had been stolen."

"What?"

"Stolen?"

Zane was stunned, but, from the looks of Tom and Huck, the shock was even worse for them since they'd been planning and expecting to reunite Jim with his family.

"They were nearly in tears," Judge Thatcher continued. "Jim's wife, Ovelia, and the two kids had become almost like family to the Albertsons. Horace said he and Constance had agreed to give them up for the price I'd first offered, but they wouldn't consider selling them to anyone but me, knowing I'd reunite the three of them with Jim."

"Oh, Daddy, that's awful!" Becky gasped.

"How did it happen?" Tom asked. "You sure they didn't just run off?"

"They didn't run off. The Albertsons treated them very kindly. You'd have thought they were salaried employees," the judge said.

"Who coulda done it?" Huck asked.

The widow sat silently observing from the other end of the table. Apparently, she'd already heard this news from the judge.

"Jim's wife and kids had gone to a church revival on Sunday evening," the judge continued. "Long about midnight, the black preacher come knocking on the door and said a dozen armed white men came along on horseback with a wagon and forced about ten slaves into the wagon and drove off. Jim's family was among them."

"That don't make no sense," Huck said.

"Funny thing about it is this," the judge said, standing up with a glass of wine and pacing around the room. "The preacher said the blacks seemed to go willingly."

"Of course they would," Zane chipped in. "Their captors had guns trained on them."

"That wasn't the reason. The preacher wasn't close enough to hear what was said, but it appeared to him, the captives were given plenty of opportunity to go back into the church building. The white men had holstered their pistols and put their long guns into the wagon and were just talking, like they were trying to persuade the slaves to leave."

"Reckon it was some kind o' charm?" Huck asked.

"Mebbe they was mesmerized," Tom said.

"Jim would probably say witches had something to do with it," Becky added.

"The Albertsons seem to think these whites were abolitionists," the judge said.

"If they was, why didn't they take the whole passel o' slaves?" Huck wondered. "Likely spun a mighty convincing yarn, like the king done to fool them folks at the camp meeting down in Arkansaw."

"You boys have grown up with slaves and played with them," the judge said. "But have you actually put yourselves in their place? Have you really imagined what it would be like to be owned by someone, the same as a dog or cat or a horse, required to work for free, getting only basic food and shelter in return?" he asked. "No matter how nice you are treated, you are still another human's property. If an abolitionist came along and told you he was going to return your freedom so you could be your own boss, wouldn't you be tempted to go with him? Maybe not return your freedom, but give it to you for the first time, if you were born into servitude?"

The boys looked at each other.

"Do you think these men were abolitionists?" Zane asked.

Judge Thatcher shrugged. "Why else would black slaves go willingly with a group of white strangers? It's as good an explanation as any." He took a sip of wine and set his glass on the mantel over the fireplace. "The last two days, I've been pondering this and also did a lot of checking around and looking up recent news articles. I found scattered news items in our village newspaper and the files of the paper in Palmyra and in Keokuk that told of slaves missing from various towns and farmsteads in Missouri and Kentucky during the past few months. Not a great number, mind you, but more than could normally be accounted for by runaways. The reporters seemed to think it was due to an increase in abolitionist activity, sponsored by wealthy men and freemen's societies in New England."

The youngsters looked blankly at each other. Zane had not lived in slave society very long—just five months, and he was baffled. Apparently, the others were as well.

"Apparently the patrollers here in St. Petersburg have kept the village safe from abolitionists," the judge continued. "I checked with Sheriff Stiles and he's had no reports of missing slaves in this county."

"Does Jim know about this?" Tom asked after a minute of silence.

"Not yet," the widow answered, "unless he's heard rumors of it through the black 'telegraph.' "

"How we gonna break the news to him if nobody knows who or why his family was took?" Huck asked.

" 'Taken,' " the widow corrected him.

"Yeah, they're gone," Huck affirmed.

The widow sighed, apparently resigned to the civilizing task that remained ahead of her.

"Since Becky and you boys are good friends of Jim's and have shared many dangerous situations, I thought I'd leave that to you," the judge said.

Zane felt very sorry for Jim. Nothing in Zane's experience could compare with the pain this kind man would suffer when they broke the news to him.

"Shall we tell Jim now?" Tom asked.

"No," the judge said. "Let him get a night's sleep before you give him the bad news."

"I agree," the widow added. "I'll give Jim time off tomorrow if he needs it."

"The main thing we have to do now is find out where his family was taken and how to get them back," Judge Thatcher stated in an upbeat tone as if the resolution of this problem were just a routine matter of setting one's mind to it.

Simple enough, Zane thought. *But how?*

"I'm in a position to make inquiries among my colleagues on the bench. I'll try to find out if there is some new effort by these abolitionist societies to capture as many slaves as possible and spirit them into free states before the Fugitive Slave Act is passed—which seems to be a certainty within in the next few months."

"What's the Fugitive Slave Act?" Tom asked.

Zane had read about it in history but was fuzzy on the details.

"The bill is being debated right now," the judge said. "If passed and signed, it will prohibit anyone from harboring an escaped slave. Any fugitives, even those who've made it to free states, would have to be returned to their rightful owners or anyone hiding them could be prosecuted, fined, and jailed as a criminal."

"Why in the world would any politician vote for a bill like that? Don't make no sense atall," Tom said.

"Because there is a strong Southern faction in the U.S. Congress that is pushing it and might have the votes to pass it."

"But the president could veto it," Becky said, apparently knowing more about civics than Tom and Huck.

"True enough," her father said. "But it could be overridden by a two-thirds majority. Even some right-thinking Congressmen look upon this legislation as a way to placate the South and prevent the Southern states from breaking off and going their own way."

"Who cares if they do?" Huck asked.

"The United States would then be in grave danger of falling apart altogether. It's all very complicated and mind-numbing and is wrapped up in a compromise about California being admitted to the union," the judge said. "But getting back to the subject at hand, I have thought of a few ways you youngsters can possibly help." He pulled a folded paper from the pocket of his black frock coat. "Here is a list of three names and locations of owners who've had slaves stolen in the past month. They reported the thefts but I want you to visit these owners and see if you can ferret out some pertinent details the reporters missed or didn't think important. Ask questions, look around for wagon tracks, any physical evidence and so on."

Tom's eyes blazed at the prospect. "You can bank on us, Judge. Me and Hucky got lots of experience as detectives."

"Figured this might be your flavor o' coffee," the judge nodded with a slight smile.

"Where'd these blacks get stole from?" Huck asked.

"I picked out three places that front on the river between here and St. Louis—two medium-sized plantations and a farm of about two hundred acres. You shouldn't have any trouble locating them. Feel free to take a steamboat 'cause each of them has a private landing. Don't let on you're snooping into their business. You've had plenty of practice embellishing plausible stories, but don't stray too far from the truth. You can bet the owners'll be cooperative if they think the law is trying to track down their property."

Tom, sitting next to Zane, took the paper and spread it out on the tablecloth. In the judge's precise hand were written Barnabas Miles, Henry Slocum, and Clay Finley, proprietors of Elmwood, Riverbend, and Cypress Forest, respectively. Alongside each were details of river miles from St. Petersburg, islands and other recognizable landmarks.

Tom's face suddenly clouded. "How we gonna get outa school? We already tasted the hick'ry for playing hooky all week."

"Mister Dobbins told me about that when I asked his permission for you two to assist me. Told him the court needed you for a special favor. He was reluctant to let you go, but I assured him you'd make up any work you miss."

Tom groaned. "Aunt Polly won't be so easy."

"The widow and I have already spoken to her and she's fine with it," the judge said.

"When do we start?" Tom asked.

"Tomorrow—right after you talk to Jim."

"Can Zane come along?"

"Certainly."

"What about Becky?"

The judge hesitated. "Maybe another time."

"Oh, Daddy!"

"Let me put it this way: If you boys find anything useful, I . . . I'll think about letting Becky go if this leads to other developments—providing it's nothing too dangerous."

It was the nearest he would come to giving permission.

As Zane drained his coffee cup, he felt glad he and the boys and Jim had not told anyone about their Halloween adventure downriver to the Grangerford house. Becky had wondered why the boys had missed school, but Tom had just told her they'd been on an outing. It was a tale Tom would likely relate later to make her envious and eager to share future adventures.

"Well, that settles it then," the widow said, with a tone of relief, pushing back her chair. "Did everyone have enough to eat?"

A murmur of assent and thanks sounded as they rose to go.

Zane actually felt overstuffed. Maybe his stomach was riled from the tension of the news and the uncertain prospect of their assignment, both coming on top of a full meal. He wondered how adults like his own father could hold business luncheons. Surely, that wasn't good for a person's digestion.

CHAPTER 9

Arminta Lucinta Fayberest was cold, tired, and apprehensive. She had spent two predawn hours huddling in the darkness of an arched brick doorway near the Keokuk waterfront, waiting for the steamboat ticket office to open.

More than an hour earlier, she'd eaten the hunk of dry bread and cold chicken leg her mother had packed for her. But now she was thirsty and longed for something hot to drink. A full canteen of water was suspended on a strap from her shoulder and she sipped clean water from it. Certainly, there must be fresh water aboard a steamboat, but she'd never ridden a commercial boat before and had no idea what to expect.

At last, dawn began to streak the eastern horizon. She gave thanks to the Almighty for the end of the long night. Light brightened the sky, minute by minute, until she was able to distinguish the treeline on the Illinois shore. What time was it? Daylight came later on these autumn days, so perhaps it was time for the villagers to begin stirring and face another dreary November day. Unlike them, she was headed south into warmer, brighter weather. Slowly the letters on a sign a half block away became legible. The board swung on an iron bracket over the boardwalk, proclaiming the location of the steamboat ticket office. She could stand the waiting no longer. Picking up her small bundle of clothing rolled up in a gray blanket, she started across the street, stiffened limbs glad for the exercise.

Just concentrate on getting aboard a boat and don't think of what you're leaving behind, she told herself. She bit her lip to get control of her surging uncertainty and loneliness. The hood of her cloak hid her face from any passersby, and her right hand, thrust inside her deep pocket, gripped the carved walnut butt of the small Colt. Better to be overcautious and prepared for anything now that she was on her own.

The ticket office door was locked, but through the glass window, she could see the big hands of the wall clock. It was two minutes until seven. She looked down toward the river where a half-dozen small boats lay at the landing. Only two steamers were tied up, one apparently a ferry. She saw no activity around either boat. She hoped there would be a southbound packet along soon so she didn't have to wait. She longed to lie down somewhere and rest—somewhere safe and warm.

As she rattled the doorknob, the minute hand moved straight up to twelve and the soft chiming began. As if it had triggered a mechanism, a lean, balding man appeared from the back room, wiping his mouth on a cloth napkin. He removed a ring of keys from a peg and unlocked the door.

"Good morning, miss. I was just finishing a bite of breakfast." He hung up the keys and moved behind the counter. "What can I do for you?"

"A one-way ticket to New Orleans on the next boat."

He glanced at her. "If you're traveling alone, I reckon you want first-class cabin passage?"

She nodded.

He pulled out a sheaf of tickets and selected one. "If you change boats in St. Louis, it's a bit cheaper. But you'd have about a twelve to twenty-hour layover."

"Why so long? Aren't there lots of boats in St. Louis?"

"Certainly. Coming and going all the time, both on this river and the Missouri. But schedules have to be loose to allow for delays caused by weather, river conditions, and breakdowns."

"How much cheaper?"

"You'd save twelve dollars."

She hesitated.

"Might be worth it if you're not in a hurry."

"I'll take a straight-through ticket," she decided firmly. It was already a long trip and she didn't want to lengthen it. She tried to come across as worldly wise and mature. By keeping her cloak close about her and not throwing back her hood, perhaps she could pass for a rather short twenty year old.

The clerk tore off the ticket, then stamped and initialed it.

"What boat is this for?"

"It's good on any boat. If it ain't used, it expires in sixty days."

"When's the next boat due?"

"The *Morgan* should be here from Dubuque in about two hours. It's a through packet to New Orleans."

She groaned inwardly, already tired of waiting. The wagon train was leaving this morning, her mother had said. What if Hiram Lester discovered her missing? He was determined to have her. This steamboat office in nearby Keokuk would be one of the first places he'd come looking.

"Is there a café close by?" she asked.

"Sure is. One block west on the corner. Nelly's place."

She turned away from his gaze and retrieved a worn leather coin purse from an inside pocket, selecting two double eagles to pay the fare. She placed them on the counter and accepted her change, tucking it into her coin purse. "This ticket doesn't have the name of the boat on it."

"Where boats are running continuously, tickets are issued for the destination—not for a particular vessel. That piece of cardboard is good for a first-class stateroom on any boat you choose, as long as they have room."

She dropped her eyes, embarrassed she didn't know that, and

slipped the ticket into her pocket with the pistol. In this outside world, money melted away like a sandbar in swift water, she reflected. The cost of the journey had already eaten up nearly half the gold her mother had given her. But from here on her expenses would be minimal, so she wasn't concerned.

At half past ten Mint stood on the landing, watching barrels being rolled down the gangway as the *Morgan* offloaded its freight. She'd wait until the roustabouts were done before she boarded. No one was debarking, nor were any other passengers waiting to board. Apparently, a slow day for travel. Then she had a sudden thought that maybe all the cabins were already occupied. Would she have to wait for the next boat? But the worry and concern she'd experienced in the darkness of the previous night had vanished. She was full of hot coffee and confidence, youthful energy rejuvenated by flapjacks and eggs.

When the last boxes and sacks were carried on, she walked aboard, her rolled blanket over her shoulder, and stepped off the gangway next to the seated purser who was checking the freight.

He stood up, tucking his pencil behind his ear. "Who're you?" He looked her up and down.

"Here's my ticket. I'm going to New Orleans."

"This boat's not taking on passengers."

"What?"

"This is a special run. We're hauling only freight and cordwood."

"I just bought this ticket for a stateroom and the man in the office up yonder says you're going to New Orleans." She was tired of waiting and she could feel her face flushing at the blunt rebuff by this handsome upstart mixed-race young man. "I mean to ride this boat downriver."

"Catch the next one." He turned away. "Should be a boat

later today or in the morning."

Two deckhands were poised to heave up the heavy gangway.

"Hey, you! Hold on a minute!" she cried, startling even herself. "If you got an empty cabin, I'm taking it." She was on her own now and had to stand up for herself.

"No, you're not. Get off this boat, or I'll throw you off!" The purser turned to face her.

Her hand gripped the pistol in the pocket of her cloak in case he made an overt move toward her.

"What's the problem here?" a rough voice demanded. A short, deep-chested man was descending the forward iron stairway. He was hatless and wore a dark-blue wool coat with the high collar turned up. Thick, grizzled hair covered his head.

Mint didn't know who this was, but he was older and seemed to be in authority. "I bought a ticket to New Orleans and he says I can't ride this boat."

"I explained we're not carrying passengers," the purser said, stepping back out of the way.

"That's right, miss."

"Are you the captain?"

"No, I'm the first mate, Conrad Winger."

"You got room, and I ain't hurting nothing by taking one of your rooms. I won't be in the way."

"Actually, you will be in the way," Winger said, looking at her in that appraising way most men regarded her lately.

"How's that?" she demanded, still irritated.

"We're scheduled to take on three or four dozen passengers forty miles below St. Petersburg," Winger said, placatingly. "We'll be full up."

"I can scrunch up and make room 'til a few o' them get off later."

"They're all going down to N'Orleans," Winger said.

"You haven't got a closet or a storeroom I can sleep in?"

Mint asked, her voice almost pleading. "I can't wait for the next boat."

"Why not?"

"I just can't, that's all. It ain't possible. I got good reason." She was desperate. "This is sort of an emergency. No . . ." she corrected herself, "this is an emergency."

The first mate was still looking at her closely in a way that made her uncomfortable.

"Well," Winger said at last, "maybe we can make an exception in your case . . . as long as you have your ticket and all, and seein's how you're already aboard."

"Thank you." She couldn't keep the relief out of her voice.

The mate turned to the purser. "Enter her name on the passenger manifest."

"It's Mint Fayberest." She spelled it for the clerk.

"Mint?" Winger raised his bushy eyebrows. "Like 'mint julep'?"

"No. I ain't a Southerner. I'm from Illinois. My full name is Arminta Lucinta."

"Pretty," remarked the mate. "Like it's owner." His hard features softened slightly in a brief smile. "Assign her to number one stateroom. That'll put her closer to the galley." He nodded. "I'll see you later." He walked aft.

CHAPTER 10

"That's what I said," the burly overseer snapped. "They was all took at once. The ones left behind said a few white men came up with guns jest after daybreak on the back side o' that twenty-acre field and hustled nine of my best field hands right off into the woods. Ain't seen hide nor hair of 'em since."

He pushed back his broad-brimmed hat and regarded Tom, Huck, and Zane. "The master gave all this information to the sheriff already." He handed back the wrinkled letter from Judge Thatcher. "Why is a judge from another county sending boys to snoop around asking more questions about this, 'stead of getting on the trail with detectives or armed bounty hunters?" He snorted in disgust and answered his own question. "I reckon 'cause the law ain't got no idea who up and took these blacks." He gathered the lines of his ground-reined horse and prepared to mount. "I tell you what—the loss of them field hands has put a crimp in the master's operation. If he has to replace them, the market value would be well over thirteen thousand dollars. Lucky it didn't happen right at harvest time or this plantation woulda been in a fix for sure. But the master is still hot about it, and he's been taking it outa my hide and my wages for not payin' closer attention to keeping them field hands in check. Reckon he figures it was my fault, so I best be getting back to work."

"Mister Sheffield, sir," Tom ventured as the overseer put his foot in the stirrup. "Did any of the hands think maybe them nine went without being forced?"

"Hell, no! I told you the whites had guns."

"The judge come across information in another case that the slaves was cajoled to go off with them raiders sort of like the whites had come to rescue them," Tom hastened to add before the plantation overseer could get away.

"Well . . . one woman who was standing close by did say them nine didn't take much persuading with the guns," Sheffield admitted. "But the master don't take no stock in what she said, 'cause she's got a reputation for lying. We treat all our blacks good here. Plenty to eat, and they ain't overworked. I try to keep a close eye on 'em, but even so, they don't have any reason to run off. Even if they took it into their heads to run, where they gonna go?" He swung into the saddle and pulled his horse's head around. "If they didn't have kin or abolitionist friends in these parts, they'd be run down right quick with the horses and dogs and brought back here to be made an example of. We scoured miles around for a couple o' days, but the dogs tracked them to the river and the trail disappeared. You tell that to the judge." He spurred away toward a distant field where the boys could see several dark figures walking behind mule-drawn plows turning under the stubble remaining from harvested corn.

The three boys turned away, scuffing along the dusty path through the weeds toward the river nearly a mile away.

"This job ain't going like I figured it would," Tom said, sounding dejected.

"A detective is kinda like being a door-to-door salesman," Zane opined. "Mostly get doors slammed in our faces."

"Even with that letter from the judge, ain't no rich plantation owner going to pay no attention to three boys like us," Huck said.

"Yeah, we need an adult."

"We shoulda brought Jim, instead of leaving him with the

boat," Zane said before he thought.

"Naw. That would be worse," Tom said. "These folks wouldn't respect nothing Jim might say. He's black. No overseer or owner would talk to us at all with Jim along, unless we could persuade them he'd been rescued from the white raiders and had some valuable information. And he don't."

They quit talking until they finally reached the river and silently climbed into their yawl.

Jim rose from sitting on the grass and stretched mightily. He blew through the stem of his pipe, slid it into a side pocket, then untied the painter from a thick sapling. Shoving the boat off, he climbed in, wetting one shoe in the process. But he didn't seem to mind the cold water, Zane noticed, even when both his feet were wet. This former slave had been toughened to discomfort, if not to severe pain.

Zane settled at the tiller and Jim shipped a pair of oars and stroked away from the shore to put the boat in the current.

"Fine any mo' clues 'bout dem runaways?" Jim asked.

"Nothing we didn't already know," Tom said. "No wagon this time. Same as before—a few white men with guns stole nine field hands, slipped away through the woods down to the river, and left 'afore anyone missed them. And the field hands didn't try to get away."

"Must be sumpin' mo' goin' on," Jim said. "Dat don't seem right, no how."

The boys had not initially thought to include Jim in this venture. But the day after the dinner at the widow's when they broke the news to Jim about his family disappearing, he reacted as if he'd been punched in the stomach. He gasped and staggered back a step or two. In a few seconds, the enormity of the news began to sink in and Zane felt a pang of sorrow when tears welled up in the big man's eyes.

"Mebbe ah won't never see m' wife and chil'ren again," he

muttered, wiping a sleeve across his eyes.

In order to soften the blow a little, Tom hurried on to tell him the judge and the sheriff would do all they could to find them.

"Judge Thatcher is sending me and Zane and Huck downriver to three different plantations to see can we snoop around and find out more about slaves that was stolen from them places, too," Tom said.

Jim was all ears and eagerness. "Ah'll go wif you."

"I don't know, Jim. You should probably stay put in case the judge gets some news while we're gone," Tom said.

"Ah can't stands de thought o' staying 'round heah. Ah couldn't get no work done fo' thinking 'bout dis. Ah gots to be doing something. Ole Jim could help row de boat an' make camp, an' stan' guard and cook and such. Besides," he added, "you boys likely be getting in some kind o' trouble and ole Jim be dere to help, like all de other times."

Tom and Huck looked at each other and nodded. "We'd be glad to have you come along, Jim," Huck said. "Iffen it's okay with the widow."

"Dis be my family missing wid de others. She gots to let me go."

And she did, willingly. Zane thought she felt nearly as bad about this as Jim did.

"Maybe we shoulda brought Becky, instead o' leavin' her on that island to fix supper," Zane said as the boat gained the middle of the river and Tom and Huck began to hoist the sails to catch the slight breeze.

"Not likely they's gonna tell us anything much with her around," Huck said. "Them overseers would jest be ogling her."

"Well, I guess we should be grateful the judge finally relented and let her come with us," Zane said. "Guess he figured she'd be well protected with all of us around."

"You know, maybe there isn't any more to tell," Tom said. "I dunno what we was supposed to learn from these plantations. The slaves was just stole by a few white men with guns. In the case of Jim's family, they was spirited off in a wagon. Here, the dogs jest tracked them to the river where they got took away by boat."

"Wonder what kind of boat?" Zane said. "A big steamer or two or three little boats?"

"More 'an likely skiffs or punts if they only took nine slaves," Tom said. "Somebody at that plantation likely woulda spotted a big steamer and it coulda been stopped, or at least be traced later."

"Well, where to now?" Huck asked. "We ain't learned nothing new so far, and that Riverbend Plantation was the second place the judge give us to visit."

Tom pulled the map from his jacket pocket. "The last place is Cypress Forest, a farm owned by a man name of Clay Finley. He had six slaves stole."

"How far is Finley's?" Zane asked. "We been at this three days already."

"Hmm . . . Looks to be another forty-five miles or so."

Zane had been assessing the purpose of their mission. "Boys, you reckon the judge just gave us this job to keep us out of the way for a week or two?"

Tom and Huck looked startled.

"Why would he do that?" Tom asked.

Zane shrugged. "Maybe so he and the other adults and the law could work on this without us bothering them."

"I can't figure the judge would do nothing that sneaky," Tom said.

"Yeah. The judge always been straight with us," Huck agreed. "When he says 'yes' he means yes, and when he says 'no' he means no."

"Yeah, but we ain't been straight up with him," Zane said. "I was just thinking that we pulled a conspiracy over on the whole village, including the judge, with that Bigfoot hoax last summer. Maybe the judge is just doing the same to us."

"The judge never found out about the whopper we told," Tom said. "Unless Becky leaked the plot to him."

"Then maybe we're like the 'Baker Street Irregulars,' " Zane said.

"What in tarnation is that?" Huck asked.

Zane thought for a moment. More than forty years would have to pass before Arthur Conan Doyle would write and publish the Sherlock Holmes stories. "In the future, some stories will be written about a detective in London named Sherlock Holmes who lives on Baker Street," he explained. "There's a bunch of street kids in that big city who can go unnoticed where adults can't go and who can find out details and pick up clues about things that the detective can't. Holmes hires these boys to scour the city and find out information that will help him solve cases. This gang of street urchins and orphans are called 'The Baker Street Irregulars.' "

Tom grinned. "That's right clever. So you think that's what we're doing? Finding clues that adults can't find?"

Zane shrugged. "Possibly." He thought maybe this comparison would restore Tom and Huck's pride in their menial assignment.

All of them were silent for several minutes.

"Reckon we'll reach the Finley place before dark?" Zane asked.

"Hmm . . . not likely," Tom said. "Especially after we backtrack a mile or so to pick up Becky and eat some lunch. I know she fixed sumpin' good. Besides, it gets dark early this time o' year. Probably take us about eight hours to get there." He looked at the map again and the instructions the judge had written. "The name of this last place is Cypress Forest. And the judge shows there's a swamp along where the plantation fronts on the river. A swamp with lots of cypress trees. Gonna be a bit tougher to find our way ashore."

"Nothing is ever easy," Zane observed. "But there has to be a steamboat landing along there somewhere." He shoved the tiller away from him to put the boat on the starboard tack across the current. Their camp and Becky were upstream about a mile.

"I struck an idea," Tom said suddenly. "Since we didn't get nothing from the first two plantations, why don't we slip up on this place and not let nobody know we're there. Instead o' rousting up the overseer or the owner, let's go 'round a back way and see can we find some field hands away from the house and let Jim talk to them." He turned to the big man who was stowing his oars as the breeze and current moved the yawl. "What about it, Jim? If they know anything, they'd likely tell you afore they'd tell the law or a bunch o' white kids, mebbe hoping their fellow slaves would get clean away."

"Dat be a fust rate notion," Jim agreed.

"Good idea," Huck nodded. "Jim, you didn't have no trouble making friends with them slaves at the Grangerford place when we was there. You give 'em a bit o' money to get our raft back, and they liked you for that. They even hid you in a dry spot in the swamp and brought you food every day."

"And all along dey lets me know what you was doin' at de big house," Jim finished.

"Then it's settled," Zane said. "After lunch we'll make good time with a fair wind and the current."

CHAPTER 11

Mint Fayberest turned the inside door latch of her new quarters in the forward cabin and drew a deep breath, relieved to be safe at last. The room looked bright and cozy. A bunk of her own—what luxury! The cabin was even furnished with a small table and chair, washbowl, pitcher, and towel. Sunlight slanted through the louvered window, reflecting off the white-painted woodwork.

Tossing the blanket bundle atop the upper bunk she sank wearily onto the straight wooden chair. This certainly was a far cry from sleeping on a hard wagon bed or shivering over a smoky campfire—her fate for several weeks since her parents had joined the Mormon wagon train. She uttered a silent prayer of thanks for her mother's wisdom in urging this escape. Mint looked forward with longing to their reunion at her aunt's boarding school in New Orleans.

She sat there in the quiet sunlight, tension of the past day sliding from her like a physical weight. People were meant to be happy in this world, regardless of circumstances, her parents had always asserted. She forced herself to assume a new attitude, to anticipate a wonderful and exciting adventure. She had endured, but never enjoyed, the winter season in Illinois. Thoughts of wind-driven snow and bitter temperatures made her cringe when she recalled numb fingers and toes, a runny nose, and coughs of the grippe, lying feverish in bed with a mustard plaster, smelling wet woolen mittens steaming dry on an iron stove. This would be a journey in comfort to the Deep South where winter did not visit.

After a cold, tense night, the quiet sunshine and warmth of the room gradually worked its spell and she stretched out on the lower bunk, pulling her cloak over her.

Sometime later, a sharp rap on the door startled her out of a deep sleep.

"Lunch in the cabin, miss," a voice said.

She rolled over on the bottom bunk, throwing off her cape. "All right," she managed to mumble, hearing footsteps receding. She sat up and rubbed her eyes. The sky had cleared and the angle of the sun told her she'd slept at least two hours. Her forward cabin was far from the steam engine, but she felt a slight vibration through the floor. How long had the boat been underway?

Standing up and stretching, she glanced out the window at the red and gold autumn forest sliding past. She was feeling a bit more relaxed and rested. Now for some food.

Only three or four crewmen were eating and talking at one of the small tables. The mate had indicated the boat had no passengers yet, and this strange situation seemed to be the case. The steward set a bowl of steaming food before her. She was not used to being waited on but dismissed the thought as she dug into the hot mixture of meat and potatoes and carrots. At least its main ingredient was not squirrel, she noted with relief.

The first mate, Winger, was not in sight—a good thing. For some reason, he made her squirm. On the surface he was courteous and businesslike, but she sensed a brutality lurking behind those eyes—eyes that sized her up as if she were a slave. It was a way many men looked at her now so maybe this craggy-faced mate was no different. As she grew into womanhood carrying the burden of great beauty, it was something she'd have to get used to.

The meal was topped off by peach cobbler, a luxury she had not tasted in many a day.

Sipping the last of her coffee, and dabbing at her lips with a cloth napkin, she breathed a contented sigh. This was more than she'd ever hoped for. This would be a vacation to remember.

She felt the boat slow and change direction as the pilot swung the vessel inshore. Was this where the promised group of passengers was to board?

Going quickly to her cabin, she threw her cape around her shoulders, then opened the door to the catwalk just in time to see the boat nosing into a landing at a small village.

The sky had cleared but a brisk north wind made her flip up her hood and hook the cape at her throat.

She leaned on the railing and took in the sight of the deckhands offloading several boxes and barrels of cargo. One strode down the gangway with a limp mail sack over his shoulder and an armload of small parcels.

Where were these promised passengers? No one was waiting to board. She knew nothing about commerce, but how could a boat make money carrying only a few items of freight and no passengers while paying a pilot, cook, deckhands, steward, and purser?

Her eyes swept over the scattering of townspeople along the levee, most of them only curious spectators watching several muscular young men lugging aboard a few wooden crates of cargo and gunnysacks stenciled Blodgett's Rice. A horse-drawn dray was pulling away from the levee.

She again wondered why the mate had allowed her to take passage at Keokuk. Except for the crew, she had the boat to herself. Not likely a good thing if she had to call for help fending off advances of the mate—advances she felt sure would come.

In only a few minutes, the deckhands were heaving up the gangway and the pilot gave a blast on the steam whistle to signal departure. She started to turn back to the warmth of the saloon when she glanced down and noticed a boy about her own age staring up at her. His thick black hair needed a trim and he was holding a shabby coat close around him. He was young, but she'd seen street urchins in Chicago even younger. Two things arrested her attention and caused her to pause—he was wearing spectacles, which a tramp probably couldn't afford and most youngsters didn't wear, anyway. And he had an Asiatic look about him. Her curiosity was piqued. Thin frame obvious under the wool coat. Maybe a hungry student seeking a handout for food or boat fare. If he's waiting for someone to get off this steamer, he'll be disappointed.

She dismissed the thought and went back inside.

Mint spent the next hour exploring the boat, fascinated by the steam engine. Standing near the starboard pitman arm, she listened to the strong quiet sighs of the long strokes driving the paddle wheel at the stern.

The deckhands fed cordwood into the blazing fireboxes to keep steam up. As she passed them on her way back to her cabin on the boiler deck, she wondered briefly why they were all white. Wouldn't steamboats employ free blacks to work some of these main deck labor jobs? There must be some good reason she didn't understand. At least with winter coming on, the fires would keep the deckhands reasonably warm while they worked in the open every day. Did they have enclosed quarters to sleep when not on duty? Concern for their welfare was something that came naturally to her; she hadn't always been a privileged passenger.

There was nothing to read to pass the time, so she sat near

the window in her room and watched the wooded shoreline slide past, thinking of her mother having to explain how she had disappeared or run away.

Presently, bored and sleepy, she lay down on the lower bunk for a nap, her youthful stamina not yet fully recovered from the cold and sleeplessness of her escape.

She awoke in late afternoon, feeling rested. The boat had again tied up along the starboard shore. From her window she could see no sign of a village. Maybe this was a woodyard. As she looked, she heard a murmur of voices—many voices, like a swarm of bees—and suddenly from the forest trail a stream of blacks began to appear, walking along casually, conversing. Two white crew members, one of them First Mate Winger, were directing them onto the gangway where they streamed aboard. They had no baggage that she could see. A few did carry small bundles under their arms, and several women had possessions slung in shawls. The crowd kept coming—women, children, and mostly young, healthy-looking men with good physiques.

So this was the promised group of passengers. She had no idea who these people were or where they'd come from or where they were bound, whether slave or free. Their clothes were worn and shabby and some were shoeless. Not a single one appeared to have enough money to buy a bowl of soup, much less a deck passage on this steamer.

She'd never thought of herself as any higher class than a poor white girl. Yet, she was the wealthy, comfortable queen of England in contrast to this miserable-looking group of blacks. A sense of injustice and grief stabbed her stomach at the comparison.

Somewhat chilled, Mint stepped back inside and threw back the hood of her cape. How would there be room on the lower deck for all these people? But she didn't wonder long. The five dozen or more, led by the mate and purser and one of the pilots, swarmed up the fore and aft stairways.

"Okay, divide up and take any of these empty cabins," Winger directed them. "No more than five or six to a room."

There was a buzz of excitement as they looked at one another as if they didn't believe this could really be happening. The murmuring became low exclamations of surprise and delight as they opened the cabin doors.

"The rooms are all furnished with water and slop jars, and towels," the young purser added. "All the cabins are the same, so it don't make no difference which ones you choose."

One black woman with an infant in her arms stopped and faced Winger. "Sir, you sure dey ain't some mistake?"

"No mistake," he said gruffly. "Spread out and make yourselves t' home." He waved at the numbered cabin doors lining both sides of the saloon.

Mint watched from the forward end of the room as the sixty or so people dispersed into the cabins.

"Get cleaned up as best you can," Winger raised his voice to be heard above the general hubbub of their selecting rooms and deciding who would go where. There was still an air of disbelief as many of those in the crowd hesitantly glanced at Winger and the purser, as if the mate's directions would be suddenly rescinded. But no negative order came. They gradually became convinced they were to actually occupy these first-class cabins, with clean bunks and sheets. Only then did they hurry to make their choices and get settled in.

"The dinner bell will ring in two hours. Everyone will eat out here at these tables," Winger thundered above the excited voices. He turned and strode forward, looking at Mint as he passed. "I'll see you tonight in your cabin, missy," he said in a low voice. "We have a few things to discuss."

CHAPTER 12

Much to Mint's relief, Winger never showed up that night because just at dusk, the boat ran hard aground on a submerged sandbar. For the rest of the night, the mate was required on deck to direct the efforts by torchlight to free the steamer.

It happened at half past six when the tables in the saloon were crowded with the sixty-odd black passengers who were talking, laughing, and putting away bowls of stew and ripping apart fresh loaves of bread to sop up the juice. Mint thought it was like a family reunion or a picnic with a festive air. She stood at the forward end near her cabin and watched for several minutes. The captain and the mate were overseeing the operation as two stewards bustled about among the tables, ladling out stew from buckets, setting baskets of fresh bread on the tables, and refilling pewter water mugs. Even the purser was pressed into service as a waiter, and two deckhands who could be spotted by their rough clothes and clumsy attempts at this unfamiliar job. Many of the diners acted rather subservient and Mint guessed they'd never been waited on in their lives. Mint wondered why the passengers didn't just form a serving line; it would have been much simpler.

Since all the tables were crowded to overflowing, she filled her bowl and retreated to her cabin to eat.

Luckily, her bowl was empty when the boat struck, throwing her out of her chair onto the floor. The water pitcher sloshed its contents over the tabletop and her bowl rolled under the bunk.

A sudden burst of startled screams and shouts blended with the crashing of crockery and furniture.

She struggled to her feet and went to see what they'd hit and if the boat was sinking. The jolt felt severe enough to bash a hole in the hull.

Above the yells, and the tumult of spilled food and water, bells jangled as the pilot rang down to the engineer.

"All right, all right!" the captain was shouting, waving his arms for attention as he set up an overturned chair and climbed on it to be seen. "We just went aground on a bar of some kind. Happens all the time. Nothing to get excited about. Go on eating. We'll take care of it." He jumped down and followed the mate out the door and down the forward stairs.

Mint stepped out onto the port walkway and looked aft. The paddle wheel had stopped, then started again in reverse and thrashed the muddy water for a minute, then fell still once more.

She went back inside. Apparently, the boat was stuck fast. This was going to take some time. It was none of her business. She was only mildly irritated that her trip south was being delayed. But she quickly forgot all about the inconvenience when she spotted the chocolate cake near the coffee urn. She helped herself to both and carried them back into her cabin. Dessert was something she almost never thought about; during her childhood, it was only a rare treat.

Hours later, Mint wondered what was keeping her awake. Possibly it was the two cups of coffee she'd drunk with dessert. But mostly, she decided, it was the clatter on the main deck as the crew worked to free the steamer from the grip of its sandy prison. Gone were the sleep inducers—the smooth swishing of the paddle wheel, water sliding alongside the moving hull in the darkness. It was replaced by shouted orders, banging of wood and metal, and the light flashing through her louvered windows from pine knot torches in iron baskets carried about below.

She knew it had to be after midnight when she finally gave up trying to sleep. Getting up, she wandered out to the galley to return her empty dishes.

The coal oil lamps in the overhead chandeliers had been turned down. Only a handful of the black passengers were still up—several men talking in low voices at a table aft. One lone woman occupied a table near the forward end of the saloon.

Mint was aware of the social barrier of a white girl approaching a strange black anywhere in Southern society. But she was bored. Since she couldn't sleep, and this woman was alone and no one else was around, she approached the table. "Would you like a cup of coffee?" she asked.

"What?" The woman, who'd been staring into space, looked up.

Mint repeated her offer.

The woman appeared to be shy of forty years old, wore a plain cotton dress, and held a knit shawl about her shoulders against the chill of the night.

"I . . . uh . . . thank you, miss, but no."

"Mind if I sit down here a minute?"

The woman quickly glanced about to see if they were alone.

"I don't mind. Please sit."

Courteous, but uncomfortable, Mint thought.

Mint pulled up a chair. She didn't know how to proceed, so they sat silent for the better part of a minute. Finally, Mint said, "How long do you reckon it will be before we get off this sandbar?"

"Don't rightly know. I haven't been on a steamboat in many years."

"This is my first time."

"Are you traveling alone?"

"Yes. Going to stay with my aunt in New Orleans."

"All of us are going there, too. But, they tells us we have to transfer to another boat downriver somewhere."

"What?" Mint was taken aback. She'd purchased a ticket through to the southern port and had turned down the option of changing boats in St. Louis. "Then somebody gave me wrong information. I was told this boat was going straight to New Orleans."

"Maybe 'tis, but all of us been told we have to get on another boat. Leastways that's what the men in charge say."

"So, all your group are traveling together?"

"We are now. But we's—most of us anyway—from different places."

"Is this some kind of church group gathering for a revival or something?" Mint was confused.

"They cautions us not to talk about it, especially to strangers, but I can't see no harm in it, long as we're on the way now."

Mint waited for the woman to go on. Instead, she pulled the shawl closer about herself and leaned forward, looking intently at Mint across the table.

"Chile, how old are you, iffen you don't mind my askin'?"

Mint didn't want to admit to her age, but instinctively trusted this woman. "Don't say nothing about it, but I'm past fourteen."

"Not long past, I'll wager."

"Almost eight months."

"It's good that your auntie is going to meet you at the boat."

"I hope she is." Mint had no idea if her mother's letter would arrive before she got there. "You never did say where your group is going," she went on, shifting the subject away from herself.

The woman didn't reply at first. Then she said, "I don't think I should say."

Mint wondered what the big secret was; she was just making polite conversation.

"What's your name, chile?"

"Arminta Lucinta Fayberest. Folks call me Mint."

"That's a very pretty name. Where is your home?"

The woman had neatly shifted the subject back to Mint.

"I come from Illinois. Up toward Chicago."

"Are your parents living?"

Mint related how her father had sold his business and the family had started west on a Mormon wagon train.

"But he took sick with fever and died a few weeks back. I was able to escape from that train, but it wasn't because of any sickness," she said in a lower voice. Then she went on to detail how her mother had spirited her away from all the converts and the lustful wagon master at Keokuk.

The woman nodded, solemnly. "It's plain enough to see how an old man like that would want you," she said. "I hear tell part of that religion is about bein' Christian, but they hauled off and added a lot to the Bible and some o' the men takes more than one wife, like rich Jews did in olden times."

"That's so."

"Well," she said, leaning back in her chair once more, "I ain't about to judge nobody by what they claims to believe. To each his own, says the old lady who kissed the cow."

Mint burst out laughing.

The four men at the back table looked up, then went back to their conversation.

"You didn't tell me your name or where you're from," Mint said. "Or if you have a family."

"My name is Ovelia."

"Ophelia?"

"No. My folks didn't know how to read and write and they just named me a name they'd heard and somebody else wrote it down for my christening as Ovelia."

"Then you got your own name and don't have to share it

with nobody else." She smiled, becoming more comfortable with this woman. "Do you have any family?"

"My husband, Jim, but we ain't seen each other for quite a spell. No trouble betwixt us," she hastened to add. "He's a free man who lives over in St. Petersburg. Works for a widow there and sends us money when he can."

"Us?"

"Me and our two kids. Johnny and Lizbeth. Eight and ten years old. They's asleep in the cabin back there."

"Then I take it you're not free?" Mint asked in a low voice.

The woman heaved a great sigh. "Not yet, but it won't be long."

She didn't elaborate. Finally Mint said, "If you don't think it's none of my business, I won't ask, but I'd sure like to know your story."

Ovelia looked around again to be sure they were alone. Then she leaned across the table. "You seem like a young lady who's had a good upbringing. Can you keep a secret?"

"Certainly."

"No, I mean really not say anything to anybody until we're all off the river in New Orleans."

"Cross my heart and hope to die."

"Then I'll tell you. All of us—every one of our group—is a slave. We been snatched away from our owners by these folks on this boat who work for a group up north, called the Holy Redeemer Freedmen's Foundation."

"Abolitionists?"

"Yes."

"Then why are you traveling south?"

"They explained that to us. The captain of this boat said that slave catchers expect runaways to be taken straight over into Illinois or up to Iowa or Canada. But he said the foundation had a better idea to keep us from being chased or run down by hounds and caught. They would take us all down to New Orleans and out through the gulf on a ship. By sailing around Florida and up the coast to New York and Boston we'd land in the free states up that way and wouldn't have to take the risk of traveling overland. Once at sea, we'll sail off the coast a long ways to keep the law from spotting us. And most bounty hunters can't afford to hire ships to chase us." The dam of her pent-up excitement burst and the words of the plan came tumbling out.

"Really?" Mint's eyes widened as she stared at this woman whose courage far exceeded her own.

"That's the plan," Ovelia nodded.

Mint didn't know what to say. This woman and the other slaves were risking a lot more in their escape attempt than she, herself, had done in escaping the clutches of the Mormon leader.

"Did your owner beat you?" Mint felt embarrassed asking this, but she'd heard lurid tales of whippings, starvation, overwork, and other abuses by slave owners.

"Oh, no, chile," Ovelia said, seeming reluctant to call Mint by her given name. "A nice couple name of Albertson owned me and the kids. We belonged to them since Lizbeth was just a little tyke and Johnny a babe at the breas'. We worked hard but they treated us well. We had to help out in the fields onliest at harvest time. I generally boiled the clothes, built the fires, and did most of the cooking and cleaning and all such as that." She paused with a faraway look as if recalling those times. "That old couple even broke the law when they taught me to read and write on the sly. I been trying to pass that along to Johnny and Lizbeth. That'll be mighty helpful once we're free." She hesitated and then went on, "I might near didn't go with these white men when they come to the church that night with tales of freedom. But freedom is a powerful likker. And the idea just made my head spin. No matter how good that old couple treated us, we was still their property to sell if they took a notion."

Mint nodded, though she could never really understand the feeling of being enslaved.

"Just don't mention this to anyone until we're long gone."

Mint made a cross on her compressed lips as she and her girl friends had done when swearing each other to keep mum about some silly secret. Now that she knew what was going on, Mint almost regretted having asked Ovelia to share this burden of knowledge with her. She would still have to pretend ignorance.

"Do you need any money?" Mint asked after several seconds of silence. "I don't have much, but . . ."

"No, chile," Ovelia put out a restraining hand as Mint reached for her coin purse. "They give us all we need. No place to spend money on this boat, nohow."

Mint felt the paddle wheel begin to churn. Was the boat floating free? No. They weren't moving. She glanced back toward the stern and saw the wheel turning in reverse.

"I s'pect they's driving water up under the boat to wash away some o' that sand," Ovelia said. "If it works, that'll save hours of trying to pole across."

Just then, a young man came through the saloon, throwing a curious glance their way. He proceeded to the galley to help himself to a mug of coffee.

"See that fella?" Ovelia said quietly.

"The purser?"

"Well, he's going to cause trouble afore we get to the foot of the river."

"How so?"

"He was one of the men sent to meet us all back there in the woods before we come aboard."

Mint nodded.

"Well, his name is Clarence Davis; he's a mixed blood. His mother was a quadroon."

Mint took another look at the man who was striding out with

his coffee. She wasn't sure what a quadroon was. "I thought he was white."

"He passes. Story goes his father was a plantation master in Mississippi."

"Why is he trouble?"

"He's right haughty. Likely 'cause he ain't exactly white and he ain't full black, neither. Got a foot in both camps you might say. Seen his kind before. Handsome as all get-out and knows it. Tries to let on he don't need nobody. It's the devil that shines through them black eyes. And he's turned his eyes on Cynthia Simmons."

"Who's that?"

"A girl I been knowing about a fortnight whilst we were all being gathered and hid and commencing to meet this boat. She come from a plantation in southern Missouri, and is 'most as white as he is, and flighty. He's gonna make a play for her before this crowd gets off the boat at New Orleans if I'm any judge. Problem is, two or three o' them big field hands are tryin' to get her attention, too, and they resent this 'Clank' Davis, as they call him. There's trouble a'comin' for sure. I just hope it don't upset the plan for the rest of us before we get out to sea."

Mint let out a deep sigh. Was there no peace from strife anywhere? Was this what she could expect from being a grown-up?

"Guess I'd better try to get some sleep," Mint said, stretching and yawning. The noise on the main deck had diminished.

"Me, too. Those kids will be up early and full of vinegar I expect, and I won't be worth shootin' if I don't get any sleep." She smiled at Mint for the first time. "Once we get off this bar and down to the mouth of the river, I'll be breathing free air for the first time in my life. I wonder will it smell fresh and sweet as clover?"

CHAPTER 13

The yawl with the four youngsters and Jim was making good time with a fair wind, and a four-mile-an-hour current in the channel, but Zane and Tom didn't think they'd arrive at the Finley plantation of Cypress Forest before dark.

Tom consulted the map, which was only an approximation of actual distance.

"The way this here river twists and snakes back on itself, we could probably walk across some o' these oxbows and get there sooner," Tom said, disgustedly folding up the map and tucking it inside his shirt.

"Not likely," Huck said.

Jim also nodded solemnly, apparently taking him literally. "And plowing through all dem woods and vines and sloughs would take de tuck right out of a body. Dis way be longer, but de yawl's best. Slow and steady win de race."

Zane wondered if Jim had somehow heard about Aesop's fable of the tortoise and the hare.

"What's the hurry, anyway?" Becky put in, looking back over her shoulder at the red glow of sun that had dropped below the treeline. "We sure don't have no timetable. Anyhow, this beats sitting in Mister Dobbins's classroom all day long."

"We'll have to camp overnight," Zane said, " 'cause those field hands won't be working by torchlight." He knew nothing about plantation life but thought this probably made sense unless it was harvest time and weather threatened.

"That's right," Huck said. "We'll find a good campsite, maybe sleep in the boat and start fresh in the morning."

Being a relative stranger to this big river, Zane wondered how they'd recognize the plantation's river frontage if darkness overtook them before they arrived. They could sail right past it. But he said nothing. Best to wait and see.

As it turned out, there was still some lingering light in the clear sky when they saw a dense thicket of cypress trees on the starboard side, their broad, unique roots thrusting up from the quiet swamp. The place looked gloomy and foreboding, silent and deserted. No fish jumping, birds all gone for the day.

With sunset, the fair breeze had died and they were ghosting along with only the current.

"This gotta be the place," Tom said, breaking the hush that had fallen. "Wonder how deep that goes back in there?"

"Maybe we could row between the trees until we come onto solid ground," Zane suggested.

"Yeah, give it a try," Tom said.

Zane pulled the tiller toward himself and the boat swung into the stand of trees. As they slowed, Jim broke out the oars and stroked slowly, Zane steering. Even so, it was a tight squeeze through the dense stand of trees; now and then Jim had to raise his oars to maneuver between two big trunks, or push off from a cluster of upthrust cypress knees to keep the bow from striking.

"Why not light a lantern?" Becky suggested. "Shutter it so won't nobody see it. We need some light to get through here."

Huck dug out one of the coal oil lanterns in the bow and struck a match to the wick. The yellow light lit up the flat black water for several yards, just enough to navigate.

What they hadn't figured on was the stumps left after someone had cut a large section of timber at the waterline. Cypress was a favorite soft wood for coffins, piers, and canoes.

As long as it stayed wet it was resistant to decay.

Thump! They all lurched forward as the hull hit a submerged stump and slid off to one side.

What appeared to be an area of open water was really littered with unseen stumps. The yawl continued to strike them, scraping and tilting, sometimes balancing atop one until they rocked the hull violently to free it.

Jim rested on his oars. "Dis ain't no good," he muttered. "We's gonna bust up dis fine boat."

"Let's go back to open water," Zane said.

"Yeah. This cypress swamp can't be too big. We'll row downstream a mile or so and get on past it," Huck said.

They turned the yawl and Huck dropped the gaff-rigged sail to keep it from hanging up or being torn on a low limb. Jim carefully maneuvered back into the river, then began stroking smoothly with the current.

Becky doused the lantern, but they all stayed alert for steamboats.

As Huck predicted, the cypress forest thinned out and disappeared within a half-mile.

"Ain't no telling if we're still on the Finley plantation," Tom said. "But no matter. We'll hunt us up a good dry spot to camp."

"Hope there ain't no snakes," Becky said.

"We've had too much cold weather," Tom said. "They's likely gone underground somers." He looked at her in the gathering dusk. "But just so's you'll feel comfortable, you can sleep in the boat."

They bumped along the dark shoreline, until they found a dirt and sand bank that was three feet above water, level and dry with only a scattering of weeds. Fifty yards farther inland they could just make out a dark wall of forest, so felt safe from being spotted once they kindled a small campfire. In ten minutes, they'd gathered dead brush washed up by the last high water and had a cheery fire going.

Zane always marveled at how being warm and dry and sitting by a blazing fire gave him a sense of well-being. He was not really a night person. Even in his other life, he never stayed up past midnight, doing homework or even watching a movie.

Apparently, the fire worked its magic on the others as well, because they became more talkative and generally more optimistic in their prospects for the coming day, brightly predicting they'd find Jim's family.

On his penciled map, Judge Thatcher had only roughed in the general boundaries of the three plantations he wanted them to visit. The judge had included no topographical features, probably because he was unaware of them. The judge's detectives were on their own when it came to the details of finding their way.

They ate slices of smoked ham with some corn pone and talked. After supper, Huck and Jim broke out their pipes.

"Ah gots a good feeling 'bout dis place," Jim said, black eyes shining as he stared into the flames.

Zane wondered what this comment was based on. Maybe only a gut feeling, some kind of premonition, like prophecies he got from a hairball.

"I think we'll find out something important, too," Zane agreed, to keep up the good spirits.

"Sometimes, after things been going bad for a time, you just know good news is coming by-'n'-by," Huck said.

"Bad news don't last forever," Becky added. "Providence will give us a boost soon."

"Becky, as I recollect, we ain't told you about our little adventure downriver Halloween night whilst we was playing hooky from school," Tom said.

"No, you didn't. And I been meaning to ask you about that."

"This might be a good time for you to hear the tale," Tom

said. "Here, let me fill up your coffee mug so's you'll be warm and comfortable, whilst you listen. Jest pretend they ain't no ghosts or witches flying 'round outside our little circle o' firelight here," Tom smiled, returning the coffee pot to a flat rock by the fire. "After all, this is a pretty lonesome stretch o' river."

"Tom Sawyer, if you think you're going to scare me with all that nonsense about the supernatural, you're mistaken," Becky said, leaning forward, hugging her knees and sipping her coffee. "You recollect I been through a lot worse things than listening to a ghost story."

Tom, with a glance at the others, began to relate the adventure, beginning with the fact that October was a blue moon month, the second full moon falling on Halloween, the most active night of the year for spirits of the dead.

Then he proceeded to give a dramatic version of their adventure, throwing in all kinds of embellishments until Zane had trouble recognizing some of it.

"Since then we been doing some detective work trying to discover what them rascals was plotting," Tom finished. "We know it has to be something illegal, especially since Chigger Smealey was in with them."

"One of these days, you boys're going to get yourselves kilt, messing around with things that don't concern you," Becky opined.

A sudden illumination flashed through Zane's mind. "Wait!" He sat forward on the blanket and held up a hand to interrupt. "I got it!"

They all stared at him. Jim puffed out a cloud of smoke and gave Zane his complete attention.

"It just came to me. Ever since we recognized Smealey's voice that night, I been trying to recollect one of those other voices—the man who was in charge and giving orders." He paused. "It just hit me who that was."

They waited.

"It was the river pirate who came out of the fog that night on the island."

"What?" Huck's mouth fell open and he nearly dropped his pipe. "The one who had the dog and stopped that stray bullet, and give us that little poke o' gold?" Huck said.

"That's the one," Zane affirmed. "I'm sure of it. He had a unique way of speaking—not slangy or anything, like he'd had educated parents."

"Lordy!" Tom whispered. "We never learnt his name, but maybe we was right—he is a river pirate."

"We were kind to him and his dog, gave them food," Becky said, as if trying to recollect the details of that night several months earlier. "And all of us helped when he got shot in the leg. Tom got the bullet out and Jim put a poultice on it. Then we helped him get away."

"What do you reckon he's doing with the likes o' Smealey?" Huck wondered. "He seemed a good bit smarter than Smealey."

"Probably why he's the boss," Zane said.

"Well, that's a most interesting clue," Tom mused. "Now we know two of the men in on this plot o' theirs." He paused. "But jest now we got bigger fish to fry. We got to help the judge find what happened to Jim's family and all the rest o' them slaves that got stole."

The talk and speculation ran on for a while longer until everyone began to fag out. Conversation lagged, then ceased. Zane stared into the coals until he felt his eyelids falling shut. The others were doing the same and, by unspoken consensus, they roused themselves up and decided to retire. Jim and the boys wrapped up in their blankets around the fire, using their rolled-up jackets for pillows, while Becky climbed into the yawl that was tied up a few feet away. She used a boat cushion for a pillow and wrapped up in a woolen blanket that was as heavy and tightly woven as a horse blanket. In fact, that's what it was—two bright green and white horse blankets sewn together that had never seen the back of a horse. Her father had decided this was the only thing adequate to keep his daughter warm if she insisted on sleeping outdoors this time of year. Except for her shoes and coat, she slept fully dressed.

Fair as she was, Becky looked even paler in the gray light of dawn, Zane thought as he watched her frying breakfast catfish over the rebuilt fire. Everyone was rather quiet, getting the sleep out of eyes and limbs. Zane was glad for her company. The boys tended not to cuss when she was around, and were generally on their best behavior, going into the woods in place of an open privy.

Breakfast over, they stowed their cleaned utensils away in a canvas sack in the boat and set off, north by west toward the line of trees that marked the normal high-water mark of the river. Their strategy was simple—strike through the woods until they spotted signs of a plantation—domestic animals, out buildings, and any cleared, tilled fields being worked by slaves. At that point all of them but Jim would vanish into the underbrush. Jim was to slide up to the field and see if he could catch the attention of one of the hands. Although Jim carried the widow's pocket pistol, he would go unarmed in case something went wrong. The slaves would certainly not have weapons.

It sounded like a simple plan, but Zane wished they had some idea of how this plantation was laid out. As they tromped through the woods in the early, misty chill, making little noise in the damp leaves, Zane kept looking back to orient himself so that in the unlikely event they had to make a run for it, he'd know the direction of the boat. He kept an eye on the bleary sun through the fog. Two miles passed under their feet—all level ground thickly forested with hardwoods. But Zane wasn't too sure they'd been able to track a straight line.

Then they spotted a clean edge where the forest abruptly stopped a hundred yards ahead.

They paused and moved forward more stealthily. A cleared field of at least twenty acres spread out before them.

"There!" Tom whispered, pointing at six blacks moving about at the far left side of the field. "What're they doing?"

"Shh!" Jim said, holding up a hand. " 'Pears they's storing sweet p'taters fo' de winter in dat dirt bank over yonder."

They crept forward again, all eyes and ears.

Zane caught the unmistakable smell of pigs. Worse than a skunk, he judged. Hogs would be kept on this plantation for a supply of pork. And the animals were likely within easy walking distance of the main house for convenience of feeding and watering. So the main house would not be far from here.

Jim crouched at the edge of the treeline with the others gathered close behind him.

"Ain't no sign of de overseer." He scanned the field. "Lot's o' open groun'. I'll see can I slip 'round to de lower end and come up on dem field hands from the closest piece o' woods." He straightened up and stepped behind a tree. "You young folks stay back outa sight. Dat sun gwine to burn off de fog d'rectly and dey ain't much brush under dese big trees. If you goes to moving 'round, somebody'll spot you, sure, 'specially wif dat bright yallah frock o' Becky's."

Becky pulled her coat closed to partially hide the bright dress.

"We'll hunker down so low and quiet, even the squirrels won't know we're here," Tom assured him.

"We just wanta stay close enough so's we can see you," Huck said.

Jim nodded. "I'll see what de hands got to say 'bout dem dat got stole." Without another word he moved away, catfooting on the damp leaves. Within a minute he was out of sight.

Zane and the other three crept to the edge of the woods and lay down on a patch of green, soft moss behind the bole of a giant oak tree.

A long ten minutes later, Zane saw Jim emerge from the woods on the other side of the irregular field. Though they could hear nothing from a distance of two hundred yards, the slaves seemed agitated when a strange black man suddenly appeared from nowhere.

"They gotta be thinking he's a runaway," Zane said in a whisper. Their movements seemed agitated. Several of them were looking around.

"They figure there might be more," Becky said.

"Or they're making sure the overseer ain't close by," Huck said.

Zane wondered what kind of story Jim was telling them—or more important, what he was hearing from them.

Suddenly, Jim vanished into the woods and the slaves began to look busy as a horseman approached from the direction of the main house.

The man in the saddle kicked the horse to a trot, his bulging belly bouncing. He stopped near the small group of slaves and was gesturing with a riding crop.

"Let's get on back in case that man comes this way," Zane said, as he scooted backward before standing up behind the tree. "Go on. I'll keep watch until you're out of sight." He heard the others scuffling away behind him. Zane guessed the man on the horse was the white overseer.

The horseman finally moved away at a walk, staring into the adjacent woods on the opposite side of the field. He must have seen Jim from a distance, Zane thought, stepping away and then taking lightly to his heels in pursuit of his three companions. The slaves probably swore there was no one there, but the white man kept his head turned toward the thick forest. Zane hoped Jim was well hidden. "He ain't about to get off that horse, and go searching," Zane muttered to himself as he bounded away, trying to be as silent as a wild deer. "With that belly, walking must be a chore."

Zane saw Tom, Huck, and Becky hurrying through the woods a hundred yards ahead of him. He soon caught up to them and they easily finished the mile-and-a-half walk to the boat.

Becky climbed into the yawl, sat down, and pulled her coat close about her.

The three boys had everything ready to shove off when Jim finally jogged up twenty minutes later, out of breath. He gestured for them to go, and tumbled into the boat as the boys shoved the bow back and jumped in.

Zane scanned the woods in the distance, fearful of seeing the chubby horseman in pursuit, but the woods appeared empty.

It wasn't until the boat was in the current, and the mainsail up, that Jim spoke. He sat on a thwart and leaned forward. "Well I foun' out why dem field hands went off wif de white men," he said. "De whites say dey was from an abolitionist society o' some kind and was rounding up as many slaves as wanted der freedom. Same as other abolitionists, but dis bunch promise to take 'em all downriver to New Orleans to get on a ship and sail outen de gulf and up de coast to New York."

"Then Judge Thatcher guessed right about them being abolitionists," Zane said.

"But why didn't they all go?" Tom asked.

"Some reckoned it was too dangersome. If dey was caught it'd be de whip and maybe bein' sold down de river to cotton plantations in Loosiana and Mississippi—de wust hell dere is." He paused to take two deep breaths. "The woman who tole me dat say she woulda left, 'cepten her chile was up to de big house being treated fo' croup by de black housemaid so she warn't about to leave her baby behind. A young man say his mother was down sick wif swamp fever in one o' dem cabins, and he couldn't take off. Besides, de white raiders only had room for a dozen or so, and wanted de biggest, strongest men. Dem abolitionists was in a big hurry afore de overseer spotted 'em and peppered dere backsides wif buckshot."

"Did you let on what you were doing?" Becky asked.

"I wuz kinder vague about it. Dey figured I's a runaway too, and I went right along wid dat notion. Said I'd heard talk of abolitionists and dis big roundup goin' on and I come to see could I jine up."

"Well, I consider our detective work a success," Tom gloated. "The judge will be proud of us."

"Well, now that we know where they's all bound, we don't have time to go home and tell Judge Thatcher," Huck said. "It's good your wife and children will be getting their freedom, and all," Huck said. "But we got to head off that steamer and get you aboard with your family."

"I ain't got no cause to go up north," Jim said. "I's free right here and likes working fo' de widow."

"Then we'll catch that boat and take your wife and children off and bring them home," Becky said. "And my father can finish buying them from that old couple, the Albertsons." She brushed away the wind-whipped blond hair that was blowing into her eyes and burst out with a radiant, sunny smile. "Everything is going to work out just perfect."

CHAPTER 14

The stern-wheeler *Morgan*, aided by a slight rise in the river, was finally freed from the sandbar with no apparent damage to the bow and wooden hull. But they didn't get underway until the boat had tied off at a nearby woodyard to inspect the prow and sound the bilge for leaks before proceeding downstream.

Mint Fayberest spent most of those hours in her cabin, resting and making plans for her immediate future, but mostly to avoid the mate who was paying her increasing attention. She knew she'd found a friend in the black woman, Ovelia, but did not approach her to socialize when there were other blacks or whites around. Mint watched her from a distance in the saloon during breakfast and lunch the following day when Ovelia was at a table with her two children and several other blacks.

Mint ate by herself or took the food to her cabin. Even if the white crew and officers were from an abolitionist society, she felt uneasy around them. She wanted to stay clear of this morally right, but technically illegal activity that was taking place on a grand scale. Sixty slaves stolen from their owners and spirited downriver toward freedom. Would anyone try to stop this escape as the boat churned along with the twisting current through the heart of the South? Local law enforcement along the way could certainly stop the boat and take all the slaves off. The only way this evasion scheme could work, she reasoned, was if it were kept secret. But surely, with many people knowing of it, somehow word would leak out. No wonder all sixty blacks were to transfer to another boat somewhere above St. Louis. Ovelia didn't know why, but Mint assumed it was to throw off any possible pursuit by Southern authorities.

If this boat was trying to maintain any kind of schedule, being aground on a sandbar for a night and the better part of a day had probably thrown it completely off. Since this boat did not tie up for the night, it ran the risk of another grounding, but the crew of the *Morgan* showed no signs of stopping after supper as the early autumn dusk began to close down.

Mint felt a need to talk to someone so she waited near her cabin door in the forward part of the saloon as the purser lighted the lamps in their sconces along the port and starboard bulkheads.

The slaves, after two or three days aboard this vessel, were acting more relaxed. Not as many were looking suspiciously over their shoulders or staying out of sight in their cabins, only coming out for meals. This night, about fifteen of them lingered in the saloon, playing cards and talking as evening advanced.

Ovelia even motioned for Mint to join her and introduced her children, Lizbeth and Johnny. The children were shy and hardly spoke as they eyed this black-haired white girl, apparently not quite knowing what to make of their mother's familiarity with her.

Before the steward had bussed the tables, Ovelia snatched two thick slices of white bread and coated them with honey.

"Now, off to bed with you two. Don't forget to clean your teeth and say your prayers."

Taller, thinner, and lighter-skinned than her brother, Lizbeth looked at Mint with big eyes as she took the treat and shyly retreated.

Ovelia watched until the cabin door closed behind them. Then she turned to Mint. "They're getting big enough now they question things I tell them to do."

"Really?"

"Lizbeth more than Johnny. Not long ago, she asked me why we should pray to a God who let us be owned by other people. I told her there was slavery in the old times, too. Even more then. But that didn't mean we should forget God who made us. He let folks stew around with lots o' troubles so they could struggle to rise above 'em and prove worthy of heaven. Someday, God willing, we'd be free on this earth, too." She paused and toyed with her coffee mug. "When they were both younger, I just made it simple for them and said we worked for the Albertsons and they fed us and took care of us. Kinda like indentured servants. Then I had to explain what that was."

Mint smiled, amazed at the steady endurance of this woman.

"But now, freedom's 'most in our grip, and I want to keep calm about it. If I tell 'em the Almighty's delivered us from bondage like the chil'ren of Israel from Egypt, and then something goes wrong, they might lose faith in the Lord, sure enough. I got a nervous feeling somethin's gonna happen t' spoil all this. It seems 'most too good to be true. But, then, I don't want to go looking a gift horse in the mouth as the farmers say."

Mint chuckled. "If it all works out as planned, will you try to get word to your husband in St. Petersburg?"

Ovelia nodded positively. "First thing after I get a place to hunker down with the chil'ren somers up north. Been studying on how to do it. I'd write him a letter, but last I heard, Jim couldn't read. But I'll figure some way. If I send it in care of the widow he works for—I think her name is Douglas—he'll get it all right. I spend hours jest thinking and planning of how it will be. Um . . ." She shook her head, smiling eyes registering the anticipated joy of reunion.

"You been apart quite a while, I guess?"

"Years, chile, years. But it's all gonna be better soon. You can count on it."

They went on chatting and the talk turned to things like cooking and recipes and shortcuts the older woman had devised to save her owners money, so the Albertsons would not become hard up and have to sell her and the children.

"The black preacher say he heard tell a judge from St. Petersburg come 'round the place just lately making an offer to buy us. It give me the willies to hear that, but leastways there weren't no talk of them wanting to split us up. That's why, when them white abolitionists showed up, scouting 'round prayer meeting that night, I jumped at the chance to go with them. I figured if the Albertsons was down on their luck not able to work no more, I sure warn't about t' hang around and tempt them with all the gold they could get for us."

"Good thing you ran when you got the chance," Mint agreed. "Just like I did." She scooted her chair back. "I'm having another cup of coffee. Would you like one?"

"Lordy, girl, I don't want you waiting on me. I feel like the Queen of England."

Mint laughed. "That's something you better get used to, 'cause it won't be long before you'll be like everyone else."

Mint brought back two cups of coffee, sweetened with honey, and then lost track of time as the two continued talking for a considerable long time. Several of the other blacks in the saloon drifted away to their cabins, and a short while later Mint heard the clear brass bell on the hurricane deck being struck to signal the change of the watch. Surely it wasn't midnight already? It was good to have someone to pass the time with.

She paid no attention as a cabin door opened and closed and a light-skinned black woman locked it behind her. Her steps made no sound on the carpeted deck as she flowed along the side of the room and stopped at their table, gripping Ovelia's shoulder. "I need to talk to you—now!" she said in a low, husky voice. She barely acknowledged Mint's presence.

" 'Scuse us a second," Ovelia said, rising and following the woman.

Mint saw them retreat to a corner out of earshot of anyone else. The young woman whispered something in Ovelia's ear and then waited for a reaction but there was none that Mint could see. The light-skinned girl was extremely agitated about something.

Finally, Ovelia put a hand on the young woman's arm and said something. Mint could hear their voices as a low mumble, but the younger woman was anything but placated by Ovelia's calm demeanor. They spoke for another half-minute and then Ovelia pointed in the general direction of the cabin the woman had come from, and apparently gave her a command or a firm direction. The woman started back the way she had come.

Ovelia rejoined Mint at the table, her face troubled as they both watched the young woman unlock a cabin door and go back inside.

"Trouble?" Mint asked.

"Just the kind of thing I feared might happen." She blinked away tears. "Lordy, if what she says is true . . . we're all in terrible danger."

Mint waited silently for an explanation.

"You recall the other night I asked if you could keep a secret?" Ovelia said.

"Yes. And I have."

"Well, this time, I don't care who you tell because the word will be all over this boat before morning."

"What's happened?"

"I told you about that purser, Clarence Davis, who's the quadroon?"

Mint nodded.

"Well that woman is the one he's after, Cynthia Simmons.

They're in that cabin together—and drinking, too. I could smell brandy on her breath. Well, I guess he got so drunk he let a secret slip about this boatload of slaves." She paused and took a deep breath. "Cynthia said he passed out on the bunk so she locked the door and come running to tell me."

"Tell you what?" Mint couldn't imagine what could be this dire.

"She said Clarence offered to let her in on a big secret if she promised to run away with him as soon as this boat landed. She agreed, thinking it was just some silly thing, that didn't amount to nothin'." She paused again, as if reluctant to divulge some horrible truth. "He said he was hired to reassure any of us who'd suspicion a white man's word about where we were going. He said we're headed to New Orleans, right enough, but not to sail away to freedom. We are to be sold at the slave market!"

"What? How can they do that?"

"They got a man downriver who's making up fake bills of sale so's to fool the folks at the New Orleans slave auction. They'll think we been bought all fair and legal and can be sold again by the men who lied to us about being abolitionists from the Holy Redeemer Freedmen's Foundation."

Mint nearly choked on her coffee. "Do you believe this Cynthia is telling the truth? You ain't known her long. And why did she come and tell you?"

"I been sort of like a mother to her these past weeks."

"And what about this Clarence Davis?" Mint went on. "He'd likely tell any kind of lie to get her to do what he wants."

"Lordy, chile, anything's possible," Ovelia said, biting her lip. "But Cynthia ain't no harum-scarum girl. She strikes me as down to earth, even if she is a tease and flirty. She'd never come to me with a tale like that if she warn't rock solid sure it was so. Truth be told, I had m' doubts about this whole escape thing from the start. It seemed too good to be real."

"So why did she go back into the cabin with him?" Mint asked. "I woulda run as fast as I could the other direction."

"Ain't right sure. Reckon she wants to play along for now and not let him know she told. But she begged me to spread the word, so's to get our menfolk all riled up and capture this crew. The men in our group is mostly field hands and don't have no knowledge of running a steamboat, not even working as deckhands. But they can steer this boat as long as it takes to ram it into the bank and let us all scatter and get away."

"Where are we?" Mint asked, her mind racing. "If we're still alongside Illinois, you can get into a free state. If we're already south of that, most of you won't have a chance, once word gets out and they put the tracking dogs to work, and men on horseback come with guns."

Ovelia took a deep breath. "Never mind what comes later. We's got to figure out what to do right now. That Clarence Davis is passed out drunk in there. Iffen he wakes up half sober directly and recollects he's done let the water moccasin outen the bag, there's gonna be hell to pay. To save his own skin, he might be desperate enough to kill Cynthia, and say she made up the whole story."

Mint's heart was pounding. She and Ovelia stood silently looking toward the door of cabin 13 where Cynthia Simmons and Clarence Davis held the fate of everyone on board in their hands. Something had to be done—fast.

CHAPTER 15

The previous day, Tom, Huck, Zane, Becky, and Jim had a problem. They had not the slightest idea the name or description of the southbound steamboat that carried Jim's family. Was it a stern-wheeler or a side-wheeler? It could have already reached New Orleans by now, or even passed that city and be far down into the delta heading for a rendezvous with a ship in the gulf.

While they discussed the situation, they had beached the yawl on a towhead and decided to stretch out in the warming sun, build a fire, and cook up some catfish for lunch.

The November weather had turned benign for at least one day and sunshine flooded the river. There was still a chill wind out of the north, but as long as they selected a sheltered spot, it was almost pleasant.

Hungry as they were, they didn't bother to go far for driftwood, but only collected what little brush was caught in the nearby willows. By the time the small fire was blazing on the sand, Huck had skinned and filleted the fish.

Becky and Tom spread out the blankets and brought out the tin plates and cups.

"How far downriver are we from St. Petersburg?" Zane wondered aloud.

"Too far to go back in one day," Tom stated.

"The way the river twists around, that north breeze would be a fair wind a good portion of the way," Becky said.

"That's right. We wouldn't have to beat up agin it all the way in slack water," Tom agreed. "But it's still at least a two-day trip—maybe longer."

"Too bad we ain't closer," Huck said. "We need the help of the judge and the sheriff to get the law to stop and search every downbound steamer."

"You know, what they's doing is illegal in slave states," Tom reminded them. "This ain't just a matter of handing over Jim's family, or any other slaves. Them abolitionists will think any lawmen with guns stopping their boat is going to arrest them and take all the blacks into custody to return 'em to their owners. That crew would likely fight off anyone trying to come aboard."

They paused to help themselves to the steaming fish and cold corn pone.

Outdoor weather and exercise were the best thing for a good appetite, Zane thought as he sat down to eat. The coffee water was just beginning to boil.

They all stopped talking as they fell to and demolished the sparse meal.

Shortly after, they were all relaxed, warming their hands and the ends of their noses with steaming tin cups of coffee sweetened with molasses. Jim sat on a log smoking his pipe while the others lounged on the blankets.

"We's got to decide what to do now," Jim said, voicing the question that was in everyone's mind.

They all looked somber and no one spoke. Even Zane could think of nothing practical they could do at the moment.

After a long period of silence, Tom, who was a plotter, planner, and more capable of convoluted thinking than the others, finally spoke up. "You know," he began slowly, as if trying to piece a puzzle together, "when we was down to the Grangerford house and heard Chigger Smealey, the river pirate, and that other fella plotting, didn't they say they was hauling loads of something down the river? They said they'd make one or two more runs before winter set in hard and put a stop to it because cold weather would ruin their cargo."

"Yeah," Zane spoke up. "Smealey said he wanted to get out now and not push their luck because he and his last partner had lost it all when they didn't know when to quit. He musta been referring to him and Gus Weir who wound up losing the gold back to us and almost getting themselves killed by the Sioux to boot."

"But the river pirate said they'd already contracted for one or two more loads from someone named Wilson in Keokuk, and he didn't want to quit now and lose the payment he'd already made, or something like that," Tom followed up, beginning to get excited. "What if that load he was talking about was a load of slaves?"

"Sure," Zane said. "Humans would be froze by the cold if they were riding on deck, so their 'cargo' would be ruined."

"These two plots is likely related, sure enough," Huck said.

"I was too far away t' hear dose men talking dat night," Jim said, "but de two plots gots to be one and de same."

"Umm . . . Something doesn't sound right about that theory," Zane put in. "Can you imagine Smealey or the river pirate being part of an abolitionist society which is all about helping people and doing good works and freeing slaves?"

"That don't sound like Smealey, sure enough," Huck said. "His old partner, Gus Weir, hunted runaway slaves for the rewards. And Smealey jined up with him."

"But I don't think Smealey cared about that part of it," Tom continued. "He was in it for the ransom money—our gold—and he wanted to punish us, 'cause he thought it was his and Injun Joe's to begin with. Smealey ain't got no lofty principles. He'll join any scheme so long as he thinks he can get a good chunk o' gold out of it."

"You mean he could actually be working for a do-gooder society for wages, and don't care who he's helping or hurting?" Zane marveled.

"Yeah."

"That's why they was all secretive about their scheme," Tom said, "because around here stealing slaves and sneaking 'em off to the free states can get a man hanged or jailed." Tom said. "Who'd a figured it? Cheap, low-down crooks and thieves working for them religious folks because it pays as good as crime." He shook his head.

They all pondered this possibility silently, while Zane strained to recall all the words he'd overheard at the Grangerford house. "Right toward the end of what we heard, when Smealey gave in and dropped his objections, he said something about 'we funnel 'em through here, same as usual,' or words to that effect. He musta been referring to the Grangerford place."

"Makes sense," Huck said. "What better place to use for their headquarters? Any squatters who mighta been considering taking up lodgings there would have to figure on dealing with a lot more ghosts than anybody wants to get used to now that the feud has kilt off most o' the two clans. But the uneasy dead don't seem to bother them abolitionists none, nor the folks who work for them."

"So, I guess the only logical place for us to look next is the Grangerford place?" Zane asked, looking around.

They all nodded their assent.

"Are we upstream or downstream of that place?" Zane asked. "I'm confused."

"We's still upstream somers," Jim said. "I reckon maybe thirty or forty mile."

"He's right," Tom nodded.

"Then we can't start too early," Zane said, "or we'll arrive during daylight."

"Yeah. We don't want to be seen. Won't take us no time to sail that far with the current."

"Whilst we kill a couple hours, why don't we build up this fire so it's nice and warm and maybe take a nap," Zane said, yawning. The food and warmth had made him sleepy.

That was agreeable to everyone.

"And for a special treat I been saving," Becky said, "I got some cherry tarts the cook made up and sent along with me."

That news brought up the level of cheerfulness.

"I'll hike off to dem woods over yonder and see can I rustle up some dry driftwood logs to stoke de fire," Jim said. He got up, stretched, knocked the dottle out of his pipe on the heel of his hand, and trudged away.

The youngsters chatted and shared the cherry tarts Becky produced from somewhere in her reticule. It was a sweet treat Zane never expected to enjoy on this spartan river expedition. In his former life in the twenty-first century, he could have all the treats he wanted at any time and didn't appreciate them half as much as he did these tarts. The only things forbidden, because of a severe allergy, were peanuts and dark chocolate. In fact, this combination had caused him to become violently sick and pass out. When he awoke, still nauseated, he'd found himself on an island in the Mississippi River and it was June, 1849, more than one and three-quarters century in the past. Even stranger, he had met and befriended the living characters from Mark Twain's famous novels.

But tarts were something he was definitely not allergic to.

Before they realized it, more than an hour had passed, and Jim had not returned. The fire of sticks had burned down to only a few coals, and puffs of a chill breeze were scattering the ashes. The sky had gone from blue to opaque.

Tom and Huck began to cast worried glances toward the dense woods two hundred yards away.

"You reckon we need to go check on Jim?" Zane finally voiced the unspoken concern.

"Let's all go," Becky said. "Ain't nobody around. The boat will be safe. I don't want to stay here alone."

They all made their way around a thick stand of cane and started toward the bare trees whose tops were bending in the gusts of wind.

The youngsters were silent with their own thoughts. Without the reassuring presence of the big black man, Zane felt vulnerable, and he guessed the others were sensing the same thing.

Twenty yards into the woods, they saw plenty of driftwood, but no Jim.

"Reckon we should holler to see if he can hear us?" Zane suggested.

"Let's wait a minute," Tom said. "If there's some animal around, we'd best stay quiet. Could be a cougar in these woods."

Zane doubted that, but this was 1849, after all, and there were still many wild places along the river.

"With this wind, maybe a limb broke off and fell on him," Becky said. "Or he coulda tripped and broke a leg or twisted his ankle and can't walk."

Nearly fifty paces into the forest, they spotted a small, disarranged pile of dead wood, the ends of which showed white as if freshly broken.

"Look at this. An armload he musta dropped."

"Over here!" Tom beckoned.

"Fresh horse droppings."

They scanned the silent forest. Then each went to examining the ground. In a few minutes they had spotted the deep indentation of a heel print in the soft mud. "Looks like those big brogans Jim was wearing," Huck said, pointing. A little farther along, they spotted a few drops of bright, fresh blood on the dead leaves underfoot.

They looked their alarm at each other.

"Lordy, somebody's got Jim," Huck breathed. "I thought we was all done with hiding and running when we got off the river last year and found out Jim had got his freedom."

"It sure enough looks like somebody don't know Jim is free."

"Or don't care," Huck said. "Maybe somebody saw Jim out in these woods all alone and figured him for a runaway."

"Yeah, a fast, easy reward," Tom agreed. "Rode up quick and clubbed or shot him."

"Clubbed, maybe; we'd a heard a shot," Becky said.

Zane had an empty, fearful feeling in the pit of his stomach. "What're we gonna do?"

"You know," Tom said, looking around. "I think we must still be on that Finley plantation, or mighty close to it. See that field over yonder beyond the trees? That ain't no natural clearing. That there has been cleared and cultivated some time or other. Maybe just lying fallow now."

They heard the far-off cawing of two crows riding the wind down a leaden sky. Zane shivered at the lonesome sound.

"We got several hours o' daylight left," Huck said. "Let's go back and break camp and load up the boat. We'll get our guns and a lantern and come back here and see can we track this hoss. They's plenty soft ground around and that hoss has likely kicked up a lot of these dead, wet leaves."

It was no sooner suggested than the four broke into a run back toward their campsite. In a minute or two, the utensils were gathered up, thrown into a canvas sack, and sand scuffed over the fire. Camp broken, and the boat waiting and ready, they filled the lantern with coal oil, loaded and capped their pistols, and each pocketed several matches.

The four of them had gone from elation at discovering the

destination of the stolen slaves, to despair at losing Jim.

Grim and silent, they set off afoot in the gray afternoon. There was no talk, but Zane sensed their desperate determination and their nervousness at the unknown violence that could await them. But there was no time to go for help. Zane wished they had a hound or two to sniff out the fresh trail. None of them was a tracker, but they'd have to do the best they could. Jim had been missing less than two hours. Speed was critical if they were to find him.

CHAPTER 16

As it turned out, Mint and Ovelia were spared from making a life or death decision. They were both still staring at the door of cabin 13 when Cynthia Simmons came out again and locked it behind her, pocketing the key. She saw them standing at the end of the saloon and hurried toward them.

"You gonna spread the word?" she asked, terrified eyes wide in the dim light of the wall lamps.

"Cynthia, I don't know about this . . ." Ovelia said, placatingly. "Let's wake up a few of the men and decide the best course. Are you sure Clarence is telling the truth?"

"I can read men—especially this one!" Her voice was low and urgent. "When I told him I'd go with him, he said this boat would arrive early in the morning before daylight where we'd be put on another steamer and that's when he wants me to run off with him whilst the crowd is all moving around by torchlight. He's drunk, or he wouldn't o' taken the chance o' telling me none of this. He wants me bad and said he had a boat at this landing."

Before Ovelia could speak, Cynthia went on, almost breathlessly. "Lookee here, we ain't got no time to waste discussing this. We got to wake up everyone and take over this boat before we get to that spot. No telling how many men with guns or dogs might be meeting this boat in a couple hours."

"Girl, these grown-ups been slaves all their lives. You wake them up in the middle of the night with this wild tale, most of 'em ain't gonna believe you, 'cause they don't *want* to believe you. Even if every word you say is true, you ain't gonna be their friend by wrecking their dream of freedom." Ovelia paused and took a deep breath. "I tell you what—you go 'round to the cabin doors on this side and I'll take the other side. Just rap quiet and wake someone in each cabin. Don't make no fuss or noise. Tell 'em the bad news but caution 'em to stay quiet until this steamer comes to a landing. Be ready to make a break on-cet the boat has put in and tied up. If the crew tries to stop us by force, then so be it. Warn our people to be ready for anything and punish anyone who gets in the way. It'll be a riot, but maybe some of us will get away in the dark. Could be there's a few small boats at the landing we can snatch. Might give some of us a better chance than the woods. Horses would be even better. I don't know if this is a woodyard, or towhead or an island. Did Clarence say?"

"No. I was so upset by the story, I didn't ask."

"We'll just have to wait and do whatever we can." Ovelia paused for a moment. "I don't know none o' these men too well, but there's one named Leon who seems like he's sort of a take-charge giant of a man."

"I know him, and a couple others who could take the lead," Cynthia whispered eagerly. "We need some weapons."

"I seen a couple axes hanging on the wall down on the main deck. But we don't want no bloodshed if we can keep from it. Best tell them to try for some handy clubs offen that pile o' cordwood below."

Mint was in shock. None of this seemed real. The older woman had recovered quicker than she had and was thinking and planning ahead. But Mint was caught in the middle. She was white and would not be detained, even if the officers and crew forcefully tried to stop the escape. There would be bloodshed, she was sure of it. Mint wanted no part of this. If

Clarence had lied just to get this girl to run off with him, and the white crew really were abolitionists, they'd be stunned by the mass rush for the shore and the woods, but likely wouldn't try to stop it.

"Oh, poor Johnny and Lizbeth," Ovelia moaned softly as Cynthia started toward the nearest cabin door. "They ain't never gonna know no peace or freedom." She turned to Mint.

"Chile, this ain't none o' your affair. You best go hide in your cabin til it's all over and then look for a way to escape yourself. These are evil men, and they ain't gonna let you go off and spread the word to the law about who they are."

"Southern law ain't gonna care what they done to a boatload o' slaves!" Mint burst out, surprising even herself. She knew nothing about the law, but it just fit with all she'd heard.

"No, chile. They's some good whites in the South, too, who won't stand for murder. Now, go 'long with you and hide out until this is over."

Mint gave Ovelia an impulsive hug, then fled to her cabin, choking back tears.

CHAPTER 17

There was no evidence of other human traffic when Tom, Huck, Becky, and Zane reached the spot in the woods where they judged Jim had been taken. Everything was just as they'd left it nearly an hour before.

Huck had the big Colt Dragoon pistol, and Tom was armed with a small Smith & Wesson .32. They assumed Jim still had the widow's Colt pocket pistol if it hadn't been taken from him by now. Becky carried the unlighted lantern and Zane, except for a stout piece of wood a shade over three feet long, was unarmed.

They took their bearings on the pile of dropped firewood and the blood spots on the scuffed dead leaves.

"The hoss was headed thisaway," Tom said, pointing and taking the lead. "Don't make no noise and keep a sharp lookout. This horseman musta come up quiet on Jim and caught him unawares."

Huck followed close behind Tom while Becky and Zane moved off to either side and kept watch for any danger on both sides and behind them.

There was no beaten trail, and the horse's tracks in the dead leaves and bare mud were easy to follow. The leaves were so scuffed up, Tom at first thought there might be two horses, but then Huck said, "Jim's a big man. He sure ain't riding double up behind whoever got him. I'd bet he's got his hands tied to the saddle somehow and is just scuffling along with his feet on

128

the ground, likely with his head bleeding from being clubbed."

"You're right!" Tom said. "Lookee here, this hoss ain't going fast. See—these tracks is too close together for a gallop."

"That means they ain't making any fast time," Zane said.

"We'll catch 'em up soon," Becky added.

"We got to be careful we don't come up on 'em too quick when we ain't expecting to," Tom said.

They proceeded at a careful walk.

A half-mile later they paused at the edge of a cleared field.

"We forgot the spyglass," Tom said.

"Them tracks go right across that soft ground through the dead cornstalks," Huck said, "but if anybody's on the other side in the trees, we'd be spotted right off if we was to try crossing over that." It was a quarter-mile to the other side.

"We got to figure out where they's headed," Tom said, biting his lip and surveying the surrounding woods and open field.

"Don't you reckon whoever has got Jim would be taking him to the master in the big house to show him off?" Becky said.

"Yeah, he'd report to the boss first, and wait for instructions," Zane agreed. "And where is the big house?"

"If you're right about this being part of the Finley plantation, the house is probably back toward the river," Zane said. "Isn't that what we figured out when Jim was talking to those field hands?"

"Yeah, we did."

They stood, irresolutely.

"Hey, let's do it this way," Zane said, finally. "You three slip around in the woods toward the river and see if you can spot the house or any sign of Jim. There don't seem to be anyone hereabouts, so I'll creep across this field and follow the tracks."

"Too dangerous," Becky said. "What if you're shot?"

Zane shrugged. "It ain't likely, but if that should happen, maybe it'll just send me back to my own time."

"We done lost one of us in this operation," Tom said. "We don't want to lose another."

"I'll be careful. Besides, I'd bet anything nobody's within shouting distance of those far woods. Whoever is dragging Jim along, ain't got any reason to be watching his back trail way out here." The more he talked, the more Zane was convincing himself.

"Okay, then. You sneak across the field and we'll slip around and try to find the house and see can we spot Jim. You'd best take my pistol, just in case."

Zane shook his head. "I don't have any experience with a handgun. This club will have to do—if I need it."

"What kind of signal we gonna use?" Becky asked. "We gotta have a signal so we don't lose each other."

Tom thought a moment. "How about a whip-poor-will? Can you do one o' them?"

"I'm not sure."

Tom demonstrated. "That's a very natural sound," Zane said. "You use that and I'll use a rain crow. I can do a rain crow."

"Let's go, then," Tom said. "We'll watch you all the way across afore we start out."

With a last look around, Zane started jogging across the rough field at a steady pace, his footfalls in the dead weeds and mud making almost no sound. The horse and the dragging man—if that's what it was—made a rough furrow through the soft earth and corn stubble nearly as plain as a plow.

He reached the other side without incident, and paused, panting, to wave at his friends who were watching.

While catching his breath, he plodded ahead and shortly the tracks turned onto a well-worn path where he had to look closer to discern the hoof marks and the scuffing of Jim's shoes in the pine needles and brown leaves. He proceeded carefully, all eyes and ears.

A movement in the woods made his heart leap, but then he relaxed as a deer bounded away soundlessly some thirty yards from him. It was good to know that if he could sneak up on a wild creature like that, he could approach a horseman who was dealing with a captive and wasn't nearly as alert. But then he remembered that, unless his quarry had stopped for some reason, the horseman and Jim had at least a one- to two-hour head start, so there was little likelihood of catching up to them.

Zane guessed it was nearly a half-hour later he spotted a white clapboard house through the bare trees. He was wearing dark clothing that would help disguise his approach as he slid silently from tree to tree, taking cover behind a few small cedars. A place like this often had hounds around the house as guard dogs, for coon hunting and tracking escaped slaves. He prayed the north wind would carry his scent away from any such dogs.

He held his breath and listened. At first all he heard was the thumping of his own heart in his ears. Then he detected the steady chunk! chunk! of an axe in wood.

He got down on hands and knees and crept along until he could lie flat on his belly behind a fallen log and observe the back of the house and a couple of outbuildings.

And there was Jim, swinging an axe, splitting firewood. A few yards away sat a fat man in a wicker chair, a shotgun across his knees.

No one else was in sight.

Jim had torn off part of his shirttail and had it tied around his head. Zane thought it was to replace his hat and absorb sweat, but then noticed the blue cloth was stained with blood.

While Zane watched, another man came around from a side yard. He wore a wide Panama hat, white shirt and close-fitting tan vest, and black riding boots.

Zane guessed it was probably the owner. The fat man in the chair rose and said something to him, their voices coming to

Zane as an indistinct mumble.

The exchange was brief, and the plantation owner left, after gesturing and apparently giving instructions to the overseer.

The overseer said something to Jim, who wearily buried the blade of the axe in the chopping block and grabbed his old coat lying on the woodpile.

The fat man gestured at a two-wheeled handcart nearby that contained a one-man crosscut saw. Jim slipped a wide leather band over his head and diagonally across his chest and began pulling the cart toward the woods. He moved very slowly as if stalling, or fatigued and sore from the rough treatment.

The white man gathered up the reins of a saddled bay that was cropping the still-green grass nearby. Without taking his eyes off Jim, he shoved the shotgun into a saddle scabbard and then mounted.

Evidently, Jim had been ordered to take the cart and saw and cut more firewood to add to the stack in the yard.

Zane scuttled backward like a crawdad until he felt safe enough to get his feet under him and make a crouching getaway. Should he try to signal the others with his imitation of a cooing rain crow? Not now. He had to find a hiding place. Besides, he doubted the soft call could be heard at any distance.

He jogged around a long bend in the trail and stopped after about sixty yards when he spotted a small, bushy cedar tree that could conceal him. Zane heard the cart rattling toward him, then Jim hove into sight, leaning into the chest harness. Horse and rider followed at a slow walk a few yards behind. Zane noted the deadly shotgun remained in the scabbard. The overseer slouched back, his bulk filling the big plantation saddle, weight pressing on the horse's kidneys, the picture of sloth and arrogance.

Zane still gripped the gnarled club that was about three-and-a-half-feet long. His heart was pounding and he was trembling.

Here was the perfect chance to rescue Jim, but did he have the courage to take that chance? He had only one shot at this. If he didn't disable the rider on the first try, he'd likely be cut down by a blast from the shotgun. He'd never struck an adult before. Violent confrontations were always to be avoided, and his previous experience consisted of only a few childish rough-and-tumble fights with boys his own age and a bloody nose from punches thrown.

He gripped the club, perspiring under his jacket in the chilly afternoon. In his former life, in spite of his slight build, he'd been a better than average hitter on his Little League baseball team. This crooked club was not an aluminum baseball bat, but it was all he had, and he'd picked it up only for defense. But Providence had put this opportunity in his path, and it would likely be his lone chance to help Jim escape.

He took a deep breath and let it out slowly, trying to calm himself. Then he stretched his arms and flexed his shoulders. He dared not swing the club to warm up as he would have in an on-deck circle.

Jim plodded past the cedar tree, head down and pulling the cart.

Watching through the evergreen branches, Zane knew his best chance was to swing from the side. If he waited until the horse passed him, he might not be able to reach the rider.

The horse sensed his presence and began to shy just before Zane sprang out of hiding. At the last second, Zane judged that the horse's movement took the overseer's head just out of his reach, so he altered his swing to aim for the ample belly. He put all his strength into the level swing and felt the club sink in as if he were pounding a foam pillow.

"*Whoof!*" The rider's head snapped forward and his hat flew off.

The horse jumped sideways and the fat man, who was already

lounging back, tumbled off the far side. Zane snatched for the dragging reins and missed, but Jim pounced, cat-quick, grabbing the horse by its halter.

Zane caught a glimpse of the fat man rolling on the ground, gasping, clutching his midsection. Zane flung the club away, leapt for the horse, gripping the forward edge of the hornless saddle, and vaulted up. The horse was plunging, trying to jerk free of Jim's grasp of his headstall, but to no avail.

"Jim! Climb up!"

The saddle seat was so broad, Zane was sliding around on the slick leather, trying to keep from being flung off.

"Stay up dere, Zane. I'll jump up behind you," Jim gasped, pulling the horse's head around to the left as his foot sought the wooden stirrup.

In a matter of seconds, Jim was seated in the wide, deep saddle, clasping Zane in front of him and the horse went thundering down the trail, carrying them back toward the fallow field and, beyond that, to the river and safety.

CHAPTER 18

"Why didn't you signal us?" Becky frowned at Zane an hour later when the boys were preparing to untie the painter and shove the bow off the sandy shore.

"When you hear a mourning dove, wouldn't you swear it was away off yonder somers?" Zane asked, falling into the local vernacular. "It sounds so soft and far-off and lonesome."

"Yeah."

"Well, most of the time it ain't far atall—maybe less than fifty feet away. You just don't see it setting quiet on a nearby tree limb."

"I reckon that's so," she acknowledged as Zane took her hand and helped her step over the gunwale into the yawl.

"I couldn't have made you hear me," he continued. "Besides I didn't hear no whip-poor-will calls from Tom, but I figured all three of you were out there somers. And I was out of breath and mighty busy trying to save Jim."

"Maybe we shoulda had you yip like a coyote," she laughed.

"Coyotes generally don't make no noise in the daytime," Huck said, shoving the boat out into the current with one long oar. "Anybody hearing that in daylight woulda knowed it was fake."

"Well, the job got done and Jim is rescued," Tom said, sounding satisfied. "What about that hoss?" he asked, pointing at the bay that was dragging its reins and cropping the grass.

"D'rectly, dat hoss'll figure out he's got left, and he'll head on back to de barn where dey's food and shelter and other animals," Jim said, moving aside as Tom and Huck heaved on the halyard, hoisting the gaff and the attached mainsail. "We gots to make ourselves scarce afore someone up t' de house misses dat overseer and his hoss."

"Jim, you still got the widow's little pistol?" Huck asked.

"Lawdy, no, Huck. Fust thing dat man done after he busted me 'longside de head, was turn out my pockets whilst I was laid out and woozy. Mebbe ah gets de judge to buy another one if I gives him some money."

"I'll take care of it," Huck said.

A gust from the starboard quarter boomed out the big sail and the twenty-foot yawl heeled to the pressure. Zane eased the mainsheet and the boat righted itself. They shot out from the shore, a wave curling away from the cutwater.

"Zane, aim for the main channel," Tom directed. "With that northwest wind behind us, we'll be around the next bend and outa sight afore you can say 'scat.' "

"Jim, you hurt bad?" Zane called out over the wind noise.

"Ah don't think so, Mars Zane." He fumbled with the bloody shirttail bandage. "Ah reckon m' head's pooty hard."

"What did he hit you with?" Becky asked, cringing as Jim uncovered the bloody, untreated wound on the side of his head. Then she reached for a canteen and a handkerchief and began trying to wash off the dried blood.

"Ah can do dat, missy," Jim said, taking the folded cloth from her, seeming embarrassed that a young white girl was fussing over him. "Reckon it was a hunk o' wood or likely de shotgun barrel, but I didn't see him coming. Ah was fixing to carry dat armful o' dead limbs back to camp. By de time ah heard dat hoss coming up on dem thick pine needles, he was right on me."

"That's what we figured."

"You got any other wounds?" Becky asked.

"Nuthin' you'd notice," Jim said, flexing his arm. "Mostly just bruises and such. He might near pulled my arms off when I was tied to de saddle and dragging along beside dat tall hoss."

"Well, them that does stuff like that deserves what Zane give him," Huck said. "He's likely got a busted rib or two and you sure enough scrambled his insides so he won't have no appetite for supper."

"Did he say anything to you, Jim?" Zane asked.

"It's jest like you youngsters figured—he thought I was a runaway from another plantation, and he wanted to get all de work outa me he could afore m' owner come looking to claim me. Den he and dat Mars Finley say dey's gonna split any reward was on m' head. Finley say it be de least he could get for having his slaves stole."

Jim moved to lay down on a cushion in the bottom of the boat.

"You dizzy or anything?" Tom asked.

"Just a tad swimmy-headed. But hurts right smart when I move my eyes quick."

Zane didn't say anything, but assumed the big man was suffering from a concussion—how serious he had no way of knowing. But he began to regret he hadn't knocked the overseer unconscious—especially since the fat man had likely gotten a look at him before he and Jim made their escape. *But it won't matter,* Zane reasoned. *He'll never see me again.* He wondered what the outcome of this clash might have been had he accepted the gun Tom offered him. Would he have used a deadly weapon on the overseer? No. He'd never shot, or even shot at, another human and didn't think he could have done it, especially from ambush. But if it were the only weapon at hand, he would've had to shoot and at least wound the man, or let Jim stay in captivity. And the shot could easily have accidentally killed the overseer. He shivered at the thought. A remark attributed to Mark Twain came to him: If the desire to kill and the opportunity both occurred simultaneously, who would escape the hangman?

But pondering these "might have been" situations was futile and he turned his attention to the boat. No one spoke for a few minutes as the yawl bowled along downstream.

"Sun finally come out," Huck remarked. "But she'll be going down afore long. We need to cipher out a plan."

"What about that steamer with the slaves aboard?" Zane asked, directing his question to Tom. He knew Tom would have some idea what to do next—good or bad.

Tom nodded. "If they's a connection with the Grangerford place like we figured, I'd say that's the onliest lead we got and we'd best use it and get on down there."

"Jim, you said earlier you calculated we were thirty or forty miles upstream from that house," Zane said.

"Dat's near as I can figure," Jim said, from the cushions near the bow.

"We're making good time," Becky said, pulling her coat about her throat, and sliding down onto the floorboards out of the wind.

"I have a feeling we need to hurry," Zane said. "No time for supper." He pointed at a sack of provisions under a thwart. "Can somebody tear off a hunk of bread for me, and maybe cut a piece of ham, too? I'm mighty hungry all of a sudden."

Tom reached for the cloth bag. "Busting the bellies of overseers always works up a monster appetite," he opined with a straight face. "Let's all have a snack."

The yawl sailed at near maximum speed for the next two hours, with the additional aid of a favoring current. While there was still some daylight, Tom and Huck took turns using the spyglass to scan the bank, but couldn't identify anything familiar.

The sun set in a welter of red and gold as if to apologize for being absent most of the day.

An hour later they pulled close to the Missouri shore to allow a well-lit upbound steamer to plow past them, bucking the main channel in the dark. The wake rocked their yawl a minute after the boat was around the bend and its lights winked off.

They continued downstream with only the current, since the wind had died at sundown.

As time rolled along, Zane thought Jim's estimate of the distance was very likely too conservative, but he said nothing. Jim and the boys knew this river a lot better than he did.

The moon had not yet risen, and Zane kept them in the channel as best he could. When no steamers were within earshot, they let the current carry them along in the dark without a running light; hoisting a lantern a few feet up the mast interfered with their night vision.

It must have been past ten o'clock. Zane was fatigued from the excitement and stress of the day. His head continued to droop as he fell asleep at the tiller.

"Zane!"

"Huh?" He jerked up his head.

"We need to stay in the channel."

Zane saw they were sideways to the current and drifting down on a barely seen white sandbar.

"Here, let me take the tiller for a while."

Zane slid aside and let Tom take over. The moon was just beginning to rise.

"I been watching and we're in the second oxbow where the river loops back on itself," Tom said. "It's right along here somers that the Shepherdsons's property's located," he said, peering into the darkness.

"Seen any lights?"

"No. I reckon most o' that clan is gone to their rewards, too, on account o' the feud."

"So, what did they gain by all that fighting and killing?" Zane wondered, shaking his head. "I'm about as tired as a corpse, myself," he added.

"Let's tie up someplace and get a few hours sleep," Tom suggested.

"I'm all for that." Zane smelled tobacco smoke and saw a tiny red glow when Huck drew on his pipe.

"Hucky, can you give us a few strokes with the oars to move us along a little quicker?" Tom suggested.

They heard Huck move carefully, stepping over Becky and Jim, who were asleep. He managed to ship a pair of oars and began stroking smoothly without disturbing them.

"In about thirty minutes we should be near the Grangerford graveyard," Tom said. "I recollect they's a good spot below the mouth of the crick where we tied up before. It's all hid by brush and trees. We can stop there."

"Good."

Zane tried to stay awake long enough to watch for the Grangerford place. Directly, he spotted a single white light where he thought the house was located, but he could see nothing else and he heard nothing.

By the time Tom pulled the yawl in alongside the bank and Huck tied off the painter to a small tree, Zane guessed it must be close to midnight. He and Tom and Huck wrapped themselves in blankets and found spaces in the twenty-foot boat to stretch out on the long seats and floorboards to rest.

CHAPTER 19

Zane was slowly rising from a deep sleep and dreaming he saw a big diesel locomotive rumbling toward him along a railroad track. As it approached the crossing where he stood, he heard the shouts and screams of a fearful crowd nearby and saw panicked people leaping from the open boxcars of the moving train.

Then he awoke to the boom of several shots and realized the roar was not a train but the deep-throated bellow of a steam whistle over the shouts and screams of voices.

"What be all de ruckus?" Jim struggled to a sitting position, holding his head.

"Tom! Huck! Sounds like a riot!" Zane said, half awake.

"Up there somers," Tom pointed upstream.

Shouts and curses, the shiver of shattering glass, another gunshot blasted the night air, a woman's scream heard over the hollow thundering of feet on a wooden deck.

"Near the Grangerford house!" Huck said in a shaky voice.

"De feud done started up again," Jim said. "All dem kilt folks be taking it out on one another just like dey done befo'." He stood up in the boat, and leaned over the gunwale, trying to see around the thick brush on the bank.

"I never heard no dead people make that much noise," Becky said. "Nor blow a steamboat whistle or shoot guns, neither."

"Besides, it ain't even near a full moon tonight," Huck added. "If ghosts or shot clan members was to come out and go to haunting around where the feud was, they'd a done it on Halloween when the moon was big and orange as a punkin."

"Dast we light a lantern?" Tom wondered.

"Mebbe best we jest lie low and keep mum," Huck said. "We don't want to get mixed up in no war."

"Couldn't be no war," Tom said. "They's gotta be at least two armies to have a war. Could be a revolution, I reckon."

"In the night and out here?" Huck scoffed. "Who's revolutionizing agin what?"

They paused and listened to the increasing cacophony. Zane guessed it was about two hundred yards away—in the vicinity of the Grangerford house.

"We could jest slip away and drift on downriver, and wouldn't nobody see us," Jim suggested.

Having been a slave, he was likely all about avoiding strife and conflict, Zane thought. Besides that, he had suffered a concussion only a few hours earlier and wouldn't have been eager to repeat that experience.

Zane's stomach contracted; his whole being recoiled at moving toward the sound of that violent uproar. But then he heard himself say, "Didn't we come here to find out what we could about the plot to smuggle slaves down to the gulf?"

Silence greeted his question.

Finally, Tom said, "Yeah. What kind of detectives are we, anyway, if we run away from the sound of a fight? Leastways we have to go see what it's all about. If it ain't got nothing to do with the plot or the kidnapped slaves, we'll skedaddle."

"Well, light that lantern so we don't break our necks in the dark," Becky said. "We'll go have a look-see."

Tom and Huck pocketed their pistols and a minute later all five of them were forcing their way through the heavy brush tangled with driftwood that clogged the shoreline. The crashing they made was completely drowned out by the rumpus upslope from the graveyard. Zane led the way with the lantern, while Jim brought up the rear, mumbling something about foolish youngsters being "drawed to trouble like moths to a candle."

They finally reached the creek where their yawl had been moored Halloween night. Zane found a narrow spot at the upper end where they could step across on flat rocks to keep from wading in the cold water.

The moon had waned so Zane had to keep the lantern partially unshuttered near their feet in order to see their way across the open field to the graveyard.

As they neared the first clump of sycamore trees, Zane caught his breath and jumped back, colliding with Tom.

"What's wrong?"

"See that?"

"What?"

"Somebody there in the graveyard." A darker shadow had glided out of the trees and moved behind the scattered wooden crosses. Now it was gone.

"Naw. Just a shadow."

And, truthfully, Zane now saw nothing, and wondered if he'd imagined it. There was no wind so it wasn't a tree limb moving.

"Let's go," Huck whispered. "If it's a ghost, he'll slide outa the way." His shaky voice betrayed his cocky words.

They edged in among the mounds and sunken graves, Zane holding his breath, realizing he was unarmed.

The uproar a couple hundred yards away seemed to be subsiding slightly, but there was still shouting and the clatter of running feet and doors slamming.

Zane had to move carefully. He held the lantern low to light the uneven ground. The open grave they'd found on Halloween was around here someplace and he didn't want to fall into it. No sooner had the thought crossed his mind than he caught a toe against the mound of dirt that bordered the hole.

"Oooh!" a breathless voice moaned three feet away.

"Arggh!!" A cry of pure terror burst from Zane; he recoiled, a chill sweeping over him. For an instant his heart froze and then gave a mighty leap and began pounding wildly. He was on his hands and knees, gasping.

Someone was alive in the grave.

The lantern had clattered to the ground and rolled down the side of the dirt pile, plunging the scene into semidarkness. Zane's sudden fear blocked out everything else and he barely heard the gabble of voices when the others crowded up to see what'd happened. Tom snatched up the still-burning lantern and held it aloft.

A giant bat as big as a human swept its black wings around itself, crouching away in the hole, away from the light.

"Oh, lawdy, lawdy!" Jim groaned, groveling on the ground. "We done loosed a creature o' darkness."

Becky, Tom, and Huck were speechless.

"Please don't hurt me," came a quavering voice. "I ain't done nothing."

"Why . . . why . . . it's only a girl in a blue cape," Tom finally stammered.

Zane crept up the dirt mound to the edge of the grave and looked, his pulse still racing. The human mind could certainly play tricks on a person, he thought. Before Tom spoke, Zane, too, had seen nothing but a bat-winged devil.

"Who are you?" Tom asked. "What're you doing here?"

"Hiding. You ain't from the steamboat, *Morgan*?" she asked, looking at Jim and then at the younger people. "No, I can see you're not."

"We come off our own yawl downstream," Huck said. "What's all that racket up yonder?"

The girl stood up in the open casket that still rested in the bottom of the hole. "Slave revolt. About five-dozen blacks made a break to get off that boat soon's it landed. Some o' them's likely been shot."

"What?" Becky sounded aghast.

"Yeah. Get me outa this hole. I have to get away from here, so's that mate don't find me—nor none o' the crew."

"We're friends," Becky said, apparently glad to see another girl for a change. "We'll help you."

Jim reached down, clasped her outstretched hand in a big grip, and yanked her up to level ground in one quick motion as if she weighed no more than one of the spirits they'd mistaken her for.

"We need to get up there and see can we do something to help," Huck said.

Zane was not so sure. He was relieved when the others voiced a negative response.

"We be sticking our nose into a hornets' nest," Jim ventured.

"Best we reconnoiter first," Tom agreed.

Reconnoiter? Where did he get that word? Zane guessed Tom had picked it up from one of the books about medieval battles he was constantly reading in place of schoolwork.

"What's that?" Huck asked.

"Find out who's fighting and why," Tom explained.

"Douse that lantern, and let's go back down to the woods along shore and hear her story," Zane proposed.

The girl glanced toward the Grangerford house, throwing back the hood of her cloak that had kept her face in shadow. "I just hope my friends got away safe." She turned back to face them just before Tom shuttered the lantern, and Zane caught a quick impression of one of the most beautiful girls he'd ever seen.

They all shuffled away through the graveyard and then hurried across the open field to the brush and trees bordering the small creek.

Making sure they were well hidden from anyone, they un-shuttered the lantern, turned down the flame, and set it on the ground. Then they all sat or hunkered down around it near enough so they could just see each other in the dim light.

Mint nodded to each of the five others as Tom introduced them. Her gaze lingered on Zane. "I've seen you before, and not long ago. But I don't recollect where."

"I know your face, too," Zane said. "Oh, I know! I was on the levee at St. Petersburg and you were on a steamboat that stopped there briefly a few days ago." Zane started to add that he wasn't likely to forget a face as pretty as hers, but held his tongue.

"That's right," she smiled. "I was wondering if you were some poor foreign student."

He chuckled. "What's your name?"

"Arminta Lucinta Fayberest," she said.

"That's a mouthful," Tom remarked.

"That's why everyone just calls me 'Mint.' "

"Tell us, quick-like, what's going on up yonder," Zane said.

"I'm not involved in any of that," she hastened to explain. "I'm just a passenger going to New Orleans—or was a passenger. I'm not anymore." Then she quickly told why she was aboard, the taking on of the sixty black slaves, then how she'd been caught up in the violence when the real purpose of the trip was revealed. "I still don't know which of the stories to believe," she concluded. "But once the word was spread, nearly all the blacks figured they were being flimflammed and decided to make a break for it and get away as soon as the boat docked here."

"How did you get loose?" Huck asked.

"Nobody was paying me no mind. Soon's the gangway was down, there was a big rush to get off. At first the mate and the crew didn't know what was happening, but then they caught on and begun firing their guns in the air and shouting for them to come back. I waited a minute until the crewmen were all busy, then slipped out of my cabin and made a run for it. The gangway was too jammed up so I jumped off onto the muddy bank in the dark before they could get the torches lit. I didn't know where I was so I just ran as fast as I could and got into some woods and away from the river. Slaves were running past me in every direction, kids crying for their mamas, women screaming, people tripping and falling in the dark, men were being hit with clubs and one or two I saw were shot when they tried to swing axes at the crew who were looking to stop them. Lots of yelling and cussing—a real battle."

"Oh, how terrible!" Becky breathed.

"After running a ways, I found myself in that graveyard," Mint continued. "Had to hide somewhere until it was all over. Stumbled onto that open grave and jumped down in there to stay outa sight. Whenever the noise died down, I figured to slip out and start walking—maybe find some help come daylight. Couple minutes later I heard you moving along and saw the light. Thought it was someone from the boat, searching for escaped blacks, so I just scrunched down, hoping I wouldn't be spotted. You know the rest."

They were all silent for a minute.

"Do you reckon I could come along, and you could drop me off at the next town or village where I could catch another steamboat to New Orleans? I'd be ever so grateful," Mint said, glancing at each one of them.

"Sure." Zane thought he spoke for his group.

Another silence, as they all wondered what to do next. Could they just walk away from this—maybe report it to the next sheriff or constable they could find?

"You know . . ." Tom said very slowly. "We jest found what we been looking for—the stolen slaves."

147

"The ones we thought were being smuggled out of bondage through the gulf," Zane added.

They all looked at each other.

"My wife and chil'ren musta been on dat boat," Jim said. "If dey got away, they could be out dere in de woods somers."

"Then we can't leave until we search for them," Zane stated. "That's the main reason we're here."

"Can't see nuffin in de dark o' de moon," Jim said. "But jest dis minute I feel de night breeze fanning over de water, so daylight be onliest a short way off."

"What's your wife's name?" Mint asked.

"Ovelia. And my chil'ren's Johnny and Lizbeth."

"Oh, my!"

They all looked at Mint.

"I met your wife and had several long talks with her," Mint said. "A wonderful woman. She spoke about reuniting with you, Jim. I saw your two kids, too. Ovelia told me Lizbeth's hearing has come back so she can understand what people are saying if they speak slowly and plainly."

"Thank de Lawd!" Jim, who usually presented a stoic face to the world in spite of misery or joy, smiled so wide his eyes nearly disappeared in the crinkled folds of skin. "Providence done its work and brought us close. Now ah has to finish de job and find 'em."

CHAPTER 20

"Listen!" Huck put a finger to his lips.

They all fell silent.

Not a sound.

"What?" Tom whispered.

"The racket has stopped. They musta all got away."

"More'an likely, some got away, some were killed, and some beat up and herded back onto the *Morgan*," Mint said.

"Well you was there, so you got to know more about what happened than we do," Tom said.

"Now that they all know they're headed for the slave market instead of to a freedom ship, the crew'll have to keep them locked up and under guard until they reach New Orleans," Becky said.

"There are enough of the crew to keep them confined," Mint said. "I thought it was kinda funny all the deckhands were white. And they all had guns. Guess they were in on the plot. Even if some o' the slaves can somehow slip out on deck in the dark, I can't see none o' them doing something crazy like jumping overboard into that cold water to escape. They'd drown or die of exposure."

"Yeah," Tom agreed. "They were all slaves before and they didn't bolt then. Why would they do it now? If I was one o' them and didn't get away tonight, I'd wait, figuring there'd be a better chance, by'n'by."

"How's your head, Jim?" Huck asked. "You feeling up to

sneaking back there and finding out what's going on?"

"M'head don't matter none. Ain't nuffin' gonna get in de way of finding m' family."

"Well, even if you don't have the widow's gun no more, me and Tom got ours, in case we need 'em," Huck said.

"And I got mine," Mint said, pulling a small pistol from the deep pocket of her cape.

"Oh," Becky's eyes went wide when she saw the small revolver.

"It was my father's. Mama made me take it for protection when I slipped off from the wagon train. Trouble is, it has only five shots. The extra powder and balls were left in my cabin I was in such a hurry to get off the boat."

"No matter. We likely won't need no guns atall," Tom said. "If everybody's ready, let's go. Just go mighty quiet and cautious. Don't make no noise." He reached for the lantern and shuttered it, so that only a few tiny slivers of light showed around the cracks. "This here's the predawn blackness that's like the pit of hell with the fire out," he said, "but if we go slow, we won't stumble. I got eyes like a cat, so I'll lead."

Zane smiled at the exaggerated boast. But better overconfident than timid. Zane chose to walk near the back with Jim, Becky, and Mint next ahead of them, while Tom and Huck with drawn pistols were in the lead, Tom carrying the darkened lantern.

The six crept out of the brush thicket with a minimum crunching of twigs and dead leaves and moved slowly across the open field toward the graveyard.

"They's a wagon track to one side of the graveyard up here," Huck said. "Let's walk on it so we don't have to go over them sunken graves. Don't step in no ruts and twist an ankle."

They veered slightly to the right and moved ahead another fifty yards.

"Hssst!" Tom put out an arm to hold back those behind.
"What?"

"I hear sumpin'. Sounds like a horse galloping."

Zane strained to hear. Then he detected the faint staccato thudding of hooves.

They waited, breathless, and the noise grew distinctive as it approached. Somewhere ahead a horse was coming fast.

They hurried to move off to one side into knee-high dead weeds.

A horse snorted and the galloping slowed to a trot, then to a fast walk as the horseman approached them.

"Hold it right there, mister!" Tom cried, jumping into the road with pistol leveled and lantern unshuttered.

Zane was startled; Tom just bet their whole stack of chips without consulting the rest of them.

The horse shied, walling its eyes at the bright light and sudden movement. The black-caped rider reeled in the saddle, leaning drunkenly to one side.

"Who're you and—" Tom stopped. "Oooohh!" All of them stared at the rider. Blood covered the front of his shirt. There was nothing above the flared collar of the cape.

His head was missing.

The shock stunned them into gaping silence. A head was staring at them from the pommel of the saddle, tied to the rider's belt by twists of long black hair.

A chill went up Zane's back, and his stomach clenched.

The horse turned nervously in a circle, breathing heavily, no hand on the reins. The body leaned far over to the right, and finally toppled to the ground, one foot catching in the stirrup. The horse walked a few steps and stopped, impeded by the dragging weight. The rider's cape was scuffed up over the shoulders revealing two crossed poles that had held the body erect in the saddle.

Making a wide circle around the body, Jim came up and took the horse by the bit so he wouldn't run off.

Zane stepped forward, yanked one of the props loose, and used it to turn the body over onto its back, while Tom tried to wrest the booted foot from the wooden stirrup.

The staring head rolled loose from the belt and stopped, sightless eyes regarding Huck. "Gashly!" Huck shuddered and turned to examine the nearby ground as if looking for a place to throw up.

Mint took the lantern Tom had set down and crouched to gaze closely at the face.

"Oh, no!"

"You recognize him?" Zane asked.

"His name is Clarence Davis and he was the purser on the boat." She rocked back on her heels and stood up, sucking in a deep breath. "He's the one who got drunk and let out the secret of this whole plot."

"Reckon he won't do *that* again," Huck said.

"But who chopped off his head?" Tom voiced the question for all of them.

"My guess would be the mate, Conrad Winger," Mint said. "When that man came close to me, I could feel the presence of evil, like the devil was near. If it hadn't been for pure luck or the interference of external events, like that grounding and the slave revolt, he'd have forced himself on me for sure."

"It warn't luck," Tom said. "It was Providence ordering events to protect you."

"Well," Mint said with a grim smile, "if Providence hadn't been on the job, I had Daddy's Colt to speak for me."

And Zane could see that she meant it.

"Why would anyone do such a horrid thing as decapitate this man?" Becky wondered, blue eyes wide in the lantern light.

"Mos' likely t' scare de slaves," Jim said, somberly staring at the sickening sight. "Mos' niggers ah knows kin stand up to beatings and danger and even guns, but you go to lopping off a man's head, like killing a rooster, black folks gets pooty skittish."

"Who wouldn't?" Tom said. "It ain't natural to separate a man from his head."

"They didn't fool around with this Davis for wrecking their plot. And, like Jim says, this would make any slave think twice about further resistance," Zane reasoned.

"The headless horseman," Tom muttered, finally twisting the body's booted foot out of the wooden stirrup and dropping the leg. "Just like 'The Legend of Sleepy Hollow.' "

"I never read it," Zane muttered. Huck and Mint shook their heads as well.

"I have," Becky said. "Washington Irving wrote it."

"Yeah," Tom said. "That story ain't likely to even tickle your terror bone after this." He took another look at the gory sight. "I reckon citizens of Paris got used to this kinda thing during the French Revolution," he continued, examining the body and head with a clinical interest, "when they whacked off a slew o' heads with the guillotine and the streets jest ran knee-deep in blood like spilt red wine."

"That's enough o' that!" Becky snapped. "This ain't the French Revolution and it ain't no headless horseman story; it's real."

Jim ground-reined the horse and stroked its neck, calming him until the lathered animal finally dropped his head and began cropping the nearby grass. While he soothed the horse, Jim was looking this way and that into the woods all around, apparently watching and listening for any real danger.

"Lookee here." Tom pulled the smoking remains of a burnt torch from the empty rifle scabbard on the saddle. "I thought I smelt something scorched. It was the purser's pants leg. I bet whoever done this propped Davis up here, tied his head in his lap, and lit this here torch. Then they hied the horse off into the woods, the animal tearing along like crazy to get shut of the flames that was burning right alongside. Any slaves seen this sight, they'd a froze or run back toward the river, figuring the forest was plumb full o' caped headless devils lighting their way outa hell with buckets o' fire. You can bet slavery seemed like a Sunday school picnic compared to what was in them woods."

"That's right," Huck nodded. "Whilst the runaways was shaking and confused, that crew likely jumped right in with guns and clubs to corral the ones left and herd them back to the boat."

"Mebbe we ought to drop the body and head in that open grave," Zane suggested, trying to refrain from cringing. He attempted to appear calm and reasonable but, truthfully, he'd been terrified to the point of nausea twice in the same night.

"Not yet. We need to get up yonder and see can we help any slaves that might still be loose," Huck said.

"Did you notice this saddle?" Tom continued, still playing detective. "It's one of them old-timey saddles with a high, curved pommel and a high cantle, and no horn. Looks jest like pictures of the saddles knights rode when they was jousting and such. It's even all fancied up with silver screws and doodads. Don Quixote likely rode one jest like this."

"So, what does that mean?" Zane asked.

"Mebbe this headless horseman did come from hell, riding the saddle he was on when he lost his head five hundred years ago."

"Not unless he was resurrected earlier," Mint said, "because that man was on the *Morgan,* wearing his head in the right place and very much alive no more than five hours ago. In fact, he was planning to run off with a beautiful slave girl as soon as the boat docked and the escape commenced."

"I want to hear that story," Becky said.

"Later," Zane said. "We got things to do." He fell in with Jim and they moved away, Tom and Huck leading the way.

"Leave the horse here," Becky said. "He's okay for now. If he's like my pony, he'll find his way back to wherever he came from."

Tom shuttered the lantern once more and they proceeded slowly up the road in near total darkness.

The Grangerford house was shuttered and still.

"Huck, how far away wuz de log church you tole me about?" Jim asked in a husky whisper a few minutes later.

"I dunno. Couple three miles I reckon. We had to go horseback when I was here. Why?"

"Dey be a light coming from cracks in a do' over yonder back o' de house."

They all turned to look.

"That's the smokehouse."

"Why would anybody be in there this time o' night?" Tom wondered.

"Likely getting a ham for breakfast," Huck said, as if that were the most logical thing to be doing in this situation.

"Oh, please!" Becky groaned.

"How can we find out?" Tom asked.

"Ain't no windows," Huck said. "Reckon we could throw a rock at the door and see who comes out."

"No. We want to go unnoticed as long as we can," Zane said. "We don't want to stir up any confrontations. Let's work our way down toward the river and see if the *Morgan* is still here."

Suddenly they all jumped as the smokehouse door opened, spilling yellow lamplight across the ground. Two men came out, conversing.

The six skulkers slid back behind the front stoop of the Grangerford house hardly daring to breathe as the pair approached and passed within eight yards of them.

"I printed up enough bills o' sale, so you'll have a few extra," a lean black-haired man said. "All you need to do is take a pen and fill in the names and descriptions and sign them at the bottom as owner, then have a couple crewmen sign as witnesses and . . ."

"I done all that before!" the stocky man cut him short. "If those forgeries don't pass inspection, I'll come looking to blister your hide."

"Yessir. No need to get upset. I guarantee these documents will get by the auctioneer. They always have. I know how to handle a printing press. These are dead ringers for the real forms. Even the paper is legal size and pale blue. I stole a stamp of the state seal, so these documents would even fool me, if I hadn't printed them myself. You can write in the names of a few remote parishes. Whoever's running the slave auction ain't gonna care so long as the documents look official."

"We cut it short, so this is our last load of the year, and everything has gone smooth up to now. If we get 'em sold before word o' this here uprising gets downriver, I reckon we'll be out of danger. We can scatter, then get the captain to hide the boat in some bayou until it's disguised with a new name and some changes." He folded the documents and tucked them into an inside coat pocket.

"How many slaves got away?" the lean man asked.

"Smealey did a rough count. Half a dozen maybe." The stocky man stopped and produced two cigars. "Here . . . have one. Might be a bit early to celebrate, but a couple o' good smokes clears my nose of the smell of blood."

The two men paused, barely ten yards from the crouching listeners. The printer struck a match and put fire to their cigars.

Zane heard Huck gasp beside him as the brief flare lit up both faces. Mint also stirred slightly when she saw the pair.

"At least two of them are dead we figure," the first man said. "You'd best pack up that printing press and get ready to leg it. Could be some fishermen or farmer across the river heard all that shooting and whooping and the steam whistle blowing. Likely be hell to pay when the law shows up."

"Yeah," the lean man said. "Sounded like the Battle of Waterloo. I'll dismantle that small press and pitch the parts into the river. Too heavy to carry on horseback. If I can't round up the horse that purser was riding, there's a mule back here in the barn I'll saddle up." He snorted a laugh. "That was a right smart idea, lopping off his head like a rooster for Sunday dinner."

"Yeah," the stocky man swore a profane oath. ". . . squirted blood all over me. I'll have to get into some other clothes. But that killed two birds with one stroke—eliminated a snitch and scared them slaves damned near as white as I am."

"If they changed color, you might have trouble selling them," the printer said, chuckling at his own joke. The men moved away.

"It's coming on to daylight. I have to get aboa . . ." his voice trailed off to a mumble.

None of the lurkers moved or spoke until the men were well away into the trees toward the river.

Huck straightened up from where he'd been hunkered next to the wall. "Jim, did you see who that was?"

"Ah sholy did. Lawdy, we still ain't shut o' de duke. But he don't look jest de same as befo'."

"Those big pink splotches on his face and neck look like healed burns. Hot tar will do that to a body. I seen it before."

"You never told me the king and the duke went in for murder," Tom said.

"They warn't nothing but frauds and humbugs when we was having to put up with them," Huck said. "It was that other fella

157

there who said he done the killing."

"Who was that other man?" Becky asked.

"That was the first mate, Conrad Winger, I told you about," Mint replied. "The one who gives me the creeps."

"With good reason, too," Zane said. "Talked about chopping off a head like he was discussing the weather."

"I heard he used to be an overseer on a plantation down south," Mint said. "Don't reckon this is the first person he's killed—white or black."

"The duke was kowtowing to him, being mighty careful not to offend. Likely figured he could get a dose of the same medicine."

"Wonder where de king got to?" Jim said.

"He was old," Huck said. "Likely threw in his hand while wearing a thick coat of hot tar and feathers. Or, mebbe passed over from what Doc Robinson would call, 'the immoderate use of bust-head whiskey.' "

"Let's git on down to the river and see can we somehow stop that boat from leaving," Tom said, urgently. "Once she gets clear and starts steaming south, we ain't got much chance o' stopping her."

"Mars Tom, ah wants to stop her wurser den you do," Jim said as they moved quietly toward the river. "But how's we gonna bust up agin all dem armed men?"

"Providence will show us a way," Tom assured him.

Two short blasts on the steam whistle signaled the boat was ready to shove off.

Dawn had crept up, unnoticed, until Zane was suddenly aware he could now see the slate surface of the broad Mississippi through the sparse trees.

They paused behind two big oaks to watch. Conrad Winger cursed the deckhands for hoisting the gangway before he was aboard. Then he took a short run and leapt from muddy bank to the deck, falling forward on the planking with another oath. The duke stood looking after him, his back to Zane and the hidden watchers.

"Two boats!" Mint whispered. "That's the *Morgan*." She pointed to the one on the right. "The other one wasn't here when we landed."

In the pale gray light, Zane could read the name, *STYX*, in large, filigreed letters stretched between the smokestacks of the boat on the left.

"Ovelia said they were told they'd be changing boats," Mint said quietly.

The paddle wheel began to churn slowly in reverse and smoke billowed from the stacks. The *STYX* took leave of the shore and began backing out into the stream.

"Dere goes my Ovelia and de chil'ren," Jim murmured. "Jest when we was mighty near to hooking up again."

Zane's heart sank when he thought of all the modern inventions that could have intercepted this boat and prevented its murderous crew from reaching New Orleans and selling all these poor souls into slavery once again. If only he had a telephone, telegraph, a computer with email, or a handheld device to text. Even a fast motorboat and several assault rifles. But it was not to be, he realized, as the *STYX* backed away from the landing and began its escape downriver.

CHAPTER 21

"Come with me!" Tom said, *sotto voce*. "Quick! I got an idea."

They catfooted back into the woods and Tom led them down the rutted road toward the graveyard, bounding past the headless body still sprawled on the ground, and running so fast the others could hardly keep up.

Zane noticed the horse was gone.

Off to their right, the *STYX* was gathering forward momentum and swinging in toward their side of the river to catch the main current on the outside of the bend.

Tom plunged into the heavy brush near the mouth of the creek and worked his way to the shoreline. The steamer was just coming toward them, possibly fifty yards distant.

"Huck, gimme your pistol. You take my little Smith & Wesson. The rest of you lie down flat in case they return fire."

"What's you gwyne t'do, Mars Tom?"

"See can I puncture the boilers with this here .44 soon as she turns broadside to us. That will stop them."

"De boiler plate be too thick fo' dat lead ball," Jim said.

"I gotta try, anyways."

"Dey got steam up," Jim continued. "Even was you to punch a hole in it . . .."

"The boiler would explode and kill 'most everybody aboard," Huck finished.

"Not if I hit the pop-off valve."

"You ain't that good a shot in this light and distance."

"You got any other ideas of how to stop 'er?"

Nobody did.

Tom gripped the gun with both hands and took careful aim as the stern-wheeler swung broadside and closer to the bank.

Boom! . . . Boom! . . . Boom!

Clouds of white smoke billowed from the muzzle and began to drift away on the slight breeze.

Boom!

Zane heard the last shot whine off the curved surface of the metal boiler.

Nothing happened, and the boat continued on course. A gabble of voices came across the narrow strip of water.

A few seconds later, two shots rang out from the boiler deck. Apparently, someone was returning fire at the white smoke, which had drifted to the left.

Tom waited until the boat had passed them and then fired twice more to empty the cylinder. If he hit anything but the retreating paddle wheel, it was not apparent.

Zane was glad the boiler hadn't been punctured. He knew nothing about the physics of steam engines and had no idea if the boiler would have exploded or not. Perhaps so, because he'd heard of airliner cabins being depressurized by a small hole that caused air to rush out violently and blow an even bigger hole in the fuselage. Steam pressure had to be much greater.

"Well, that didn't work," Becky remarked, standing up and brushing herself off. "Any more thoughts?"

"I didn't hear you coming up with no plan, Miss Smarty," Tom snapped, exasperated. He exchanged pistols with Huck.

"What do we do now?" Mint asked as if she were getting comfortable being part of their group.

"I just had an idea," Zane said, "but should have thought of it earlier. Too late now."

"What's that?" Tom asked.

"When we were eavesdropping on the duke and Winger, we shoulda jumped them with our guns and held them hostage to demand the release of the slaves. Bold and chancy move, but it mighta worked."

Tom thought a minute. "Naw. The crew aboard the boat looked like they wasn't even waiting for the mate since they'd already pulled up the gangway. So they didn't care. Ain't no honor among thieves and murderers. They woulda sailed off without him."

"Pulling up the gangway musta been a mistake," Zane insisted.

"Why?"

"The slaves could not have been sold at the New Orleans market because the mate had the newly printed blank bills of sale in his pocket."

"Hmmm . . . That's right. Providence likely let us miss that chance 'cause the mate and the duke was likely armed, too, so somebody mighta been killed if they'd decided to shoot it out. We just got to think of another way."

"We're wasting time," Huck said, moving out of the bushes. "Let's get the yawl and light out after them."

"We gwine to jest let de duke get away?" Jim asked.

"Ain't no matter," Tom said. "He's only a hunk o' burnt cornbread at a bakers' convention. Just a hired hand. The law can run him down later."

They all trooped toward the boat.

They crossed the upper creek on the stepping-stones and found their boat just as they'd left it.

The sun had not yet risen into the clear sky, but shafts of light were lancing through the trees when they shoved off in the chill of early morning. A mist rose from the river, and the STYX was out of sight around the next bend downriver. A light morning breeze puffed up out of the northeast. Tom and Huck hoisted the main and jib and Zane maneuvered to catch the fair wind on the port quarter while staying in the channel.

"If the *STYX* should run aground like the *Morgan* did and we catch up to them, what do we do?" Mint wondered.

"Same thing we woulda done if we'd delayed it by busting the boiler," Tom said. "Sail right on past as fast as we could go and stop at the next town or village that's big enough to have a sheriff or constable and spread the alarm. See could they get up an armed force to stop the boat and arrest the crew."

"You reckon any of these little one-horse burgs got the might—or the will—to go up against an armed crew?" Zane wondered. "We might have to go all the way to the next big city to find enough tough lawmen to do the job."

Becky nodded. "And that's only if the boat is delayed by a machinery breakdown or gets her bottom holed by a snag or something. Otherwise, it just steams on down the river, with us trailing a long way behind."

"Yeah," Huck added. "Those slaves might be all sold afore we get there."

"They have to stop now and then for wood," Zane said. "Won't that delay them?"

Huck shook his head. "Not long enough."

Zane had not voiced his other concern earlier, but now he did. "Just supposing the boat does get stopped by the police somehow before it reaches New Orleans," he said. "Ain't no free states on either side of the river from here on south. The law won't just turn these slaves loose. They'll find out where they came from and see to it they're taken back to their masters. So, except for the ones that got killed or got away at the Grangerford place, they'll all be back in bondage, and probably get whipped or sold down the river for escaping."

Tom looked exasperated as if he hadn't thought of that before. "Yeah, I don't reckon even Judge Thatcher could stop that from happening. Even if them slaves all lied and said they was free, the police would only have to check their descriptions against the reports by the plantation owners who had slaves stole."

"That might take a few weeks," Zane said, thinking there were no computers with such lists, and the names and descriptions of the blacks would have to be advertised up and down the river.

"Ah hopes m' Ovelia and Johnny and Lizbeth didn't get kilt back in dose woods," Jim moaned, rising up from his blanket. He was pressing a hand to his head, as if the effects of the concussion were still bothering him. The ugly wound on his temple had begun to scab over.

"Those young'uns could run fast," Huck hastened to say. "If anything, they likely got away. I can't see your missus being af-eered o' that headless horseman. She'd a knowed it was some kind of trick."

"Yeah," Mint added. "Ovelia struck me as a very smart and resourceful woman. If anybody escaped, it woulda been her and the kids."

These assurances of hope seemed to soothe Jim, and he lay back to rest on his blanket.

"My, this is a beautiful boat!" Mint remarked, changing the subject. "I've seen sailing boats on Lake Michigan, but never been in one myself. Mostly it's just rich folks who own those yachts."

"We all own this yawl together," Huck said.

"We bought it last summer when we was trying to rescue Becky from the kidnappers," Tom said.

"Kidnappers? Really?" Her blue eyes went wide.

"Yeah. It was quite an adventure," Tom said.

"Tell me about it."

"I listen better when I ain't hungry," Huck said. "I'll break out some bread and cheese and ham for us to munch on."

Jim reached up under the bow for a jug of water and several tin cups.

For the next hour as the sun rose and bathed them and the river in its warming light, dissipating the mist, Tom regaled the new girl with a dramatic telling of their summer adventures, including his and Huck's captivity, their brush with Sioux Indians on the Oregon Trail, and the later mystery of the giant hairy monsters.

During the telling, Mint never took her gaze from Tom's face.

Seated at the tiller in the stern, Zane could see everyone in the boat, and read Becky's expression as it slowly turned from solemn to scowl minute by minute while the lovely black-haired girl became more engrossed in the story and fascinated by Tom.

Finally, Becky got up, crawled over a thwart, and moved forward where she could scan the shorelines and scout ahead for upbound steamboats. She and Jim, who was propped up on an elbow, held a quiet conversation Zane could not hear.

"Wow!" Mint exclaimed when Tom had finished. "You folks live exciting lives. That's more adventures in six months than I've had in my whole life put together."

"How old are you?" Tom asked.

She hesitated slightly then said, "I'll turn fifteen next March."

Tom nodded, not offering to reveal his own age, but apparently satisfied this new girl was just the right age for him. "It took a lot of courage for you to run off by yourself like that, and head for New Orleans."

Her face flushed a bit at the compliment. "Well, I didn't have much choice. My mother is wiser about those things, but we both figured that old man wanted me for his third wife, and we weren't having none of it. I just hope he doesn't take it out on her."

165

The sun dissipated the mist and the chill from the air. The tall trees on each side of the river blocked most of the light breeze and they all removed their coats and basked in the warm Indian summer day. Now and then the sails puffed out, but mostly just flapped idly when the breeze died around noon. The current provided their only means of motion. They discussed the advisability of rowing, but decided against it.

"Dat steamer be going like a houn' chasing a rabbit," Jim said. "We won't get nowheres near it."

Lack of sleep and the terror of the previous night, along with the warm sun, lulled them into a stupor by early afternoon. Conversation lagged, and they took turns napping, sprawled in the sun on the seats and leaning against thwarts, padding their heads with jackets and blankets.

Zane dozed at the tiller until Huck, who was alert and smoking his pipe, relieved him for about two hours. "I'll make sure we don't get run down by no steamers," Huck said, correcting their course slightly as Zane slid over on the seat and lay down on his ragged coat. He dropped off to sleep within a minute and slept soundly for an hour, but his subconscious mind was still racing as he dreamt of running and shooting and hiding.

CHAPTER 22

Tired of being confined in the boat since dawn, the party voted to land on a deserted towhead an hour before dark, stretch, walk around, and discuss their next move while cooking and eating a decent meal.

"I'm sure glad you found me in that graveyard," Mint commented to the group as she stared into the fire, leaning forward on the blanket and hugging her knees. "I don't know where I'd be right now if all of you hadn't come along."

Becky and Zane were busy scouring the tin plates with clean sand and rinsing them with a bit of their fresh water.

"I'm very grateful for your help," Mint continued. "If I'd been captured by that crew, no telling what that mate mighta done."

"It was only Providence led us to you," Tom said, and the others nodded.

"I didn't think to question it until now," Mint went on, "but how come that open grave was there? It was like somebody dug it and set an empty coffin in the bottom. I thought at first I busted that lid when I jumped down on it, but then saw it was already busted."

"We ain't figured that out yet," Huck said. "We found it that-away on Halloween when we was there. Onliest thing we can surmise is that a resurrectionist got to it."

"A what?"

"Grave robber," Tom said.

"Oh."

The sun had slid below the treeline and November's night chill was settling in.

The supper plates and frying pan packed away and the blankets and coats brought out, they all huddled close around the driftwood blaze. There was nothing quite like the comfort and wonderful aroma of a wood fire Zane thought, especially on a chilly evening. The house in his former life didn't have a fireplace, and he seldom attended any picnic or outdoor event where a log fire was lighted. Mostly gas grills were used for cooking outside.

"What are your plans, Mint?" Becky asked.

"Well, I need to get to New Orleans, even though I'm not on any timetable. My aunt won't be expecting me if my mother's letter doesn't get there first."

"If you don't care about being in danger, you can tag along with us," Tom said. "I hate to dump you off by yourself at some town. We're likely to wind up in New Orleans, anyway. You could save yourself the price of a boat ticket."

"That's very kind," she nodded. "And I feel safe with all of you. Doubtful I could stretch my cash to cover even deck passage," she mused, "especially since I really need to buy a few personal items and a change of clothes. Everything I had was left on the *Morgan* except what I'm wearing and this pistol."

"Memphis is a good-sized town where you wouldn't have no trouble buying whatever you need, including a boat ticket. Tom has some extra gold he could give you," Becky offered, a bit more eagerly than necessary, Zane thought.

"How far is Memphis?" Mint asked.

They exchanged blank looks.

"Well, let's see," Tom said, apparently trying to calculate how far they'd come from the Grangerford place. "We traveled about ten hours today. I reckon we likely covered maybe sixty river miles with the sails and current. We got an old map stuffed in with our gear in the boat. But it ain't no more accurate than Huck with a loaded pistol."

"I saw a couple islands today I recollect from last year when me and Jim come this way on the raft," Huck said, ignoring the comment. "Take it all around, Memphis oughta be somers close to seventy more miles. Iffen we scarf up some hot flapjacks and coffee afore daylight and don't dawdle, we could maybe hit Memphis sometime in the afternoon."

"We need to decide what we'll do when we get there," Zane said.

"Fust off, de police gots to know what happened," Jim said, opening his eyes. Zane thought the big man was dozing, but apparently, he was listening to the conversation.

"That's right," Huck said. "But they ain't likely to put much stock in a wild story from a bunch o' kids and a black man."

"Even if they do, would they—or could they—do anything to stop that boat?" Zane wondered.

"Before we go to the law, I reckon I'll ask around the waterfront to see if anyone recollects seeing the *STYX* pass by there in the last day," Tom said. "If we're lucky, mebbe they stopped there a few hours for wood or food or medical treatment iffen anyone was bad hurt in the breakout."

"I suppose lots o' boats pass Memphis," Zane said. "If that boat is a regular on the lower river and didn't stop, I doubt anyone would have noticed. Besides, it could be passing there during the dark right now if they didn't tie up for the night."

"Worth a try, anyhow," Becky said. "We might need to buy a few supplies, too, and maybe Mint can find herself a southbound boat to continue her journey in comfort."

When Zane opened his eyes next, it was still dark, and he thought he'd just dozed off. He heard someone stirring and cracked his eyelids to see the fire blazing. Maybe Jim and Huck were up late, talking, or keeping watch. Zane wanted nothing more than to snuggle back into his warm blanket and go back to sleep.

"Time to be up and doing," Huck greeted him.

Zane smelled coffee and something cooking as he threw off his blanket and reached for his shoes, which were rolled up in his shirt nearby. "What time is it?"

"Dunno. Ain't got a watch, but the catfish're already biting. I got two fair-sized ones frying up for breakfast. Better have some and dunk a hunk o' this hard bread in your coffee. Likely be a long day without much to eat."

Zane pulled on his shirt and shoes and shrugged into his ragged wool jacket, shivering himself warm. He stood near the fire, soaking up the heat while the others were rousted up, one by one. All had slept in most of their clothing, but nobody complained as they all gathered themselves to face another day—a day of unknown adventure and danger. Zane wondered what his family in twenty-first century Delaware were doing this morning. Likely preparing for a routine day of school or work. Or did they even exist yet? Was he the only one who'd journeyed back in time, or had the whole world, in rotating, slipped a few cogs on its axis and returned to the time of his nineteenth century ancestors? If so, how come he had survived? He'd gone over this problem in his mind hundreds of times since he'd been here but had come up with no satisfactory answer.

Tom thought the whole world was existing now, in 1849, and no one was missing Zane because they weren't even born yet. Huck and Becky weren't so sure. They were of the opinion, with no evidence, that Zane had made this trip in time alone. Jim attributed the whole situation to witches. And who knows but what he was right? Hadn't Miguel de Cervantes described how Don Quixote was often bewitched? Jim had a long and powerful tradition of belief to draw on. Zane, himself, still had hopes of returning to his home and former life, but imagined himself reentering the twenty-first century at the exact point where he was plucked from it.

While all this was churning through his mind, he'd nodded to the others, and poured himself a steaming cup of coffee, wishing it was hot cocoa, or was at least sweetened with honey or cream to cut its bitterness. The brew warmed his hands and the tip of his nose as well as his insides but didn't favor much of anything in taste.

The weather this mid-November day was much like the one before it—cold, damp, and foggy overnight, giving way to sunshine and light breezes during the day, and warming to nearly sixty degrees, Zane estimated.

Within thirty minutes, they'd eaten, packed up, scooped sand over the fire, and were on their way.

It was a glorious sailing day, with a chilly northwest breeze. The wind direction remained steady, but Zane, due to the loops and bends of the Mississippi, had to tack or jibe the yawl frequently. Over the next five hours, they moved out of the channel to make way for two upbound steamers, and for three headed downstream, the yawl bouncing and pitching in the wakes as the big boats passed.

Huck's estimate was close. They rounded a bend about mid-afternoon and saw the buildings of Memphis atop a bluff a mile ahead on the port side. The river was close to a mile wide at Memphis, and Zane could see the flat fields on the Arkansas side where the river overflowed in high water and spread out as far as it cared to—dropping its load of silt over several square miles.

They nosed into the bank upstream of the main levee, which was busy with at least ten steamers, loading and unloading.

They covered everything in the boat with a big canvas and

Tom hailed a young boy who was playing with his hoop on the cobblestone street nearby.

"Hey, boy, you want a job?"

The boy paused, grabbed his hoop and stick, and cautiously approached.

"What's your name?

"Harry . . . Harold," he corrected himself.

"You outa school for the day?"

The boy nodded.

"If you wanta earn some money, I'll give you this here silver half-dollar to watch our boat and make sure nobody bothers it or steals nothing from it until we get back in an hour or so."

Harold's eyes lit up at the sight of the shiny coin Tom held up.

"I'll give it to you now, if you're honest and won't run off as soon as we leave. Can I trust you to stay until we get back? It won't be long."

"I promise, mister. I'll stick right here, and if anybody fools with this boat, I'll call a cop."

"That's what I wanted to hear," Tom said, handing over the fifty-cent piece. "By the way, I figure you're just going by, but did you notice a steamboat along here or passing downstream today called *STYX*? It's a stern-wheeler."

Harold thought a moment, and then solemnly shook his head. "No, sir. I just this minute come from school up yonder on the bluff."

"Okay."

"Will you be back by suppertime? I have to be home before dark."

"Long before then," Zane assured him. The six of them walked away and started along the cobblestone street that bordered the levee.

Tom and Zane questioned several dock workers who had

been on duty all day. Two of them knew of the *STYX*, but none had seen the boat in the last fortnight.

Rather than go the long way around, they climbed the steep, rusty iron steps to the top of the bluff.

"Now to find the nearest police station," Tom said.

CHAPTER 23

True to Zane's foreboding, they got little or no satisfaction from the local police, who eyed their little group suspiciously and apparently decided that a tale like theirs was some kind of elaborate practical joke to see if they could get the authorities all stirred up.

"We'll have our patrolmen keep an eye open for that boat along the waterfront," was the only cooperation they got, as they were shown the door.

"Well, that wasn't worth spit!" Becky said as soon as they were back on the sidewalk.

"Just a polite way of saying, 'Don't catch your tail in the door as you leave,'" Tom agreed.

"Tell you what," Huck said, "the newspapers are always looking for a good story. And the wilder it is, the better it sells papers."

They asked a well-dressed couple on the street and were given directions to the office of *The Memphis Enquirer.*

Here they were met with more enthusiasm. "Yeah, we've run a couple stories about the theft of those slaves up and down the river," an editor told them. Then he called a reporter over and the two of them began scribbling in their notebooks while Tom and Zane, as spokesmen, started from the beginning and gave the entire story in detail. Mint and Huck and Becky threw in particulars as it went along.

The eyes of the two newspapermen grew wider as the story

progressed, and they scribbled as fast as they could write, sometimes pausing to interrupt for clarification. Zane noticed the reporter jotting in some kind of shorthand.

"We can promise to publish the tale just as you told it to us," the editor said an hour later as they were leaving. "We can't vouch for the truth of it, of course, but we'll publish it and make sure the word gets out."

"We're from St. Petersburg," Zane said. "A hundred miles or so above St. Louis."

"Yeah, I know the village," the editor said.

"You got our names, and you can address any letters to Judge Thatcher—this girl's father," Tom said.

"So, when this all blows up, you can take credit for breaking the story first," Zane said.

"And we're the ones who give it to you, firsthand," Huck added.

Zane wished there was some way of contacting the authorities in New Orleans to get ahead of the crew of the steamer before the blacks were again sold into slavery and scattered. He used to take for granted all the modern devices available in his other life, never thinking how difficult it was in the mid-nineteenth century. Instant communication by telegraph was on the horizon now, but not in common usage everywhere.

Out on the street again, Zane heard a brass band playing a march in the distance.

"Sounds like a parade somers," Huck said.

"Let's have a gander," Tom said. "It's on our way to the river."

Tom and Huck were in the habit in St. Petersburg of never passing up a band, a circus, a parade, or a show by a magician or a mesmeriser to break the chronic monotony of their lives. The chase they were engaged in now was the third harrowing adventure since June, and they loved every minute of it. Though Jim was a little more reluctant participant, Becky, and now

Mint, seemed to revel in the excitement.

They homed in on the music as they zigzagged toward the waterfront. The rhythmic march grew louder and a buzz of crowd noise greeted them when they finally turned a corner and saw, filling a vacant lot, a crowd of several hundred people being entertained by a five-piece brass band seated on a flat wagon bed.

A man dressed like a circus ringmaster with top hat and tailcoat stood on a wooden platform beneath a massive gas balloon that was bouncing slightly in the wind, but held to earth by a web of ropes and ties.

The band finished their piece with a flourish and put down their instruments to take a break.

The man on the platform lifted his megaphone, allowing no time for the crowd to get restless or begin to drift away.

"Ladies and gentlemen, while the band is taking a breather, allow me to introduce you to one of the wonders of the world. This magnificent flying machine you see before you is the future of mankind. Gas balloons were first invented in France some sixty years ago, just before their great revolution. These balloons, nearly miraculous in their abilities to lift man for a time from this world of toil and sin, are constantly being improved and perfected even as I speak. I just happen to possess one of the latest, most beautiful, and safest examples of a flying machine now in existence. And, just think of it—you, yourselves, can experience the thrill of flight for only ten cents, one thin silver piece. For this paltry sum, you can slip the bonds of earth and its mean drudgery to soar aloft and commune with the eagles while viewing your magnificent city on the bluff. See it as God sees it."

He set down the megaphone and swept his arm in a grand gesture that took in everything around him.

The six travelers edged their way through the crowd to get a closer look. To keep anyone from taking offense at a big black man shouldering them aside, Zane and Tom led the way, slipping, sliding, slowly opening a way for Jim to follow close behind them, until they finally stopped about ten yards from the platform to which the balloon was tethered.

Up close, it looked enormous. Zane had to bend his head far back to see the entire balloon. It resembled an inverted teardrop with wide panels of vertical green and white stripes. The balloon was contained in wide netting that terminated in thick cords at various points on a spacious gondola. The gondola, itself, was shaped like a boat, pointed at both ends and about four feet deep and perhaps fifteen feet long. The inside appeared to consist of wicker and cork while the exterior was covered with thin wood, the seams sealed with pitch and painted white.

"How do you steer it?" someone from the crowd yelled.

"Ahh . . . well you should ask. This device is controlled by the wind. Nature guides it. It can be maneuvered to some degree, but primarily it goes where the wind blows." But then the barker raised his megaphone again and bellowed, "But its ascent and descent can always be controlled. And today, for a measly dime, I will take you aloft, but not to leave you at the mercy of this strong autumn breeze. The balloon will be safely tethered to this platform so that you cannot drift farther than a few hundred feet. After a decent interval of sightseeing, you will be hauled back safely to mother earth." He turned to survey the crowd. "Who will be the first to venture up?"

There were no takers.

The barker waited a few seconds, scanning the crowd.

"Today alone at least two dozen of your fellow Memphians have gone aloft to view your fair city as only the angels and the hawks see it. I assure you, I haven't lost a customer yet—nor even bruised one."

Still no volunteers.

"Well, it's your loss. But go home to supper and think it over. It's the chance of a lifetime. I will be here tomorrow, but then must move on to other places where many eager folks await the thrill of soaring into the heavens." He turned to see the band members again taking up their instruments. "I see the band is preparing to give you a rousing send-off. Thank you for attending our entertainment."

The band struck up a lively march and the crowd began to disperse.

"I should find a store and buy a change of clothes and something to fix my face," Mint said to Tom as the six turned away.

"Nothing wrong with your face that I can see," Tom said.

Zane saw Becky scowl behind his back.

"Sir, can you tell me the time of day?" Tom asked the balloon owner.

"Sure, son." The lean, bearded man above him pulled a fat watch from his vest pocket. "A quarter to six."

"Thanks," Tom nodded. "Mint, we don't have time to do any shopping. We told that boy guarding our boat we'd be back in an hour. It's nearly two hours now."

"Okay."

They paced quickly away.

Within a block of the waterfront, they passed a chandlery.

"Hold up a minute," Tom said, darting for the door. "Want to see if they got a good map of the river."

The rest of them paused outside. Tom was back in less than three minutes. "Besides the money the judge give us, I'm glad I brought some of our gold," he said to Huck. "Never know what extra expenses might pop up when we're far from home." He held up a cardboard tube. "Rolled up in here is all we need," he stated. "Heavy paper. Got lots more details than the map in our boat. Likely drawed by a river pilot. And I bought a pocket compass, too. Won't have to figure out directions by the sun no more, especially on cloudy days."

"Thought maybe you was gonna leave this boat to me for keeps," Harold grinned when they appeared. "I gotta git on home."

"Everything safe here?" Huck asked.

"Not a soul bothered her. Had a fella ask what steamer she come off of. Told him I didn't know."

"Here's an extra twenty-five cents 'cause we was longer than intended," Tom said.

"Thanks, mister," the boy grinned, pocketing the coin and looping his hoop over one shoulder. He dashed up the ramp toward the street above.

The short November day was closing down, a chill wind blowing off the river as they climbed aboard their yawl.

Tom unrolled his new map and spread it on a broad seat in the stern. He studied it a few minutes, measuring and making notes with a pencil on the margin. "This here map is a beauty," he announced. "Shows we still got roughly six hundred and fifty miles to go before we hit N'Orleans."

There was a collective groan. "A trip that far would be great fun iffen it was summertime," Huck said, "when there warn't no rush and we could go in a'swimming to cool off whenever we'd a mind to. Wouldn't even have to travel at night like me and Jim did last year."

"De raf' be a good home fo' us," Jim said. "But she'uz mighty heavy and hard to steer wif a sweep. Couldn't run ahead o' de current. Not like dis heah beautiful sailing yawl."

Tom bent over the map once more, measuring with his pencil. "Only about four hundred miles as the ostrich flies," he announced brightly.

"Ostriches don't fly," Huck grumbled. "And neither do we."

"But we could . . ." Tom looked at them. "If this north wind is still blowing tomorrow, that old man's balloon would take us straight down to the gulf in somers around ten to twelve hours."

Becky's light complexion turned even paler, but she said nothing.

"Let's discuss this after supper," Zane said, standing up in the boat. "Anybody else hungry?" He'd become conscious of his lean physique filling out a bit and putting on muscle in the few months since he'd arrived in this long ago and faraway place. He was constantly hungry.

"Hmm . . ." Tom thought a moment. "Probably ought to save our rations for later. Ham and corn pone, dried apricots, and pickled beets and okra ain't gonna go bad—especially in chilly weather. Whilst we're here, what say we jest walk uptown and buy dinner at a restaurant and bring it back here and eat in the boat?"

"Better yet, why not go uptown and eat inside where it's warm?" Zane asked.

"Ain't no eatin' place in Memphis gonna let Jim inside, lessen he's cooking or serving."

Jim nodded, acknowledging the actual state of things.

"Okay," Zane said. "Let's find out what everybody wants and me and Tom and Mint will go get it."

"Let me go," Becky said. "Mint, you ain't used to this kind of rough life. You rest here with Huck and Jim and watch our stuff."

The three staying behind told what they'd prefer to eat. Then Tom, Zane, and Becky started for town.

"We can't spend too much on one meal," Tom remarked as they climbed the iron stairway to the top of the bluff. "If roast beef and carrots and banana pudding and milk are too expensive, we'll substitute something else."

"Well, at least Miss Fabulous gave us money to buy hers," Becky said. "Maybe she used her face-fixing money."

"Her name is Fayberest," Tom said, puffing slightly with exertion and not looking back at Becky as he led the way up the rusty steps.

"Well, whatever. I guess she'll still have enough left for a steamboat ticket."

Tom did not reply—wisely, Zane concluded. *Is this the kind of thing I'll face when I go back to the twenty-first century?* Zane thought. But, then he realized the question was irrelevant since he had no prospects of ever returning home again.

CHAPTER 24

A solid gray overcast covered the sky at dawn when the six began to stir, threw off their blankets, and came to life in the boat, yawning and stretching. They'd discussed going to a hotel for hours of restorative, comfortable slumber, and a good wash-up, but consideration for Jim kept them in their twenty-foot yawl where they spent a cramped and chilly night.

Shrugging into his ragged wool jacket, Zane shivered himself warm. He had no hat, but his thick black hair, which had grown down his neck and over his ears, partially protected his head. A cold north wind whistled along the waterfront, snapping flags and pennons of the steamers that were nosed into the landing. As much as he wanted to overtake the *STYX* and somehow avert the sale of its black passengers, he considered the real possibility of not reaching his fourteenth birthday if they actually tried to fly to the gulf in this stiff wind. The chances of a balloon crashing were better than good, and Zane was leery of dying in this alien world of nineteenth century America without ever seeing his family again.

This weather was exactly what Tom was hoping for—if he could somehow cajole the balloon owner into taking them all on a crazy, wind-directed flight overland in the general direction of New Orleans. As Zane recalled his geography, a lot of wild, wooded and swampy country lay south of here in Arkansas, Mississippi, and Louisiana. Here and now in 1849, it was likely even more primitive and less settled. Since he'd become a pretty good sailor in the past few months, he decided he'd volunteer to stay behind and take the yawl downriver to meet up with the others in New Orleans in a few days.

The travelers were quieter than normal as they sat on the thwarts, sharing a cold breakfast of ham, corn pone, and canteen water, each entertaining his or her own thoughts.

Tom was the planner, the organizer, the one whose convoluted schemes often got them into trouble. But, Zane knew once Tom got a course of action fixed in his head, it would take nothing short of a blast of black powder to divert him.

If they were lucky, Zane thought, the balloon owner would flatly refuse such a crazy idea, or demand a price so high that the six of them, pooling their money, could not pay the amount. Owning and flying a balloon and hauling it by wagon from place to place had to be expensive.

They trooped uptown. From several blocks away, they could make out the tethered balloon, bobbing in the wind above the rooftops.

It was a workday and there was no band to draw a crowd now, so only a few scattered spectators were drifting across the open field, pausing briefly to stare at the giant airship.

The owner/barker was just finishing another effort to attract customers by shouting and wheedling through his megaphone. He paused and sat down on his stool, mumbling to himself, his face red.

Then the owner noticed the six approaching and his face lit up.

"Well, folks, how about a tethered balloon ride this morning?" he suggested without use of the megaphone, his voice scratchy and hoarse.

"How about a flight that ain't tethered to nothing?" Tom suggested boldly with no preliminary.

"Sorry, son, but it's far too windy for that. We'd be in the next county before you could recollect your grandma's maiden name. Then we'd have to land, hope the balloon wasn't damaged by a tree or something, and walk back here to get the wagon and some help to retrieve it."

"I don't see that you're being overwhelmed with business," Tom stated, looking around, apparently trying to act like an adult.

"Alas, no," the lean man said, resting both elbows on his knees, head hanging down. "I think I'm a man ahead of his time." He looked up and regarded them with blue eyes staring out from a wind-burned face.

Tom glanced at a combination weathervane/lightning rod on the ridgepole of a nearby bank building. Then he pulled out his pocket compass and aligned it while the rest watched in fascination.

"Appears the wind is directly out of the north. If I ain't too far off, Memphis is directly north of New Orleans. We got a very good reason for needing to be in New Orleans in just a few hours . . ."

The owner was already shaking his head before Tom even finished. "Oh no . . . too dangerous. We might all go down in some swamp or forest and never be found."

"I'd think a man who is a scientist and adventurer and a man who is ahead of his time, would be up for something like this. You'd be famous. I'm sure you got maps tucked away in that big basket to guide us and . . ."

"As big a wonder as this balloon is, it can't be steered, no matter how many maps I got. We'd be at the mercy of the wind."

"I been a sailor a good long time . . ." Tom said.

Five months, Zane thought.

Tom continued, ". . . and even got a twenty-foot yawl down at the levee right now. I'm a good judge of wind and weather. An autumn wind like this in November ain't likely to veer more'an a point or two in the next fifteen hours. Might wobble around a little, but its direction is gonna hold pretty steady," Tom stated with authority, continuing as spokesman. "Not like summer storms with thunder and lightning and updrafts and such." Tom could be convincing when he knew little about a subject.

The man looked at their little group, arching his eyebrows at the two girls and the big black man standing in the back.

"Who are you folks? Why do you have to be in New Orleans so quick? If this ain't no emergency, why not take your boat? You'll be there in four or five days and be a lot safer, to boot."

"We can't waste no four or five more days on a river trip. This is an emergency."

"Life or death?"

"That's right," Huck spoke up. "We have to catch up to a steamboat that's carrying a load of slaves that was stole at different places in Missouri, Kentucky, and Arkansas. The law is after them but there ain't no way to get word downriver quick enough to head them off from selling prisoners at the New Orleans slave market."

"That boat has to be stopped and the crew arrested," Becky said. "This free man's family is among those prisoners on board," she added, pointing at Jim.

"The slaves already tried to bust loose a day upriver, at the Tennessee border, and some people was killed," Huck said.

"What do you youngsters have to do with all this? You ain't the law," the owner said.

"We're acting on behalf of Judge Thatcher from St. Petersburg, Missouri," Zane said.

"Well, even if you got papers proving that, we can't take a free flight south in this weather. It's just too dangerous."

"The wind ain't that fierce," Tom said.

"I'd guess it's blowing about fifteen right now," the man said, holding up a finger. "But five hundred feet up, it's likely blowing twice that."

"What makes you think so?" Tom asked.

"Experience," the man said. "Look here, you said you were a sailor. On the edges of the river, the water scrubs against the dirt banks and the current slows down, making for slack water. But out in the middle, the current is swifter since there is nothing to impede it. Right?"

Tom nodded.

"Well, it's the same with the air. The wind is scuffing along the ground and rubs against the hills and buildings and gets slowed down a good bit. But up yonder, there ain't nothing to slow it down and old Boreas, god of the north wind, can puff up a mighty breeze."

"Makes sense," Tom agreed. "But that's even better for what we want to do. The faster the wind blows, the quicker we'll get to New Orleans." He grinned and looked around at the other five for approbation.

"What I'm trying to say is, my expensive air ship could be torn to shreds and our bodies severely scuffed at the same time—if we're not all killed in the wreck," the balloonist said.

"What I'm trying to say is," Tom countered, pulling a fistful of gold coins from the ragged pocket of his pants, "we'll pay you three hundred dollars in gold to fly us to New Orleans today."

The lean man's blue eyes went wide at the sight of the glittering wealth and his mustache twitched. That put a different light on the matter altogether.

"How long would it take you to earn that much at ten cents a ride—or even twenty-five cents for each person who goes up for a short look-see?"

Apparently, the balloonist was thinking the same thing. "Well, uh . . ." he wavered.

"Okay, you got me. Make it three hundred and thirty, but that's my final offer."

Zane saw the tall man's Adam's apple bob up and down as he swallowed hard.

"When do you want to leave?" the balloonist asked. "Reckon I might as well go out in a blaze of glory as starve to death peddling cheap rides."

"Give me fifteen minutes to get our boat secured," Tom said, handing the man a double eagle. "By the way, what's your name?"

"Oscar Bettinger. Call me Ossie." He thrust out a hand and gripped Tom's.

"Zane, come with me and we'll go rent a safe place to stow our yawl for now. The rest of you stay here and make sure he don't leave without us."

"Hey, kid," Bettinger frowned. "I'm an honest businessman. My word is my bond. I'm not going anywhere until you get back."

"My name is Tom Sawyer. The rest of you can introduce yourselves. Me and Zane'll be back afore you can smoke a pipeful o' tobaccer."

Tom shoved the rest of his gold coins into a pocket and took off down the street at a dead run.

Zane thought he was still in good condition from soccer, but he had to sprint to keep up with Tom as they flew toward the river.

CHAPTER 25

Tom and Zane were longer returning than going since they were lugging all the blankets, a sack of their leftover food, and two jugs of water. It was also a farther walk because they'd moved the yawl below the town to a small boat basin and paid the owner a month's rent.

But they finally arrived at the balloon site, panting and sweating in spite of the chill breeze.

Huck appeared to be ready for his next adventure, helping Bettinger and one hired man release the metal hooks of the dozen mooring lines holding the balloon and gondola.

The two girls stood to one side, pale and quiet. Zane glanced at Jim, who wore his same stolid expression. Except for occasional bursts of great glee or joy, it was nearly impossible to tell whether Jim was about to be whipped or given a commendation.

"Throw your duffle into the gondola and gather round so you can hear me," Bettinger said. "When you climb into the basket, split up and move to either end to balance the weight. Then I'll get in and release the last cable and we'll be off. And I do mean *off!*" He stood up straighter and smoothed his trooper's mustache, which nearly hid his mouth. "I'm the pilot and captain of this vessel. What I say, goes. Nobody is to question any order I give. Is that clear?"

They all nodded.

"If this were not an emergency, we would not be taking off in this kind of a gale," he stated.

Or if it didn't pay so well, Zane thought. Humans would do nearly anything for money, even endanger their own lives. It was the same in the twenty-first century and probably had always been so. Except for the gold strike, California would not have been settled and become a state within two years.

Zane had never flown in a hot air balloon or a blimp, much less the obsolete and dangerous dirigible, but he and Ossie Bettinger were the only two in this group who had experience in an airship—Bettinger in this hydrogen balloon and Zane in a jet airliner. But this contraption was no jet with an enclosed, pressurized cabin. It would be a new experience for him.

"Get in," Ossie said, pointing at a step stool on the platform.

Tom was the first, having a bit of trouble because all of the tie-downs except one cable had been released and the balloon was tugging at its tethers as if eager to be airborne. The big inflated envelope of gas, in turn, was jerking the gondola around on the platform.

"Don't touch those sand bags hanging over the sides," Bettinger told him. "They're for controlling our altitude."

Zane was second and nimbly threw a leg over the rim and hopped in. He and Tom reached down to hand in the girls one by one. Jim was next, pushing down on the edge of the thick wicker basket and muscling himself inside.

Bettinger turned away and said something to the hired helper, who nodded. Then the pilot quickly scissored his long legs over to join them.

"Ready?"

They nodded.

"Hang onto something. Just don't touch any of this apparatus in the middle here. That's where the chemicals are stored to make the hydrogen gas. Lots of other things in these cabinets, too."

With one last look around and above, apparently gauging the wind direction, he leaned over the side and released a snap shackle on the cable, their final contact with earth.

The balloon shot skyward as if yanked by a giant rubber band. Zane caught his breath and clung to the rim while his knees nearly buckled from the force. It was almost like being shot from a cannon. He straightened up, locked his knees, and looked down. The ground, the platform, and the hired hand were already a hundred feet below and dropping away fast.

He was suddenly aware of the cries and squeals of the girls and yells of sudden fear from Jim and Huck.

The wind was carrying them up and away from the open field.

They were all gripping the edge of the gondola or the black braided cords that tethered the net to the basket.

Bettinger was bracing himself against the control seat in the middle and looking at a gimbaled compass.

"I thought you said it was blowing hard high up. They ain't no wind atall up here," Huck managed to gasp, his voice carrying clearly in the still air.

"Huck Finn, you got all the sense of a mudcat," Tom said. "Ain't you learned nothing from that nice yawl we got? When a fair wind is pushing the boat, you don't feel it because you're traveling the same speed."

"That's almost right, young man," Bettinger said. "But a sailboat cannot move as fast as the wind due to the drag of the hull through the water. You'll always feel some breeze. A balloon does not have as much resistance, so it feels as if the balloon is moving on its own because the balloon and the wind are going approximately the same speed. If we were standing still, we'd be bracing ourselves against a forty-mile-an-hour blast."

In the relatively peaceful atmosphere, Jim, Huck, and the girls, and even Tom and Zane, let go of their secure holds and began to walk about, turning their curious gazes on the receding city below, and the mighty river that looked like a creek probably two miles west and far below. It was chilly, but not near as cold as it would have been with a wind.

They began to relax and remark how wonderfully liberating it was to be free from earth and floating in the heavens.

"If I'd a'knowed it was this easy, I'd a done it long before now," Huck said.

"I reckon the river above Niagara Falls is pretty smooth, too," Zane remarked. Nobody paid him any attention.

"This is a lot like sailing," Tom marveled with a grin.

Zane had also noted the similarity, but a sailor had better control of his craft than Bettinger did of this. It was oddly frightening to be at the mercy of impersonal nature—akin to being in the calm eye of a hurricane, clinging to a wicker basket and a few yards of fabric.

Bettinger knew the danger. Creases furrowed his brow as he continually gazed aloft at the hydrogen globe straining against its cord net, swinging the gondola and its human cargo ever higher and farther.

Zane edged toward the middle of the gondola and took a long look over the side. "How fast do you estimate we're traveling?" he asked.

Bettinger looked down. "Hard to tell from this height, but every bit of forty miles an hour."

In Zane's other world, this was relatively slow, like a car driving through the suburbs.

"Wow!" Tom breathed. "That's about as fast as a racehorse can run. And he can't keep up that speed for no distance."

"We's testing the patience o' the Almighty," Jim said, solemnly. "If folks was meant to soar like de buzzards, He likely woulda fixed us up wif wings and tail feathers."

Becky and Mint didn't seem too awestruck or worried, only

curious now that the initial shock of the ascent was over. The only way they could tell they were moving was the slight puff of a crosscurrent now and then.

"This is like setting still in a skiff on the river on a calm day," Becky said. "The current is taking you right along, but you don't have no sense of movement."

"Look," Mint finally spoke, pointing down. "Memphis is already moving away from us. Nothing but solid forest down below. Those trees look like little bitty bushes. It feels like we're standing still and the ground is moving." Her voice betrayed her thrill at the spectacle. "I can't believe I'm this high off the ground. There aren't even any mountains in Illinois to compare to this."

"We're about five or six hundred feet up," Bettinger said. "Unless we get an updraft, we're not likely to go much higher because of the weight of seven people in this basket plus our gear." He studied the overcast above. "That's a good thing because we don't want to get up into them clouds, maybe another three hundred feet. Could be ice crystals up there, and we'd lose sight of the ground. If we were to keep rising, I'd have to release some gas to stabilize our altitude."

"I can still see the river off thataway," Tom said, pointing west. "So long as that's in sight, we can't miss New Orleans." He was sounding confident. "I ciphered out it was around about four hundred miles straight down to New Orleans from Memphis," he said to Bettinger. "At this rate, how long do you reckon it will take us? That would be ten hours at forty miles an hour."

"A lot of variables involved," the captain said. "Wind speed will likely change after dark."

"We have to be up here in the dark?" Becky said, sounding apprehensive.

"Of course," Tom said. "You don't start out to cross the ocean in a ship and then dock every night at some handy island. You have to keep going if you want to get there."

"Don't matter none," Huck said. "We got a couple lanterns and coal oil, so we can see. And there ain't no wind to blow out the flame."

"We have to be very careful about using any open flame in this basket," Bettinger said. "Don't even light a pipe. This balloon is filled with hydrogen gas—which is very flammable. One spark could blow this whole thing into a huge fireball. We'd all look like crispy bacon by the time our bodies hit the ground."

Silence greeted this news. Mint wrapped her cape about herself and looked away.

"It's all enclosed safely inside that fabric up there, though," Zane ventured, hopefully.

Bettinger nodded. "I have to release some of it in order to descend or land, so hydrogen will escape. It will dissipate quickly in the air, but it's still like carrying kegs of black powder or a cargo of coal or barrels of fuel oil in a ship. In that instance, even coal dust is dangerous and can explode. Of course, static electricity is always a danger."

"What's stadeck elec . . . elec . . ." Huck fumbled the words.

"The word is static—s-t-a-t-i-c," Bettinger said. "Umm . . . how to explain it? Have you ever rubbed a cat's fur, especially in cold weather and heard and felt a crackling and stinging?"

"Sure. Just figured it was their way of hissing at me," Huck said.

"No. The cat has nothing to do with it. Have you ever rubbed your shoes on a carpet in the winter and touched a doorknob and seen a spark?"

"Sho has," Jim replied. "Ah loses a tiny spark o' my spirit when dat happens."

"No. Your soul is still intact," the captain smiled.

"I've pulled off a wool sweater over my head in a dark room and seen sparks," Zane offered.

"Exactly. The wool rubbing on your hair causes it. All those are examples of static electricity. Have any of you studied physics in school?"

They shook their heads.

"Then it's a bit complicated for me to explain quickly. You have to know about atoms—the building blocks of matter."

"I know about matter," Tom said. "That's the gummy stuff Aunt Polly has to wash out of her eyes when she first gets up in the morning."

Bettinger chuckled. "That's matter, all right, but not the same thing. By 'matter' I mean any physical thing on earth and in the heavens. Everything is made up of these tiny particles called atoms that you can't see with your bare eyes. There's been lots of speculation that even atoms have smaller particles in them, but nobody has been able to prove it so far. Scientists speculate that when pieces of material are rubbed together, it scuffs off some of the atoms. Nature likes to stay in balance, and these atoms tend to jump back where they came from— kind of like letting go of a stretched-out spring. That snapping back into balance is what causes sparks. Men a lot smarter than I am study this stuff all the time, but they aren't even certain that's what really happens. If they can't figure it out, I sure can't. They just know sparks are some kind of electricity—like tiny lightning bolts—and can set fires or cause explosions if they strike certain flammable things. You'll likely study all this in school. Maybe by then, scientists will have found out a lot more about it."

Zane started to add that a scientist in 1897 discovered even smaller particles in atoms, particles he called electrons, but didn't want to further complicate a subject he knew very little about.

"You talk like a teacher," Mint said.

"Well, I used to be a professor, but I didn't teach physics.

Just had to learn the basics when I decided to seek my fortune as a balloonist." He shook his head. "That was probably a mistake. I taught geography and history. After this experience, I might return to the classroom." He glanced again at the compass and then up at the globe above them. "But static electricity can be as dangerous as other atmospheric conditions."

"Atmospheric conditions?" Tom asked. "Like rain or snow?"

"Lightning," the captain said. "We make a nice target up this high. Lightning is completely unpredictable and erratic. That's why I don't fly much in the summer when thunderstorms are in the area. Safer in cold, stable air. Of course, we're making a beeline toward warmer weather right now. Near the gulf, lightning storms can pop up any time of year when warm, moist air and cold air get to mixing, one rising and one falling. Then there's also the possibility of tornadic winds blowing in from Texas."

Tom, Jim, Huck, and Zane all looked at each other. They knew about tornadoes, having survived one in the Nebraska Territory only four months earlier.

Zane began to regret that he hadn't been more forceful in dissuading Tom from pushing this experienced balloonist to fly when he clearly didn't want to.

Ignorance is bliss, he thought. Tom was brash and had his way most of the time, but he and the others had let themselves be persuaded without knowing all the dangers involved.

None of them had any idea where the steamboat was. It could already be in New Orleans. Or it could be broken down or aground somewhere—frequent mishaps for all steamboats. Perhaps Tom's pistol shots had caused some damage that took some time to show up. There was just no way of knowing. But one thing he did know—he would much rather have been sailing south in the yawl than flying through space, literally hanging to the tail of a kite.

But it was too late for regrets. They were all here in this wicker basket together, more than five hundred feet above the forests of western Mississippi and streaking toward the gulf at forty miles an hour.

CHAPTER 26

Zane awoke to the sickening sensation of falling. Gasping, he jerked upright and threw off his blanket. "What was that?"

"We hit a downdraft," Bettinger said, calmly, folding up his map and replacing it in a locking cabinet beneath his seat in the captain's chair.

Tom and Huck looked a bit pale in the gray light of the heavy overcast. "A downdraft?" Tom queried.

"Yeah. Currents of air flow along like water, but the streams of air are not always on a flat plane. They undulate like waves on an ocean. We just hit a sharp dip, like dropping off a steep wave."

"Dey be mo' to dis flying den my stomach can take," Jim said from where he was slouched under a blanket next to the wicker wall.

All six of the passengers had been napping, Mint wrapped in her cape with the hood covering her head, and Becky huddled under her heavy horse blanket.

Zane realized the voices around him sounded a bit dimmer than usual, and he yawned to pop his ears and equalize the pressure. He told the others to do the same if their ears seemed plugged up.

"Is the river still in sight?" Zane asked, staring off to the west. "I can't see it."

"I been watching," Tom said. "It made a big bend to the west and then I lost sight of it about an hour ago."

Zane's innards twinged. As long as they could see the Mississippi, he felt as if he still had one foot on the ground and all would be well.

"The wind has veered a few compass points to the northwest," Ossie said as both boys looked at him. "We're no longer going straight south. I been trying to orient us to the map I got, but it's pretty hard from this altitude to identify landmarks on the ground."

This information did nothing to calm Zane's fears. Lost in space. Wasn't that the title of some TV show or movie? Of course, they weren't in weightless space and would not drift endlessly until they starved. But was that worse than eventually crashing to earth and being killed? "What time is it?" he asked.

Ossie consulted his pocket watch. "Ten minutes of four," he said, winding the stem before slipping it back into his vest pocket.

"Looks later than that."

"Heavy overcast and shortening days," the captain said. "We should have covered approximately three hundred miles since we took off early this morning."

"No way to turn west to intersect the river again?" Zane asked, knowing the answer already.

"Not unless the wind shifts." The captain stared into the binnacle and then checked his watch and made a note in his log.

Zane looked at the two girls, still peacefully asleep and free of worry for the time. He envied their repose. He took a deep breath. At least there were no power lines around in 1849. These were a common hazard that had proved fatal for many hot air balloons in his own time.

"We'd best get some supper soon," he said, trying to distract his mind from their situation. Nothing bad had happened so far. Their major problem would come when they figured they were as close to New Orleans as they could get and had to start descending and looking for a place to land or risk drifting far out over the trackless, swampy river delta. But that would be sometime after dark. Even pilots in the twenty-first century didn't attempt to land in the dark in unknown country, except in an emergency. It was a recipe for disaster.

Everything would depend on their dead reckoning, since they lacked any instruments except a compass. They had no detailed charts, computation tables, or sextant, and no ability to use them if they did. Without a sun sight, even these would have been useless to pinpoint the airship's position. Right now, he'd give his best pair of calfskin baseball shoes for an accurate iphone GPS.

He gazed toward the southwest. Nothing visible but a murky, heavy gray sky. In fact, it seemed even darker than normal for this time of day. Was that a rainstorm on the horizon? The air aloft here was definitely a few degrees warmer. Or was he just becoming acclimated to it?

As he looked, lightning flickered behind a bank of clouds in that direction. He glanced quickly at the captain.

Ossie nodded. "I saw it."

Tom and Huck had their heads together in conversation on the other side of the gondola and had not seen the mortal enemy of the hydrogen balloon unsheath its sword.

"Anybody hungry?" Zane asked. "I'm digging out some food if anyone wants to join me. You realize we all missed lunch." He was hungry and determined not to die on an empty stomach. But he also wanted to distract the others for as long as he could. The thought of the escaping riverboat with its load of stolen slaves had receded to the back of his mind for now. If or when he ever got his feet safely back on mother earth again, he resolved to nail his sneakers to the ground.

Mint whispered something to Becky. The blond girl turned to the captain. "She has to use your privy."

"Over there in the far corner. Behind that curtain. When you're done, pull the lever and it empties out below us."

"You've thought of everything," Tom marveled. "I'm next."

"Someday these flying machines will even have running water," Bettinger said. "I'm hoping to be in at the beginning of this futuristic enterprise."

When everyone had taken a turn at the built-in commode, all washed their hands in a splash of water from the jugged drinking water and then sat down on the blankets to eat. Bettinger had his own food and remained seated in the captain's chair as he munched on a sandwich.

Zane was determined to distract himself and the others from the dangers of the airship and began discussing the possibilities of stopping the steamer.

"With only three pistols and not much powder and shot, we ain't got near enough firepower to stop that bunch without help," Huck said. "Even if we wasn't all kilt, that mate and crew could alus use the blacks as hostages, if they was to get in a fix with the police."

"Best thing to do is convince the law to stop them and we back out of it altogether," Zane said.

"What if it's just our word against theirs?" Becky asked. "If they've already filled out those fake bills of sale, they might fool the police into believing their story."

"I could always be a witness to what I saw and heard on the *Morgan*," Mint said.

"Yeah, and the rest of us could swear to what we saw and heard 'twixt the duke and the mate, Conrad Winger, at the Grangerford house," Zane said.

"If they want any more proof, the sheriff could hold the *STYX* in quarantine, whilst he sends a deputy up to Compromise Landing to look for that headless horseman and any other slaves that might've been kilt and left in the woods thereabouts," Tom said, slathering horseradish on a slice of ham. "I reckon the duke has pitched that little printing press into the river and hightailed it on the headless man's horse by now."

"Ooh! It's just all too terrible to even think about," Becky shuddered. "How did you stand it on that boat?" she asked Mint. "I would've jumped ship at the first woodyard." She sounded sincerely concerned. Maybe she'd put aside her resentment of this beautiful visitor for now, Zane thought.

"I was fooled from the beginning," Mint said, simply. "Wasn't even scared until Ovelia and I found out what the real plot was. And that was only about three hours before the boat landed, and the breakout started. My only concern up to then was to stay out of the clutches of that mate."

They continued to discuss plans they'd try once they reached New Orleans.

"I just hope the *STYX* hasn't arrived there yet," Zane said. "I guess it also depends on where we land and how fast we can get to the police." He didn't voice his fears of the various possibilities. For all the others knew, they would arrive safely in or near the city. If anyone but Zane realized the dangers, it was Bettinger, but all he said, as he overheard their conversations, was, "You mind telling me what this is all about? I know you gave me a brief summary of the situation before we took off, but I'd like to know the details."

They obliged him by running through their entire story once again, this time relating all the particulars they could recall.

Bettinger pursed his lips. "I can see why you were in such a hurry. The time will come in the future when flying will be routine to save precious time in perilous situations just like this one."

Zane thought of life flights to hospitals, and the Berlin Airlift from World War II, and other things he knew of, but kept silent. Now was not the time to spring his time traveling on Bettinger.

The pilot consulted his watch again and then made a few calculations on the back page of his logbook. "We'll have to start descending soon and looking for a good place to land." he said. "Near as I can figure, we'll be within a few miles of New Orleans." He pulled out his maps and spread them on the floor for all to see. Using his pencil as a pointer he indicated where he estimated they were now. "See the river, here, it's always snaking back and forth, but the general direction is south and east. But right here it takes a turn almost due east and runs along for about fifty miles before bending south again down into the delta and then the gulf. While we still got a little daylight left, I'm going to drop down to avoid the worst of that thunderstorm yonder . . ."

Everyone but Zane looked up in alarm.

"Don't worry, I been watching it for the past hour. We'll get down low, maybe a hundred feet above the trees so the wind will be lighter. I want all of you with your younger, sharper eyes to be my lookouts. We'll skim along watching for the river, which should cut right across in front of us. Depending on how far east or west we've drifted, we might see Lake Pontchartrain first, just north of the city. So, if you spot any water, sing out and we'll pick a spot and start into our landing." He got up from his chair and moved to the leading edge of the gondola.

"You been here before?" Zane asked, quietly, leaning next to him.

"No, but don't mention that to the others. I'm relying on my maps." He turned around and instructed them all to be on the lookout in all directions for any sign of water. "I'll start releasing gas so we can descend gradually." He opened the cabinet and took out a flexible hose and a coupling.

Within a minute, Zane heard a hissing sound and shortly after, the darkening landscape below seemed to come closer. He could clearly make out the trees festooned with Spanish moss as they slid silently past beneath them. They reminded him of skeletal old men wearing gray beards.

A grumble of thunder drew his eyes to the thunderstorm approaching from the southwest. It was dark and ominous, a veil of rain blocking the view of everything over a quarter-mile away. An icy hand gripped his stomach as flashes of lightning became more frequent. The lightning had progressed from dimly illuminating the cloud bank to stabbing jagged bolts into the earth.

A few minutes later, the hiss of escaping gas ceased.

"We'll cruise at this altitude until we spot the city or the water," the captain said.

Several agonizing minutes passed when nobody spoke. They all strained to see what lay ahead and on either side of them in the twilight.

Zane was eyeing the rolling thunderstorm and wondered if the approaching veil of rain would blot out any view of the lake or the river or even the lights of the city. The storm appeared to be angling across their line of flight. If it hit with heavy wind and rain, the balloon could be forced down wherever they happened to be. They'd have no choice.

Another five minutes passed, and still no one spoke. Even Tom Sawyer was unusually silent. All of them knew the situation.

Suddenly, Zane saw a dark form loom up a few yards ahead. He instinctively recoiled as the basket brushed through the top of a tall tree and floated clear.

"Whew! Didn't know we were that low." His heart was racing. He snatched off his glasses and put them in the case, tucking it deep inside a shirt pocket. Before he had time to calm himself, Huck shouted, "There's water off to the larboard side!"

"Looks like we're about a mile to the right of the lake," Bettinger said. "Wish we could steer more to starboard. Map shows all this area around here is marshy ground." He looked over the side. "The trees are thinning out. We'll . . ."

A blinding flash lit up the sky around them, hissing and crackling, for the space of two heartbeats. Then the light subsided.

All of them hit the deck, and Zane heard cries of fear all around him. From flat on his back, he saw the top of the balloon ablaze, wind driving the spreading, billowing yellow flames ahead of them.

"Hang on!" the captain shouted. "We're going in."

The burning balloon, collapsing, was still dragging the basket forward on a stiff breeze, the flames blowing out away from them. Charred bits of fabric whirled around as they lost altitude. Would the remaining lift prevent the gondola from crashing?

The basket snagged on another tree, tilted sharply, then yanked loose and plunged downward as the balloon collapsed. Zane had no time to brace his feet before the basket hit with a jarring thud, throwing a muddy spray over them. The wind dragged the remaining balloon forward, the basket scooping up mud and water for a few feet before coming to a jarring stop, tumbling them out into a cold muck.

At that moment, a solid phalanx of rain swept across the area, drowning the blaze in a hissing cloud of steam and snuffing all light.

CHAPTER 27

Several seconds of silence ensued. "Is anyone hurt?" Bettinger's voice came dimly to Zane, who raised his head from the foot-deep water and fingered mud from his right ear.

"Becky! Mint!" Tom cried. "Sing out if you're all right."

Zane struggled to his knees and heard the two girls respond, and then Jim's deep voice, "Ah's here, thank de Lawd!"

"I ain't hurt none," Huck said.

All the voices were a bit muffled by the roar of the downpour.

They got to their feet in calf-deep water. Zane felt a twinge in his left ankle when he put weight on it. After a couple of steps, he concluded it was only a minor sprain.

They splashed closer, wiping mud and water from their faces and arms. Everyone was drenched. They could hear, rather than see, each other.

"That was a near miss," Bettinger said, raking a forearm across his mustache. He spat to one side. "We were lucky to land on soft muddy ground with the rain to put out the fire."

They all reached to touch one another to reassure themselves they were all upright.

"Oh, that was awful!" Becky cried.

"I expected we'd all be k . . ." Mint said at the same time.

"This has gotta be the greatest adventure of my life!" Tom yelled over the girls' voices. "Wait til I tell Joe Harper and . . ." His voice was giddy.

"Okay, okay, that's enough," Bettinger said. "We've landed

safely. Sorry I don't have a bottle of champagne to share like the French used to do."

"What was the champagne for?" Huck asked.

"They always figured any balloon landing you could walk away from, deserved to be celebrated."

"De Good Lawd dropped us outen de sky on soft, mushy ground," Jim said, "and den put out de fire wif rain. Glory be!"

"Don't get too relieved," Bettinger said. "We're not in New Orleans yet. The city is just over yonder maybe two miles. I'll retrieve my charts. This whole area is a bayou of marshy ground, and we'll have to slog through it to reach the city." He turned to Tom. "You still got that compass?"

"Yessir."

"Get it out and be ready to get a quick look in the next flash of lightning."

Tom did as directed.

Bettinger was fumbling in the dark of the overturned gondola for his charts.

Lightning was flashing and thunder booming, but not as frequently as in a summer storm.

He and Tom huddled together, with the chart unrolled, rain pattering on it.

At the next flash of lightning that wavered for a second or two the whole miserable, but grateful, assembly was lighted in perfect detail.

"Okay, I got the direction!" Bettinger said, rolling up the chart. "Look yonder," he said. "You can just make out lights reflecting from the underside of the low clouds. That's the city. I'll lead. Just so we don't lose anyone, hang onto each other by a shirttail, a coat sleeve, or something so you can follow me single file. Don't be alarmed about anything that might be in this water to bother us. This is part brackish water and part fresh and it covers a large area around here."

"Oh, this is scary," Mint said softly.

"Don't worry," Tom said. "We're all in this together, and nothing will happen."

"Just stay calm and keep putting one foot ahead of the other, even if we get into waist-deep water," the captain said. "Don't be concerned if I have to veer off a bit from a straight line," he cautioned them. "Tom, stay right behind me with that compass handy in case we need to check our course while the lightning is still flashing. I might have to twist and turn a little if we run into some tangled growth or probe for shallower water. Might have to stop now and again and check the compass and chart. But we'll make New Orleans in an hour or so. Everybody ready?"

A murmur of assent.

"Let's go."

They hooked up, Tom second, Becky and Mint third and fourth, Zane next, followed by Huck with Jim last as the strongest in case any of the others got into trouble ahead.

The line sloshed forward, everyone but Bettinger with heads bent, enduring the cold rain sluicing over them, plastering hair, trickling down necks to chill bare skin, adding weight to the sodden clothing.

Zane could not recall the last time he'd been this miserable. Then he remembered a soccer game played on a day when a forty-degree rain was lacing a field and driven by a twenty-mile-per-hour wind. He'd stayed home sick from school the next day with a sinus infection, and a slight fever.

Now he trudged ahead, holding a fistful of Mint's cape while Huck was gripping a sleeve of Zane's wool jacket that'd slipped off one shoulder.

It seemed the ordeal would never end. He concentrated on escaping in his imagination to some pleasant place—a brightly lighted room, warm and dry with someone playing the piano.

And, of course, there was something to eat—smoky strips of dried beef and lemonade to drink.

After an eternity, Zane looked up and the lights of the city were noticeably brighter, the rain easing as the storm blew east. The water was now just above their ankles and walking was easier, lighter. Somewhere along the way, his left shoe had been sucked off by the mud and lost. Then the marshy bayou was behind them and they were stumbling along uneven muddy ground toward the flaming torches that lit up a pier a hundred yards ahead. He could make out the superstructures of several steamboats moored alongside. They had apparently reached the Mississippi River.

Next, they were falling, exhausted, onto the wet, rough planking of the wharf and loud voices were around them, two men calling for help.

The next two or three hours were a blur in Zane's memory when he thought back on it.

A freight wagon pulled by a span of mules was brought and Bettinger asked to be taken to the nearest police station, promising to pay for the help. The seven were helped into the wagon and two dock workers hauled them about three miles through a labyrinth of dark streets to a precinct station where Tom and Zane told their story to the sergeant on duty.

Unlike the police in Memphis, the New Orleans lawmen were apparently used to strange tales and took them seriously. The sergeant immediately sent a courier to fetch the captain who had gone off duty for the day.

As soon as the messenger dashed out the door, the uniformed policeman called, "Wilson, take the front desk." Then he turned to the shivering, bedraggled group. "Come with me to the back room. There's a hot stove and coffee to get your blood circulating."

Ten minutes later, all seven of them were huddled around the iron stove, sipping mugs of black coffee, clammy clothes clinging to them. Their sodden outer garments lay in a pile on the floor nearby.

"I'm Sergeant Charles Benson," the burly, rosy-cheeked lawman said. "We don't have any dry clothes here, but a patrolman is bringing some blankets from a storeroom you can wrap up in until we can find something better for you to wear."

By the time they'd finished their first cups of coffee and driven some of the chill from their bones, a well-proportioned black-haired man entered and took in the scene at a glance.

"Captain James Norris," he said. He wore civilian clothes. "Once we get you warmed up a bit, I want to hear your story in detail. From what little the messenger told me, you have a fascinating tale to tell. And if it involves the steamboat *STYX*, it's a story I very much want to hear." He shifted a toothpick in his mouth, and Zane guessed he'd probably been interrupted at supper.

Before Tom and Zane began to relate their story yet again, Norris asked them some pointed questions about when the steamboat had left the area of the Kentucky–Tennessee border. He made some quick calculations in his head, and then said, "Excuse me a moment." He went out of the room and Zane could hear some sharp, urgent commands being given.

Five minutes later, the captain reentered, and began pacing up and down near the group huddled near the stove.

"We have suspected for several weeks that the stern-wheeler you described has been engaged in illegal slave trafficking. We've even gotten search warrants and gone over their boat and their documents but were unable to find anything that we could arrest the crew for. Of course, some of the slaves blurted out they'd been kidnapped from other plantations, but we could not take the word of slaves who are not allowed to testify in court. I want you to know that I've just put out an order for a dozen armed men in plain clothes to search the docks for that steamer. If they find it, they are to immediately arrest the crew and they'll be locked up, while the slaves will be held until we can get to the bottom of this. Now that we have all of you as witnesses, I think we can finally bust up this ring of slave kidnappers."

He paused and looked at each of them, one by one. "A very unusual mixture of witnesses, I must say—a white man, a black man, two young girls, and three boys."

Norris turned to Sergeant Benson. "Send in Corporal Wilson with a notepad; we need a record of this."

Then, once again, Tom, Huck, Zane, Jim, Mint, and Becky went through their long tale from the beginning, Bettinger adding what he could toward the end.

Nearly an hour later, Captain Norris stood up, and heaved a great sigh. "Well, thanks to you, I believe we will have enough proof to put these men away for years. And this Conrad Winger and a couple of the others might even have a date with the hangman for murder. I'll send two men upriver on the next steamer to examine the site near this Grangerford house to see what bodies or evidence they can collect. And we'll try to locate Judge Thatcher as well." He turned and held his hands out to the warm stove. "Meanwhile, I would like all of you to remain in protective custody until we capture this gang. The city of New Orleans will put you up at a nearby boarding house for now. Do you have any money for clothing and incidentals?"

"I do," Bettinger spoke up. "Thanks to the generosity of these young folks for hiring my airship, I want to furnish those things."

"Well, then, it's getting late and I'm sure you want to sleep. I'll personally conduct you down the street a block to a boarding house we use a lot, run by a Mrs. Sadie Sadler, a widow who will take good care of you. Just in case, I'll post one of my men as a guard while you're there. You'll be notified immediately if we head off the *STYX* and apprehend the crew."

"What about Jim?" Huck asked. "They won't let him stay in no boarding house with us."

"Mrs. Sadler will. She's a lady of color herself. And you'll find that this city is not the strictly segregated place that most people see in much of the South. Blacks and whites mingle freely at many events with no trouble, and even their houses are not completely separated. Some Negroes own their own slaves here, many others are freedmen, and Creoles and all kinds of mixed bloods are residents of New Orleans, people all shades of color from the Caribbean and elsewhere, even a small settlement of Filipinos west of here, so don't give segregation a second thought. I believe you said Jim is a free man?"

"Yessir, ah's free," Jim said, speaking for himself. "But my wife and two chil'ren are on dat boat. Dey still belongs to some old folks on a farm in Missouri."

"Don't worry about that, Jim," Becky said. "Once we find your family, my father, the judge, plans to take care of that situation."

Norris smiled. "Then, follow me and I'll get you settled in for the night at Missus Sadler's. She sets a good table, too, and I'm sure she has some leftovers from supper."

CHAPTER 28

Captain Norris was as good as his word. Missus Sadler fed all of them leftovers, then directed them to the outside pump to wash up as best they could, shivering in the cold water. She lent them spare nightshirts to wear while they left their clothing to be laundered overnight. Missus Sadler, a tiny woman in her sixties, treated them all like they were family.

Zane shared a room with Tom while Jim and Huck shared a room and Becky and Mint the third room. Bettinger was given a tiny garret—the only vacant spot left.

Zane was so tired, he slept like a dead man.

The mantel clock in the dining room of the spacious old boarding house had just chimed a musical nine when the seven shuffled, barefoot, across the threadbare carpet and sat down at the long table next morning. The were all wearing an odd assortment of misfit, but clean, clothing—shirts, pants, and skirts—that Mrs. Sadler had scrounged for them from the bin of clothing left or lost by previous residents.

"Where are your other boarders?" Zane asked. This was his first experience in a boarding house other than the one in St. Petersburg where he'd been living for five months.

"Oh, chile, they's been up and et and gone about their business for nearly two hours."

"Thank you for letting us sleep so long, Mrs. Sadler," Becky said, with a yawn. "I was exhausted."

"That's what I'm here for, honey, to take care of my boarders. And I'm just called Miss Sadie by all m' friends."

"Miss Sadie, I was almighty tired too," Mint added.

"I'm so sorry your nice blue cape got ruined," Becky said, sounding sincere.

"Me, too. Could have cleaned all the mud off it, I guess. But even if I was to patch those three or four burn holes in it, that cape wouldn't resemble nothing worth wearing to a ratting match." She looked around and then reached into her skirt pocket. "I did save my father's hardware, though the powder is wet."

Zane figured Tom and Huck's two pistols were in the same condition.

Sadie fed them hot flapjacks and molasses, side meat, and chicory coffee with cream and sugar. Zane thought it was nectar of the gods.

Just as they were finishing up, a uniformed policeman came into the parlor and stood in the arched dining room doorway.

Zane's stomach tensed. What now? But the young man said, "I been posted as guard here all night. Before I go off duty, I'm to get a carriage and take you to the city where you can buy some decent clothes and shoes and anything else you need."

"Why we bein' treated like kings and dukes and princesses?" Tom asked.

"Captain Norris wants you under police guard until you appear as witnesses in court against those men who're kidnappers and killers."

"We're likely to be here a good while until they's caught," Huck said.

"And they have been," said another voice as a tall figure appeared and stood beside the patrolman. He wore a gray suit with a silver badge affixed to the lapel.

Oscar Bettinger rose from the table. "Captain Norris!"

"Keep your seat," the officer said. "I wanted to come here in person and surprise you with this news myself. We have captured the steamboat *STYX* and its crew. They are all in jail on suspicion of kidnapping and murder."

A spontaneous cheer went up from those at the table and a great gabble went around as they congratulated each other.

"We were waiting for them at Stearns Wharf where they've docked before. But this time we had enough evidence to arrest them. The boat was taken at four o'clock this morning when the crew tied up and were preparing to offload the slaves in wagons and haul them directly to the main slave market."

"What about the slaves?" Zane asked.

"There are fifty-two of them who have been taken to an empty hotel, the Dennison, where they will be held until the law can sort this out."

"Was my Ovelia and my two chil'ren among 'em?" Jim asked.

"I don't yet know the identity of all the slaves. As soon as you've finished eating, I have a police wagon outside to take you into the city where you can buy clothing and anything else you need, and then we'll go directly to the Dennison and look for your family."

"There was an even sixty blacks when they first came aboard," Mint said.

"Don't you recollect what that mate said when we was hiding out and overheard him and the duke talking?" Huck reminded her. "He said Smealey did a rough count and figured a half-dozen got away and at least two was kilt trying to escape. Then he also told how he lopped off the purser's head and got blood all over hisself."

"You can bet he'll swing for that," Captain Norris said, tight-lipped. "Did you folks say there was a complete separate crew who manned the *Morgan*?"

Mint nodded. "I think maybe there were a few transferred to

the *STYX.* The mate Conrad Winger was one of them."

"We'll work on getting all the details down on paper maybe tomorrow so we'll have an accurate record while all this is fresh in your minds. I've already sent two men upriver by steamer early this morning to see if they can find any sign of the *Morgan,* and to search the area around Darnell's Point where you said that Grangerford house is located."

"Yessir."

"Thank the Lord you arrived when you did; it was just in time to snatch up those rascals red-handed. My men even found several bills of sale partially filled out they hadn't yet completed with false information as if they'd legally bought those slaves from other owners in Louisiana. Later today, you can view the prisoners in a lineup and see how many of them you can identify." He paused and looked around. "Well, it appears you're about done with breakfast. No sense wasting any more time. Come with me and I'll take you to some stores where you can buy some shoes and get yourselves re-outfitted."

They all rose and began talking among themselves as they prepared to follow.

"What will happen to those black prisoners?" Zane asked.

"We will interview them to see if we can pinpoint where they came from and return them to their proper owners."

"I was afraid of that," Zane said under his breath.

"Don't worry," Becky said. "At least Jim's family will be free. You heard my father say he'd just about agreed on a price for Jim's wife and children when they were stolen. If they're taken back upriver to that old couple, the Albertsons, my father will buy them and free them."

Zane smiled at her. "Sometimes the good guys win," he said. "But many of those others who are going back into bondage will have to tough it out for another sixteen years before they are freed by President Lincoln and an amendment to the U.S.

Constitution."

"If they survive that long, it's something to look forward to," she said hopefully. "Too bad we can't just wave a magic wand and make everything like we want it to be."

CHAPTER 29

Jim's wife, Ovelia, and two children, Johnny and Lizbeth, were not among the slaves quartered at the Dennison Hotel.

Jim had been antsy during the two hours they spent buying clothes, shoes, soap, and toothbrushes, and then returning to the boarding house to change, hardly able to contain his nervousness until they arrived at the hotel. He was distracted and silent as Captain Norris showed them into the lobby where the slaves were resting.

Jim and the others looked quickly for a woman with two small children. Nothing. Then they scanned the group more carefully and began asking some of the slaves if they had seen Ovelia and the two children.

A half-dozen slaves said she was among them, but disappeared during the breakout, and they never saw her or the two children after that.

"Don't worry, Jim," Huck said. "We'll find her. Providence ain't gonna let nothing bad happen to them—not after all they been through."

The big man wiped his eyes with the sleeve of his new shirt, took a deep breath, and turned away, hardly speaking to anyone until they arrived at the police station. There they identified Conrad Winger, and Mint pointed out several of the crew who had also been manning the *Morgan*.

"Who was the captain of the boat you came down on?" Zane asked Mint.

She shook her head. "I don't see him here."

"Likely a different man," Tom said. "And the pilots would not be the same ones, either, 'cause they'd have to know the lower river."

"Do you recall the name of the captain of the *Morgan*?" Zane asked.

"Umm . . . I heard him called Captain Barjee. That's it. His name was Bit Barjee."

"Strange. Might be a nickname. What did he look like?"

"Good-sized man with a lot of black hair and a limp."

"Sounds like the man we called the 'river pirate,' " Huck said. "We never learnt his name, but that bullet in the leg coulda done enough damage to cause a limp after it was healed up."

"We overheard his voice at the Grangerford house the first time we were there," Zane explained. "Figured he had to be part of this."

The youngsters and Jim again studied the insolent faces of the prisoners behind bars.

"Oooh!" Mint shivered and turned away. "I hate the way that mate looks at me," she whispered.

Zane glanced at the grim, craggy face of Conrad Winger, who was staring fixedly at the beautiful blue-eyed, black-haired girl.

"There's our old friend, Chigger Smealey," Becky said.

But Smealey didn't act like he knew them. He slunk behind two other men and looked toward the back of the cell.

"He ain't gonna let on he knows us," Tom said as they left the police station. "Reckon he's still wanted for kidnapping us earlier this year and stealing our gold."

For the next fortnight, the air travelers remained at Missus Sadler's boarding house and were guarded by an armed, uniformed policeman. He took them everywhere they wanted to go and showed them all the sights of the city.

Jim remained glum and quiet about his missing family.

Mint asked their uniformed escort to take her and her friends to the Saint Agnes Female Academy where her aunt, Rowena, was headmistress.

Rowena Medlin, a vibrant outgoing woman in her forties, greeted her niece with a huge hug and invited them all inside her house.

Mint introduced her new friends and they were all seated in the living room while Rowena scurried around and produced some delicious, freshly baked New Orleans pastries from a bakery just around the corner. "Good timing," Rowena smiled, setting out the snacks, and a big pitcher of lemonade. "I bought these for a parents' reception this afternoon. But I'll get more." She sat down on the couch opposite them. "I got your mother's letter. But when you didn't show up, I became concerned something bad had happened—and it almost did," she added. "But then the story hit the newspapers and I was stunned. But I was proud, too, that you had a big part in helping break up this gang of kidnappers and slave runners. My goodness, what an adventure! I showed the paper to all my friends, and to the students as well."

"Aunt Rowena, I want to stay with my friends until this is over. We have to appear as witnesses in court."

"Of course, dear," she said, glancing at the young policeman. "You appear to be in good hands. How long until the trial?"

"The judge agreed to move the case up on the docket," the policeman said. "Probably another ten or twelve days, the captain tells me. Early to mid-December."

"When this is over, I want you to come and enroll in school here next semester," Rowena said, turning to her niece. "And I can't wait to see your mother when she can finally join us. Margaret and I were always close growing up."

★　★　★　★　★

"We don't have this whole gang in irons yet," Captain Norris told Tom and the others a few days later when they questioned him about the reasons for the armed guard wherever they went. "The rest of them, and maybe a couple of the leaders, are on that other boat. No telling where they might have gotten to by now. We'll check to see if the *Morgan* was leased. Likely so. I'm guessing the kidnappers owned the *STYX*. The news of this whole plot has exploded in the newspapers, and you've been identified. If they know your testimony can put away their friends for a long prison sentence or give them an appointment with the hangman, it's very possible they might send someone to this city to make sure you don't testify against them."

"What about me?" Oscar Bettinger asked. "I was more or less just the airship pilot."

"You could be a target for kidnapping and threats to get the kids to recant or conveniently 'forget' their story. Since you and Jim are the only adults in this group, I'd rather you stay with them until this is over. Even though Jim's free, and can probably testify in court, I'm not sure his word would carry the weight with a jury. He could be more of a corroborating witness."

Becky shuddered. "And I thought all the danger was over."

"Not quite yet," Captain Norris said. But he sounded confident.

Mint smiled. "I don't have any fear of being killed. Especially after what I already been through. I feel like I've lived a hundred dangerous lives since the first of the month. I'll be a gray-haired, wrinkled old woman before I'm twenty!"

Zane, his gaze again attracted by her classical features, seriously doubted this last remark.

CHAPTER 30

Five days later, Judge Thatcher showed up at their boarding house, surprising them all.

"How'd you know where we were?" Tom asked, jumping up to greet him while Becky gave him a hug.

"The detectives Captain Norris sent north came to the village to look me up. They also found two decomposing bodies of blacks in the woods near Darnell's Point and another man who'd been beheaded. Besides that, they picked up a goodly number of clues about what's been going on at the Grangerford place."

"Yeah, we know all about that," Huck said.

"But the best news of all is Jim's family has been found," the judge announced after all the hugs and greetings with Becky and handshakes with the others.

Another round of cheers and loud talk.

"They're at the Dennison Hotel with the rest," the judge said. "Since they can't leave there because they are still technically in bondage, we'll go down there in a few minutes."

"Where had they been?" Becky asked.

"They got away from the steamer that night and ran north along the river in the woods toward Compromise Landing. But when they got there, they saw lights in that little store, and knew they had to avoid it. As you know, the Shepherdsons's property is just a little ways north of that landing. Ovelia said she was on the lookout for a skiff or canoe to steal, but that land has been abandoned and she didn't find any kind of boat. Well, she can tell you all about it, but, to make a long story shorter, they spent a few days in the woods, and got so hungry they finally hailed a white fisherman in a skiff, who came and gave them some raw mussels he'd just gathered and some corn pone. Ovelia told him what'd happened and he convinced them to turn themselves in so they wouldn't be hunted down by dogs. He rowed them to the next village downstream that had a constable, and they surrendered. The constable, thinking there was likely a reward, fed them and escorted them deck passage to New Orleans since that's where the *STYX* was bound. As it turned out, there was no reward, but Captain Norris took Ovelia and the two children to the Dennison Hotel where the rest of the black passengers were being held after the crew of the *STYX* were arrested and the steamer impounded."

An hour later, Jim and his family were reunited amid tears of joy, and the young people, along with Oscar Bettinger and Judge Thatcher, went outside to give the reunited family some time to themselves.

The judge repeated his promise to buy Jim's wife and children from the Albertsons and to legally free them.

Jim was all smiles the rest of the day.

Judge Thatcher took a room at the Sadler boarding house to await the trial date of the kidnappers.

November turned to December, but it felt less like winter than ever. The low-lying city nearly surrounded by water was like a damp sponge.

Everything became moist from the warm wind off the nearby gulf, and the lake. The late autumn temperatures were in the sixties and low seventies, the skies overcast much of the time.

"This place must be like a steam bath in the summer. How does anyone live here without air-conditioning?" Zane asked aloud one day, wiping the mold out of his new leather shoes.

"What's air-conditioning?" Huck asked.

"Never mind. I'm too tired to explain it," Zane said, flopping down on the unmade bed with his shirt off. He stuck to the clammy sheets.

"Miss Sadie told me she has to take a handcart to the market nearly every morning to buy fresh vegetables and milk because it spoils so quick," Becky remarked as she came into the boys' room. "Can't dig a fruit cellar in this soil 'cause the shovels hit water a short ways down."

Oscar Bettinger and the judge were playing a desultory hand of poker at the small table.

"What are your plans when the trial is finished?" the judge asked Bettinger.

"I believe my ballooning days are over, except as maybe a sideline," the tall, blond man said. "Thinking of looking for a college teaching job and going back to the classroom. That seems to be my natural calling."

"Probably a wise decision," the judge agreed. "You're likely out a considerable sum since your balloon was destroyed."

Zane went through the living room and out onto the front porch where a warm, humid breeze was blowing. He was bored and ready to get this trial behind them and catch a steamer back to Memphis to pick up their yawl.

A few minutes later, the others wandered out and sat down in the two porch swings.

"Anyone care to walk down to the drugstore? I need to get something to help clear this catarrh outa my throat." Bettinger said. "Comes on me every winter when I get chilled. Wading in that cold water a couple weeks ago didn't help, I reckon."

"Sure, I'll go," Zane said. "Been getting hungry for lemon drops lately."

The mention of candy brought Tom, Huck, Becky, and Mint to their feet. "I could use a few licorice sticks, too," Tom said.

They were joined by the judge and even Jim, who was out of pipe tobacco.

A bell jangled when they entered the drugstore. The place smelled faintly of chemicals, mixed with a pleasant aroma of cured tobacco and peppermint. They browsed the store buying a few sweets with the pennies and five-cent pieces they had in their pockets.

"You sure this will do the trick?" Ossie asked the pharmacist as he paid for a stoppered pint bottle he thrust into his pocket.

"About as good as anything I know of," the druggist said, coming out from behind the counter. He wore an apron and his black hair was slicked down and parted in the middle. Wire-rimmed glasses gave him a studious look. "Wrote the dosage on the label, there. It's the usual whiskey, honey, and lemon juice, but I've also ground up and added a combination of herbs that make mine unique and effective. My own secret formula. Of course, nothing is surefire." He paused and smiled. "Some of my customers say that none of my concoctions are any good, and they wind up paying Marie Laveau for a cure of whatever ailment they got."

"Who's Marie Laveau?" Bettinger asked. "A doctor?"

The druggist chuckled. "In Africa she'd be called a witch doctor. In Louisiana, I call her a fraud and a fake who takes money for selling hexes and spells. If her customers are cured of anything, it's all in their heads—the power of suggestion more'an likely. She's infamous hereabouts. Some swear by her; some swear at her and avoid her."

"Never heard of her," Tom said, strolling up.

"Apparently none of you is from New Orleans," the lean druggist observed.

"Just visiting," Bettinger said.

"She's a light-skinned woman of color and middle years. Had several kids, but I believe she's a widow now. A real beauty in her day—tall and willowy, moves with the grace of a snake. She got a reputation as a voodoo priestess. Has quite a following among both blacks and whites."

Jim had crowded up with the others to listen to the druggist.

"She must have done something pretty noteworthy to have a following like that," the judge observed.

"She's no miracle worker, although there is no explanation for some of the things she does. And it's not all medical stuff, either. She'll take your money for just about any problem you got in life—lost job, rejected love, an enemy who stole from you. She even dabbles in the law by somehow getting judges to drop charges against accused men, even to commuting a death sentence."

"She's a lawyer, too?" the judge asked.

"Oh, she doesn't use the written law. If she feels a defendant is wrongly accused, she uses a charm or witchcraft of some kind to influence the judge's decision."

"Quite a woman."

"In spite of all this voodoo nonsense, she claims to be a devout Roman Catholic, and uses holy water, and burns votive candles in front of statues of the saints including the Virgin Mary. And Marie is a regular at Mass at the Cathedral. I don't know how she reconciles black magic and Catholic beliefs."

"I've read some into this voodoo," the judge said. "As near as I can tell it originated in Africa, migrated to the West Indies with the slaves—especially Martinique—and then into this country. Picked up the sacramentals of the Catholic Church along the way. A really odd mixture of barbarism, superstition, and Christianity."

"You've hit on it," the druggist said. "Apparently many cannot see the dichotomy. Doesn't the first commandment forbid 'strange gods' such as putting faith in all kinds of magic charms? But the voodoo practitioners make their gibberish sound attractive and mysterious and powerful because much of the ceremony, ritual, and song are in a patois of French Creole."

The effects of voodoo have spread a lot wider than just to the Caribbean and Louisiana, Zane thought, but kept silent. He recalled the superstitions of Tom and Huck—curing warts with stump water, a marble finding another lost marble, a spider burning up in a candle flame causing bad luck, a howling dog prophesying a death, and Jim's getting advice from a hairball oracle and attributing all kinds of unexplained happenings to the work of witches.

"What do these spells consist of?" Bettinger asked.

"All kinds of things, and I think more are being invented all the time," the druggist said. "Just a couple of examples: if Marie decided she wanted to help a defendant, she'd melt a black candle, place a piece of paper containing the judge's name inside the wax, knead and roll it into a ball, then place the ball in a tub of water. All the night before the day of the trial Marie would sit beside the tub, turning the ball with a stick. The judge would be too sick to appear in court the next day."

Bettinger chuckled.

"To get rid of a person, his name is written on a small balloon, the balloon tied to a statue of St. Expedite, and then released into the air. The person would depart in whatever direction the balloon was carried by the wind."

"I'm Catholic, and I never heard of St. Expedite," Bettinger said.

"I think he's invented and named for the word *expedite*," the druggist laughed. "There are dozens of kinds of gris-gris."

"What's gris-gris?" Huck asked.

"An amulet or incantation. The term originated in Africa. Sometimes gris-gris is used for good purposes. For sprains and swellings, she uses hot water containing Epsom salts and rubs the injured parts with whiskey, chanting prayers and burning candles at the same time; sometimes she administers castor oil while praying. Some element of medical truth in a bit of that, but mostly complete nonsense."

"Can't people see through her?" the judge inquired.

"Many are too poorly educated to know the truth from fraud. And many just want something to believe in, and they fasten on voodoo. Some of her powers are even said to reach into killing an enemy—for a price of five hundred to one thousand dollars. Not directly, of course, but through some evil incantation, to cover up the hard fact that poison is involved—and circumstances where the person responsible can't be traced." He paused and looked at them. "If your faith in her powers are strong enough, she says she can even transport you to another time and place."

"What?" Zane was suddenly all ears.

"This is usually done privately and for a high price. It's not like her public displays such as the big one on St. John's Eve in June when a couple hundred blacks and whites and mixed bloods gather at the lake north of town and she preaches, and they all sing and dance naked around a big bonfire, and then go into the water. During all this folderol, they kill a couple of small animals, including a snake, and boil them in a big kettle and then later bring out food and liquor and have a feast. It's all absolutely ridiculous. The weirder she can make it, the more people flock to her. It's only the folks with good sense who stay away and say she's capable of terrible evil, like conjuring up zombies and even Satan himself."

"Is there any proof that she can make people move around in time?" Zane asked, getting back to what he'd just heard.

"I don't know of any. The person involved just disappears and is never seen again, and she can then claim he or she has been transported to another time. Who can prove otherwise? Meanwhile, she has that person's cash payment in full."

"Where does this Marie Laveau live?" Zane asked.

"She has a little house over on St. Ann Street, not far from Rampart." He gave them directions. "I'm sure if you get close, anyone can direct you to it. You're not thinking of visiting her, are you?"

"Maybe just out of curiosity," Zane said.

Judge Thatcher arched his eyebrows. Zane was almost sure Tom and Huck and Becky knew what he had in mind.

"Judge why don't you and I go back to the boarding house?" Bettinger said.

"Are all of you youngsters bent on going down to see this Marie what's-her-name?" Judge Thatcher asked.

They all answered in the affirmative.

"Becky, I don't know . . ."

"What can happen? After all I been through . . ."

"Well, Jim, you protect them from whatever evil charms this woman has."

"Yessir, ah'll sho look out for'em. Ah been wid'em right along."

CHAPTER 31

"Zane, I thought you had better sense than that," Tom said as the group trooped back to their boarding house two hours later. "You just spent four hundred dollars of gold me and Huck give you for expenses and bought some magic potion this slithery voodoo queen swears will take you back home."

"Reminds me of those suckers in Pokeville who was swindled by the king and the duke," Huck added without mercy. "That woman 'most give me the fantods. Felt like a zombie staring at me outen them black eyes."

"Or the devil," Mint said. "She's the female version of that mate, Conrad Winger." She looked at Zane. "I wish somebody would fill me in on this story. What are you trying to do, anyway?"

"I forgot you're the only one here who doesn't know I came from a future time," Zane said.

"A what?" Mint seemed incredulous.

"I'm not sure I'm totally convinced, either," Becky said.

Then Zane pitched in and told her the whole tale of his mysterious transportation, with Tom, Huck, and Jim adding details as he went along.

Mint's blue eyes got wider as the story unfolded. "Well, I never . . ." She hesitated. "Can such a thing be true?"

"Guess you sorta have to be inclined to have faith in things you don't understand," Zane said. "If it hadn't happened to me, I wouldn't believe it, either."

"That quart bottle of stuff she mixed up and sold you is likely nothing but baking soda and wood ashes with a dollop of alcohol to make it good and strong," Tom said.

"Yeah. That way when you drink it and throw up, you'll think it has mighty magic powers," Becky said to Zane. "Maybe in your day there ain't no snake oil salesmen, so she just took you in."

"Well, I don't have much faith, but since I been here in 1849 for six months, she's the only one who even hinted there might be a way for me to go back to the twenty-first century where I belong. I want to see my family again. If there's even a small chance of this working, I gotta try it."

"Why not just try eating chocolate and peanuts again," Becky suggested. "That's what brought you here last June."

Zane shook his head. "Ain't no guarantee that allergic reaction will work in reverse to take me back. It made me really sick the first time. I'm afraid it might kill me if I try it again, or wind up in another place like the middle of the French Revolution. Who knows? No doubt there's something supernatural about this," he said, holding up the bottle of cloudy liquid. "But you heard what she said—the Almighty made my body and spirit so they are instinctively tugging me back to my place of origin—like a salmon swimming in from the ocean to fight its way back upstream in the river where it was hatched, or like a migratory bird that flies back to where it came from. She says this elixir bonds with my body chemistry and just helps along this natural process."

"Well, dat's a power o' money you let go of, Mars Zane," Jim said. "But we knows where to find dis Marie, if dat potion don't do da trick. I ain't gonna 'llow no high yallah gal to cheat my fren'. Da judge, he axed me to look out fo' you youngsters. And dat's what I aim to do."

"Maybe we oughta stop at the drugstore and see can the

druggist taste it and tell what's in it," Tom said.

So they did.

The druggist took a sip, swished it around in his mouth a few seconds, then made a wry face and spat to one side on the rough wood floor. "I think you just threw away four hundred dollars," was his opinion. "I can taste algae and ashes and bicarb, and lemon and alcohol, and some other bitter herbs I can't identify. Likely some cat urine and bat blood, too. If you had another four hundred dollars, I'd bet you even it won't do nothing but give you one helluva bellyache."

They thanked him and left, Zane feeling humiliated.

When they reached the boarding house, Zane stopped out front. "Okay, all of you watch me do this." He uncorked the bottle and sniffed the contents. "Carry me to a doctor if this doesn't work."

Quickly, before he lost his nerve, he tipped up the bottle and took three deep swallows.

"Ugh! That's terrible!" He stuck out his tongue and wiped it with his shirtsleeve.

They moved around the house and he thrust his head under the pump to rinse the nasty taste out of his mouth.

"Don't say anything about this to Judge Thatcher or Ossie Bettinger. They don't know about where I came from. It's just a secret among ourselves for now. I'm afraid they wouldn't understand. Is that agreeable with everyone?" He glanced at Jim, who was even more inclined than the rest to believe in otherworldly things.

They all shook hands, swearing to keep mum, then trooped into the house, Tom chewing on the end of a licorice stick.

In a few minutes Zane began to yawn. He excused himself by saying, "I'm going outside where there's a nice breeze and catch a few winks in the porch swing before supper. Come and wake me when it's time to eat."

The sultry, quiet afternoon was having a soporific effect. But his stomach was beginning to gurgle. He hoped that wouldn't interrupt his nap. If the concoction made him nauseous, he could vomit over the porch railing and nobody would see him. For now, he would ignore the digestive unrest. What would be, would be. Normally, his energy, alertness, and attention in late afternoon always sank to a low ebb as his daily biorhythm swung into a downward cycle.

He lay down in the long wooden porch swing, resting his head on the thick, corduroy pillow at one end, feet propped on the opposite armrest. After a little more gurgling, his stomach settled and weariness overtook him. The long, thin branches of a nearby weeping willow tree sighed softly in the warm breeze. At peace with the world, he closed his eyes and sank into a doze.

A few minutes before six, the house was filled with the aromas of baked sweet potatoes and ham, and Tom came out on the porch to rouse Zane for supper.

But there was no sign of Zane. Tom had an empty feeling in his stomach and it wasn't from hunger. He went back inside and whispered to Huck, who motioned for Mint, Becky, and Jim to come outside with him.

The screen door banged behind them and all five stood, seeing the barely moving porch swing, looking over the porch railing into the bushes, and gazing about the yard and street.

"Did he go around to the pump to wash up?" Huck asked.

They circled the house. No Zane.

"Maybe he took a walk," Tom suggested. "He knows it's suppertime. He'll be along directly." He didn't want to voice the apprehension he felt.

"Or mebbe de potion done it's work," Jim said in a deep

voice, the whites of his eyes showing as he looked at each of the youngsters.

They stood around the swing for several seconds with their own thoughts, Tom looking at the indentation in the corduroy pillow. The heavy ache of loss began to make itself felt in his chest. "Supper's waiting," he finally said. "Reckon we better go in. In case the judge or Ossie ask, I don't have no idea where Zane went. What about you?"

Becky, Mint, Huck, and Jim all silently shook their heads.

CHAPTER 32

When Zane swam up from the depths of an ill-formed dream, he cracked his eyelids and realized he was no longer in the porch swing but was lying on his stomach in warm sand.

He rolled over and pushed up to a sitting position, brushing the sand from his cheek. The sun's rays were slanting through the trees at an angle that indicated late afternoon.

Rubbing his eyes, he came fully awake, and aware that he was near his favorite creek—in Delaware.

A great sense of relief and thankfulness flooded over him. "Ahhh . . . Marie Laveau's elixir worked, and I don't feel sick," he breathed to himself. He was home! He got to his feet and glanced at his wrist to see what time it was. But his watch was missing, and there was no cell phone on his belt. Both with dead batteries were collecting dust in a drawer of his boarding house in St. Petersburg, Missouri. Not only did he not know the time of day, he didn't even know the time of year. From the looks of the trees and bushes, it was high summer. He had returned to the exact spot from whence he'd left six months earlier. What time of day had that been? As he recalled it was about two o'clock in the afternoon after a soccer game. Now it looked to be about six in the late afternoon of a long summer day.

"I knew it, I knew it!" he whispered to himself. "Tom Sawyer was wrong about the whole world moving back to 1849. I traveled back by myself, and everything here is just the same as when I left it."

Or, had he just passed out and dreamed this entire bizarre episode that seemed to last all summer and autumn? He always had very vivid realistic dreams and maybe that's what he'd just experienced. The three major adventures he recalled could have been three dreams, since most of his dreams that were fully formed seemed to last about an hour each in actual time.

Then a sinking feeling attacked his stomach. He was wearing the clothes he'd bought in New Orleans—a coarse linen shirt with full sleeves and no collar, buttons made of mussel shells, pants of gray canvas with suspenders and no belt. He looked down at his new high-top leather shoes that appeared to be made to fit either foot. He thrust a hand into a side pocket and felt a Barlow knife Tom had given him, and a few coins. Drawing out the coins, he clutched four big copper pennies, a silver five-cent piece, and two quarters. But what really caught his attention were six ten-dollar gold pieces, two fives and a two-and-a-half-dollar quarter eagle—all he had left after paying Marie Laveau the four hundred dollars for the potion. The other side pocket contained the square, three-quarters-full bottle of the potion itself.

He took off his glasses—the wire-rimmed spectacles made in 1849 St. Louis—and felt the hair curling over his ears. It was of a length it should have been after not being cut for several months. He had a clean handkerchief, but his billfold was missing.

All this added up to far too many physical proofs that this had not been a dream. But then he wondered if perhaps he was still dreaming.

He had to decide. The creek was about two miles from his house and he could walk it in less than thirty minutes. So he set off at a brisk pace in that direction.

On the way, he tried to plan what he'd say or do when his

parents noticed how different he looked.

He went up the driveway into the back yard and smelled grilling hamburgers. But his father was on the far side of the yard, breaking a dead limb off a tree.

Before Zane could slip into the house unnoticed, his father turned around. "Oh, there you are. We were wondering what happened to you after the game."

"Just wanted to be alone for a while so I walked down to the creek. I forgot we were having a cookout for the team. Let me go inside and change clothes."

"Wait a minute."

Zane stopped.

His father had a puzzled look on his face as he walked up. "What have you done to yourself? Why're you wearing a wig?" He glanced over his son. "Where'd you get those clothes? This isn't a masquerade party."

He decided to come clean. "Dad, do you have a few minutes? I gotta tell you something really weird—in private."

"Yeah. Let me take these burgers off first."

Zane led him into the house and to his bedroom, where he closed the door. "Dad, you might think me crazy when I tell you this, but I have to ask your opinion about something I don't understand that just happened to me. First, tell me the date— month, day, and year."

His father complied, a bewildered look on his face.

Zane nodded, confirming what he suspected; it was June 4th. He still had summer vacation ahead of him. Then he quickly told his parent the full story—from just after the soccer game when he sneaked to the creek and ate the candy bar with the peanuts and dark chocolate, had a severe allergic reaction, passed out, and woke up on a Mississippi River island, until finally bringing the story up to the present moment. To save time, he summarized much of the details of his tale. "Dad, I think I've somehow traveled in time back to 1849," he concluded, holding out the handful of gold coins.

His father was silent for several seconds, then frowned. "This better not be one of your elaborate practical jokes."

"Honest Injun, it ain't."

"And you never used to talk like that. I'm even more familiar with Mark Twain's work than you are, and of course we both know the characters you've been talking about don't really exist and didn't even exist in the 1840s."

"I know, but every word I told you is the truth. And I can give you a lot more details when we have time. This is no joke. And it could not have been a dream. My hair could not have grown this long in only four hours."

"Yeah," his father mused. "And you seem bigger and more muscular than I recall. And I know you didn't have the money to buy those rare coins—unless you stole them."

Zane swore up and down that he had not.

"Okay, we'll talk about this later. For now, I won't say anything to your mother. She and your little sister won't be home from Rehoboth Beach until Saturday, anyway. Maybe by then, we'll have time to sort this out. Change into a pair of shorts and tennis shoes and your soccer shirt. Let me trim that hair some and we'll go out to the picnic."

"Okay. First, I have to use the bathroom." Zane went in and closed the door. He flushed the toilet, and under the noise of the water, ducked down to the cabinet under the sink and slipped a wall tile loose in the open back of the enclosure, tucking the corked bottle of elixir into the space behind—a secret hiding place he'd used for his treasures since he was a little boy. He would somehow find a lab to analyze the contents the first chance he got. He was leaving nothing to guesswork.

An hour and a half later, Zane and several of his teammates, stuffed with hamburgers, potato salad, and baked beans, were shooting some hoops at a goal over the garage door, while several of the boys' parents lounged in lawn chairs and chatted.

The hamburger Zane had eaten was filling, but bland, even livened up with horseradish mustard. It was lacking the flavorful smoky taste he'd become accustomed to in the past few months. When he'd suggested maybe they could plan an old-fashioned wiener roast on the 4th of July with hot dogs and marshmallows and a real wood fire, he received a shrug in reply and the comment, "I guess we could, but I'll have to chop or buy some logs. Seems like a gas grill is a lot cleaner and more convenient."

He didn't pursue the matter but went off with his friends for a game of "horse."

Across the yard near the patio, Zane's father moved around the picnic table and put a foot on the bench, leaning his elbows on one knee. "Jack," he addressed an older man with iron gray hair who was sipping a cold can of beer, "you're a clinical psychologist, and I'm not trying to get free professional advice, but I desperately need your opinion about a family matter that just came up."

"Sure. Let's have it."

Nearly an hour later, the sun had disappeared. A few of the boys had gone home and the others who were spending the night had adjourned inside for a movie. They left the deepening dusk to the lightning bugs, mosquitoes, and the two adults who'd volunteered to clean up—Jack Burnam and Zane's father.

"As a psychologist I have to keep an open mind about a lot of things," Burnam was saying. "The human mind is infinite— or infinitely complex. No one in history has yet been able to completely probe its depths. I'm thinking Zane has experienced a rare, super-realistic episode of the mind."

"But what about the physical evidence?"

"The clothes could be faked, as well as the coins. The hair

could have grown that long in one afternoon through a psychosomatic event. The mind can control the body. Severe trauma can turn the hair white overnight—such as a man might experience in the horror of war. There are many instances of people dying because they will themselves to die, though there is nothing physically wrong with them. Certain Indian tribes and subcultures around the world know this to be a fact. Jesus is thought to have actually sweat blood in the Garden of Gethsemane. And there are a few historical instances of this happening to others under extreme duress. Zane is a highly intelligent boy who has an active imagination and is well read. He dreams a lot."

"So you're saying this was just all in his head—a subconscious dream of some kind, maybe dressed up as a joke?"

"Very likely. But we must not conclude that's all there was to it."

"What do you mean by that?"

Burnam paused for a few seconds and then said, "Do you know anything about Einstein's theories?"

"Not much."

"Well, he stated the speed of light is a constant in nature. What is the figure—186,000 miles per second? He said that no material thing can move faster than that, and the speed does not change depending on your frame of reference. So, if you neared the speed of light, time does slow down. If you could somehow fly in a terrifically fast spacecraft, you would age more slowly than the people back on earth."

"Meaning?"

"Meaning that time can be manipulated. As a free thinker myself, I can allow for the possibility that, with the right combination of circumstances, time travel such as Zane described, might just be possible."

The two men stared silently at each other in the semidarkness.

Life in the Rasmussen household would never be the same again.

Zane lounged on the living room floor while five of his soccer teammates were sitting and sprawled around on the divan and chairs. An on-demand movie was playing on the big TV screen. It was a fantasy, set in the past with a race of nonhuman characters—the kind of movie that had become popular. Could he write down the story of what he'd just experienced—or dreamed? He doubted he could make it real enough. It would be a great film, but marketing such a thing for the big screen or TV was mostly a matter of luck, or having the right connections, or . . . Providence. He smiled to himself.

His thoughts turned to the upcoming trial of the kidnappers. He wished he could be there to testify. Would Conrad Winger be hanged for beheading the purser? Would the others be sentenced to long prison terms? Would the law catch up with Bit Barjee and the duke? Would Mint attend the Saint Agnes boarding school? Would Ossie Bettinger go back to teaching college history and geography? Would Jim settle with his reunited family in St. Petersburg to live as "free persons of color"?

Then, with a jolt, he realized that all those things were long past and forgotten. The trial was only a mote in history and everyone Zane was associated with had been dust for generations. He struggled to wrap his mind around such a thing. The slow grinding of time that created this vast gap was frightening when viewed from his current perspective.

His mind shifted to the gold coins he'd brought back. Because of their age, barely circulated condition, and with gold prices above a thousand dollars an ounce, the coins could be sold for many times their face value online or to a coin dealer—maybe for enough to cover the first year of college.

It was going to take him at least the rest of summer to reorient himself to this modern life. He doubted he could ever accomplish it completely.

Glancing around the room, he noticed three of his five friends were not watching the movie; they had their eyes glued to their handheld electronic devices.

In spite of his father's doubts that his trip in time had actually happened, he was already sorely missing his friends of long-ago Missouri. No dream could have been so acutely real. In 1849, teens could actually make a difference and accomplish big things with little adult help or supervision. He'd found Tom, Huck, Becky, and Mint to be resourceful and courageous.

His teammates in this very room were great friends, but all seemed a bit immature to him now, all addicted to the allure of the electronic world, all closely supervised, if not inhibited, by loving parents. It was a completely different time and place. Zane was overjoyed to see his family again, but he would pay the price for growing up in this twenty-first century world of instant communication, robots, space stations, frequent senseless violence, threats of atomic annihilation, and living with widespread pollution of the planet for profit. Could he accomplish anything worth doing?

He visualized the bottle of elixir hidden in the bathroom wall. He should have poured it out while on his walk home from the creek.

Deep down, he sensed there was a reason he didn't.

AUTHOR'S NOTE

Ideas and material that can be adapted to fiction are all around us. Often a person's own experiences or family background can be modified and used to create realistic stories.

For example, years ago, my mother told me what she'd heard of a brief legend that touched our extended family. Mom was born in 1912 and grew up in the small town of Pisgah, in western Iowa. The town is only five miles south of a place called Preparation Canyon where a group of Mormons settled and lived for some years in the latter half of the 1800s. At its height, the town had more than sixty buildings and a post office. Charles B. Thompson, who founded the town, instructed his Mormon followers to refer to him as Father Ephraim, after an Old Testament figure. A property dispute arose between him and the residents—a dispute that was eventually decided by the Iowa Supreme Court. Thompson then fled the state. The town of Preparation later dwindled away. My mother recalled that, when she was a child, the canyon still contained the remains of a few buildings. The site is now a state park and physical evidence of Preparation has disappeared.

During one of the waves of Mormon migration through this area, a young girl was supposedly left behind or dropped off a caravan. My grandfather, George A. Champlin (1863–1942), had several brothers, one of whom took this girl into his family to bring her up as one of his own. Her name was Arminta Lucinta (last name unknown). Unfortunately, this is all the information Mom had about the girl. I can't say whether any, or all, of this tale is true, but I was still intrigued by it. After deciding to use this mystery girl in my novel, I had to invent a last name, physical description, age, and background for her. She became the beautiful teenager, Arminta Lucinta Fayberest, closely resembling the dark-haired women on my mother's side of the family.

Besides drawing on vague oral tradition, an author can create fiction a bit easier by using solid personal experience.

As a gift for my daughter, Liz, on her sixteenth birthday, I arranged for a free-flight balloon ride, hiring a young man who owned and piloted his own craft.

On a windy Saturday in early October, we gathered in the empty parking lot of a school in Williamson County, Tennessee. While the pilot began inflating the collapsed balloon with hot air blasted into the big envelope with what resembled a flamethrower, he said he'd considered canceling the flight because the wind was too strong to fly safely. This remark did nothing to calm my nerves.

The huge, tethered balloon was riding upright, tugging at its rope when we climbed into a wicker basket only large enough for the three of us to stand. The pilot released the clip holding us to the trailer and the balloon shot up more than a hundred feet before I could take a deep breath. For the next hour or two, at the mercy of the wind, we flew several miles over the countryside, viewing white-fenced farms and Confederate cemeteries below. Now and then, to keep us at altitude, the pilot shot a thick tongue of flame upward into the open end of the balloon to refill it with hot air. The roar of the pressurized gas flame stampeded horse herds on the fields below. In the distance, we could see the pilot's girlfriend driving the pickup pulling the trailer, zigzagging on the roads, trying to keep us in sight. My wife and mother were in a car, also attempting to follow where the wind was taking us. Busy taking photos, I didn't notice we were headed for a hill until the basket dragged us through the top branches of a tree. Luckily, we were just high enough to clear it.

Finally, late in the afternoon, the pilot spilled air from the balloon and we gradually descended, coming in for a landing in a tree-lined vacant pasture. The basket hit, dragged, tipped over, and spilled us out onto the grass. The pilot jumped up and finished deflating the balloon.

By the time the two vehicles caught up with us, we were sharing a bottle of champagne our pilot provided—an old French tradition.

ABOUT THE AUTHOR

Tim Champlin was born in Fargo, North Dakota, the son of a large-animal veterinarian and a schoolteacher. He grew up in Nebraska, Missouri, and Arizona, where he was graduated from St. Mary's High School, Phoenix, before moving to Tennessee.

Following his graduation from Middle Tennessee State College, he declined an offer to become a U.S. border patrol agent in order to finish work on a Master of Arts in English at Peabody College (now part of Vanderbilt University).

After thirty-nine rejection slips, he sold his first piece of writing in 1971 to *Boating* magazine. The photo article, "Sailing the Mississippi," is a dramatic account of his three-day, seventy-five-mile solo adventure on the Big River from Memphis, Tennessee, to Helena, Arkansas, in a sixteen-foot fiberglass sailboat built from a kit in his basement. His only means of propulsion were river current, sails, and canoe paddle.

Since then, forty of his historical novels have been published. Most are set in the frontier West. A handful of them touch on the Civil War. Others deal with juvenile time travel, a clash between Jack the Ripper and Annie Oakley, the lost Templar treasure, and Mark Twain's hidden recordings.

Besides books, he's written several dozen short stories and nonfiction articles, plus two children's books. One recent book is a nonfiction survey of world-famous author Louis L'Amour and the Wild West.

He has twice been runner-up for a Spur Award from Western

Writers of America—once for a novel, *The Secret of Lodestar,* and once for a short story, "Color at Forty-Mile."

Tim is still creating enthralling new tales. Most of his books are also available online as ebooks.

In 1994 he retired after working thirty years in the U.S. Civil Service. He and his wife, Ellen, have three grown children and ten grandchildren.

Active in sports all his life, he continues biking, shooting, sailing, and playing tennis.

The employees of Five Star Publishing hope you have enjoyed this book.

Our Five Star novels explore little-known chapters from America's history, stories told from unique perspectives that will entertain a broad range of readers.

Other Five Star books are available at your local library, bookstore, all major book distributors, and directly from Five Star/Gale.

Connect with Five Star Publishing

Visit us on Facebook:
   https://www.facebook.com/FiveStarCengage

Email:
   FiveStar@cengage.com

For information about titles and placing orders:
   (800) 223-1244
   gale.orders@cengage.com

To share your comments, write to us:
   Five Star Publishing
   Attn: Publisher
   10 Water St., Suite 310
   Waterville, ME 04901